MAY   2024

THE
FUNERAL
CRYER

THE
FUNERAL
CRYER

A NOVEL

WENYAN LU

HANOVER
SQUARE
PRESS

HANOVER
SQUARE
PRESS™

Recycling programs
for this product may
not exist in your area.

ISBN-13: 978-1-335-01693-5

The Funeral Cryer

First published in May 2023 in the United Kingdom by Allen & Unwin. This edition published in 2024.

Hanover Square Press
22 Adelaide St. West, 41st Floor
Toronto, Ontario M5H 4E3, Canada
HanoverSqPress.com
BookClubbish.com

Printed in U.S.A.

For my mum and dad,
who always think I am the best

1

Great-Great-Grandma was dead.

The whole village was touched by an eerie atmosphere, almost a strange relief. It seemed everyone had been secretly waiting for this moment to come.

She was Great-Great-Grandma to everyone in the village. I didn't know how old she was at the time; we just knew she was alive. I felt a moment of surreptitious excitement and a shameful buzz in my chest since I would earn some money from her timely death.

A young woman in a white linen gown approached me in the cramped kitchen. She was also wearing a white cloth hood. If she walked on the street like this, she would frighten little children to tears.

She read Great-Great-Grandma's obituary to me while I dabbed powder on my cheeks. Several village chefs and their helpers were preparing food amid much shouting and chopping. I could hardly move. I was surrounded by stacks of large cardboard boxes with "FRAGILE: PORCELAIN" printed on them in thick black letters.

The young woman didn't look happy, but she didn't seem too sad either. Then again, I could be wrong. What you saw was not always what was there.

"Will you really be able to remember her obituary?" she asked me.

"Yes."

"I'm just worried. If you make any mistakes, my uncle will be mad at me."

"You don't need to worry. I promise everyone will cry. Trust me."

"Let me read it once again. Just to make sure," she said. I nodded and she began.

"Dear Great-Great-Grandma lived an extraordinary life of 106 years. She selflessly devoted herself to the continuity and prosperity of her family. She suffered various hardships during her exceptionally long and enduring life and she did many remarkable things. She had twenty-five grandchildren, sixty-two great-grandchildren and sixteen great-great-grandchildren. More than thirty of her descendants live abroad. She will be remembered dearly by her family and her village. She lived the longest on record in our county, so we shall feel tremendously proud of her. Her heartbreak was that seven of her grandchildren predeceased her. Let us cry for her and keep hope in our hearts for ourselves."

I took a brief look at myself in the mirror. My face was pale, my eyebrows were painted long and my lips bright red: the perfect image for a traditional funeral cryer. There were several black and red makeup stains on my white gown, but nobody would notice them in their distress. The young woman had helped me to tie the big black cotton bow on the side of my gown. My bun was neat. I tugged some strands of loose hair along my temples and ears to cover my wrinkles. Finally, I pinned a white fabric flower carefully onto my hair.

The young woman handed me a small teacup. "Your hair looks nice," she commented.

"We've got a good barber in the village." I felt my bun.

"Your belt is nice. Look at mine." Hers was a linen rope, a symbol of bereavement.

"It doesn't matter what it looks like. You have to wear it."

"You're right. By the way, you need to eat something. Some rice biscuits?"

"Thank you. I'll keep some for the husband. He likes them."

"I'll ask them to pack a box for you. Now, shall we rehearse a bit more? It's not easy to get all those numbers right."

"Twenty-five grandchildren, but seven dead, sixty-two great-grandchildren and sixteen great-great-grandchildren."

"And don't forget: she lived for 106 years."

The courtyard was spacious but neglected, with weeds growing in the gaps between the chipped stone slabs. The guests were mostly sitting on small stools and benches. Some people were chatting, some were staring at their phones, and some were cracking sunflower seeds between their teeth. There was no sorrow or grief in the air just yet. Most people's expressions were indifferent. When a relative or friend has lived so long, after their death there is often a sense of detachment amongst the funeral goers.

A suona sounded: the musical instrument of choice for countryside funerals in Northeast China, similar to a trumpet. High-pitched, squeaky and very noisy, like a wolf howling in a gale. It stopped after a minute or so. A tape of slow, heavy music began to play. The crowd fell silent as the coffin was carried into the courtyard from the back gate. It was a redwood coffin with patterns carved onto the lid, wrapped in white silk ribbons.

I watched as the pallbearers slowly lowered the coffin onto a makeshift stage, in the middle of a display of wreaths and baskets of flowers. The stage was a sea of color.

As soon as the music faded and the pallbearers had retreated, I skipped up onto the stage waving my wide, flared sleeves high into the air. I knelt down in front of the coffin. This was my favorite part of the funeral crying. I felt like a beautiful actress on the stage.

All was silent.

I threw myself onto the ground and began to wail.

"Oh, Great-Great-Grandma, have you really left us? Have you? The sky is murky and the earth is dark because of your absence. How can you bear to leave us behind? You had a turbulent life in the old society when you were young, but you never complained. In our new socialist society, you recovered from adversity thanks to the Party, and you followed Chairman Mao's appeal to produce as many children as possible for our motherland, seven altogether. Although you were not granted the official title of Heroic Mother by Chairman Mao, what you achieved in increasing the population of a new China was glorious. You are survived by two daughters, eighteen grandchildren and sixty-two great-grandchildren and sixteen great-great-grandchildren. What a feat. Who could ever wish for more in this life?"

I paused. No one was crying.

I took a deep breath, leaned forward and slapped the floor with both palms.

I repeated, "Oh, Great-Great-Grandma, have you really left us? Have you? The sky is murky and the earth is dark because of your absence. How can you bear to leave us behind? How?"

I rubbed my eyes. "Great-Great-Grandma, are you looking down at us from Heaven? Do you know how much we miss you? How bereft we are? We will remember you dearly. We will remember everything you did for your family and for your country. We are glad you are reunited with Great-Great-Grandpa in Heaven now. We couldn't bear to think of you being alone."

Some of the mourners started to rub their eyes. I slowed down.

"Great-Great-Grandma, we hope you can see our tears."

Nearly everyone was crying by now, and I felt pleased and relieved. I deserved the money I was going to be paid.

"But life must go on. Great-Great-Grandma would now like to see us smile. We can't be happy for a long, long time, and she knows that. It is true we are mourning her farewell, but we are also celebrating her rare longevity. She brought prosperity and pride to her relatives and to our village. Her family has arranged a banquet to show her the highest respect. We can share stories of our beloved Great-Great-Grandma. By the way, don't forget to collect your longevity china bowl before you begin eating."

While everyone was still sniffing, I announced that I would sing some joyful songs to lighten the atmosphere. I didn't feel comfortable singing joyful songs at funerals, but it was the custom. The farewell belonged to the past. Life had to go on with joy and hope.

After a loud round of applause, I moved swiftly but quietly to the back of the courtyard, from where I could see attendants placing food on large trestle tables.

The aroma of the hot food filled the air. There were no signs of sadness on people's faces anymore. They started staring at the dishes and picking at food with their chopsticks. My stomach rumbled.

I looked around for any familiar faces. The village barber caught my eye. I would tell him people thought my hair was nice when I visited him next time.

The feast after the funeral was called a tofu banquet. The funeral dinner used to be a vegetarian meal with tofu as the main ingredient. Hard or soft, fried, boiled or steamed tofu, made from nutritious soya beans, showed respect for both the dead and the living. In recent years, more and more meat and fish have been added to the funeral meal, but the banquet wouldn't be complete without tofu. After all, it's white, the color of death.

I wouldn't stay for the tofu banquet, but I would be given some food to take away. Nobody would mind if I stayed, and I would stay if I had known the dead person well. Great-Great-Grandma was much older than me, so I had never had a chance to get to know her properly. I had been fond of her, but she had probably never noticed me.

The young woman handed me a white envelope while people were queuing up for their china bowls. I could feel the stack of cash inside the envelope was thick. Thick enough.

The husband would be pleased.

2

Although I lived only a stone's throw away from the reception, I was driven home by a car arranged by the uncle of the young woman. The respect they showed me reflected the filial piety they had for Great-Great-Grandma.

When the car was about to move, the young woman rushed to the car and knocked on the window. "You forgot your food." She waved a paper bag at me.

Once inside my house, I went straight to the bedroom to get changed. The husband was sitting in the middle of the bed wearing his outdoor clothes, fiddling on his phone.

"I've told you enough times. You shouldn't come home in your horrible white funeral gown. You're cutting years off my life. Stupid woman." He was angry.

I should have expected him to be home at this time. Removing my gown, I made for the bathroom.

While I was in the shower, I lathered my body again and

again, to wash off all the bad luck from the funeral. I couldn't stay here too long, as the husband would insist I was wasting water.

I was upset when the husband first called me a "stupid woman." I knew I wasn't stupid, but it had since become his catchphrase. It washed over me now.

I unwrapped the longevity china bowl I had been given and placed it in the cupboard. Now there were twelve of them, all similar, with the Chinese character for "longevity" printed on the side.

The longevity bowls were only given away by the bereaved if the deceased was elderly, a blessing for others to live such long lives.

I never use the bowls, as I worry I might break them, which is considered bad luck. But sometimes I would open the cupboard and admire all my precious longevity bowls.

I heated up the food I'd brought home from the tofu banquet and dished out two plates.

I called out to the husband, "Dinner."

He came out and sat down. "Dinner? I haven't had lunch. It's 4:30 now."

I explained, "The funeral ran on for much longer than I expected. Shall we call it an early dinner?"

"Are you going to starve me?"

"You should have gone to the funeral. Nearly the whole village was there."

"I didn't want to hear you crying and singing. You bring food home anyway."

"We can have some snacks later. I've got some rice biscuits for you."

"White rice biscuits? Funeral nibbles. I don't want any."

"They're not cheap in the shop." I knew he would eat anything if it was free.

The husband stirred the five-spice beef cubes with his chop-sticks. "How much did they pay you?"

"I didn't count, but…they said they would pay me 1,399 yuan."

"Have you thrown away the white envelope?" He frowned.

"I'll throw it away after dinner."

"Will you give me the money now?"

"I will." I started eating. "But after dinner."

He was hungry. I was hungry too.

We finished our food in silence.

When I took his dirty bowl to stack on top of mine, I noticed a couple of grains of rice on the lapel of his jacket.

While I was washing the dishes, the husband had already counted the money.

"There's 1,699 yuan," he said.

I felt contented and proud. I was paid extra when my clients were satisfied with the job I'd done, and I often got paid extra. My ability to cry and sing well had earned me a good reputa-tion. People thought it was a genuine, heartfelt performance. I didn't care how much I was tipped; the extra money showed how much trust people placed in me.

This had been a short-notice crying job. One day Great-Great-Grandma felt tired, so she lay down in her bed. Her card-playing friends went to see her because she hadn't turned up for the game. When they found her, she refused to go to hospital. She wouldn't eat. A few days later, she died.

Many deaths happen at short notice, and some at no notice at all. The family of those deceased were usually in shock as well as being grief-stricken, so they needed a great deal of care and consideration. I was ready for all scenarios; the longer-notice relatives of the deceased deserved just as much care and con-sideration.

There were stories and secrets that I would never have heard if I weren't a funeral cryer. A lot of the time, mourners needed to share their stories, and they wanted to do it with someone who didn't know them too well and who wouldn't share the stories with anyone else. Someone like me. To these people, I was usually a stranger. Most of these stories were tragic or unpleasant—I was always receptive to them, but I hardly made any comments. I was a pair of ears, that was all.

Miserable stories made me feel as if my life wasn't all that terrible; all the stories added a little excitement and life to my boring existence. My head was full of these tales, but I kept them all to myself.

The husband threw me five 100-yuan notes for housekeeping after he put most of the rest of the money away.

Over thirty years ago, when we were studying in the same classroom, he was nice and quiet. I hardly knew him then, and I never thought that one day we would eat and sleep together. I couldn't believe he was the same person I knew when I was young.

The husband always moaned that I was bringing home bad luck, but he never said the cash I made would breed misfortune. When we argued, he would casually say I smelled of the dead. However, when he removed my panties, it was a different matter.

When he was inside me, my body was rigid. Luckily, it was only a matter of a couple of minutes, so if I kept my eyes shut and stayed still, it would be over soon enough. He never knew whether I felt pain or not, because he never asked and I never said anything.

For him, it was like… I actually didn't know how he felt.

I didn't care.

3

I had been crying at funerals for a living for about ten years. It hadn't been my own choice, but there had been no better jobs available. I had to find a job, as the husband and I were both out of work.

In the village, most people around my age had no jobs. They spent a lot of time in the fields allocated by the village committee, growing rice, onions, sweet corn, potatoes and sweet potatoes. We used to have some fields, but they were confiscated by the committee on grounds of neglect. We were now amongst the very few people in the village who had to buy rice and flour. I wish I could turn back time. I would have done all the hard labor needed to keep the fields.

There were hardly any young people left in the village, as there was no future for them here. Who wanted to live in a smelly place? They had all gone to cities for education or work, including my own daughter. Some of the more ambitious young people had gone abroad.

Once young people had families, they would send their children back to live with their parents to save on childcare costs. If they earned good money, they would ask their parents to move to the cities to take care of their households. But that rarely happened. It was hard to survive in cities. Unless they happened to make a fortune, which was very unlikely for the majority. Over the years, two or three grandmas in the village had been abroad to look after their grandchildren, which caused much envy at the time.

I was born in this village. It's called xī ní hé cūn, West Mud River Village. There was enough mud in the village, but there was no river. I had asked Mum and Dad whether there was ever a river before. The answer was *no*. I then asked why *river* was in the name of the village. They said nobody knew why or cared what the village was called. But I cared. Whenever people asked me where I was from, I felt embarrassed. I hated the thought of people laughing at such an ill-fitting name.

There were two mountains that formed the backdrop of the village—one was called South Mountain and the other North Mountain. They were useless mountains. People used to bury their ancestors on South Mountain, but it wasn't in use anymore. In theory, Mum and Dad were allocated grave plots on the mountain by the village committee, but these days people would buy a plot in the graveyard instead. Then there was North Mountain. There was nothing there, apart from some rocks and maybe a handful of trees and plenty of weeds. I had never been to the mountains, and most people in the village had never been there either.

The husband wasn't home. He had snuck out when I was in the backyard.

Mum and Dad used to keep two pigs in a pigsty in the backyard. The filthy pigsty was still there, in the corner of the backyard. There was a chicken run too. We used to have our own eggs and chicken meat. We stopped raising pigs when the husband and I got married. He said it was too dirty and smelly, and it was hard work. Mum insisted on keeping the chicken run. Three years ago, after she moved to the brother's, we ate some chickens and sold the rest away.

There was plenty of room to grow vegetables in the backyard. I mainly grew what Mum used to grow, like onions, beans, snow peas, mooli, potatoes and sweet potatoes, together with some green vegetables, since they were easy to look after. Stir-fried sweet potato leaves were the most delicious.

We had always been tight for money when I was little, so being thrifty was second nature. I used to think money wouldn't be tight one day, but sadly it still often was. I would sit on the bench in the backyard admiring my vegetables. I couldn't help trying to work out how much money I had been saving. I wouldn't make a fortune through growing my own vegetables, but it was a little help.

The husband never told me when he went out. He must have taken some cash and gone to play mah-jongg. He always boasted he was better than most of his friends. Some would play mah-jongg overnight—sleeping and eating were the only other things they did, but he would at least come home for dinner. I thought perhaps he could come home after dinner, which meant I wouldn't have to cook for him, but of course I never suggested that.

People used to come to our house to play mah-jongg until I started working as a funeral cryer. They used to enjoy coming. I would prepare snacks and occasionally watch them play. They would donate a fraction of their winnings as "rent." To be honest, I didn't like to have people around playing mah-jongg, but it seemed they liked the husband and me. It was important to be popular in a village where everyone knew everyone.

I'll never forget the moment when people stopped coming to

our house—in fact, when they left. I had just been offered my first funeral-crying job, so I was excited. There were people playing mah-jongg in our house, and I told them about it. As soon as they heard the news, they put the mah-jongg tiles back in the box and started to make a move.

Now that I brought bad luck and I smelled of the dead, nobody would step into our house to play mah-jongg or chat. I didn't like mah-jongg, but I liked to have some female friends over, eating snacks and gossiping. As for the bad luck and smell, I couldn't disagree too much. You could say it was superstition, but when someone was associated with death constantly, it was understandable that people wanted to keep away from them. I wouldn't go to a funeral cryer's house myself.

As I was home alone, I was able to practice my singing. The husband complained that my singing sounded like a ghost howling, so I wouldn't sing when he was around. I guessed he'd forgotten that he used to tell me I was a good singer.

I didn't need to practice, since nobody at funerals would care about the quality of my singing. The clients would prefer to have a cryer who could sing well, though. The funeral goers paid money to go to "eat tofu," so it made sense that they would like to return home satisfied, as if the whole experience had turned into an occasion for entertainment.

I hated singing at funerals, even though I was paid to do it. After everyone queued up and bowed to the body in the coffin, the calm and solemn funeral turned into chaos. No one needed to show their grief anymore. Some funeral cryers would bring a random band to play loudly, and often out of tune, but I would never do that. Having to sing joyful songs was bad enough.

There was always some pressure for funeral goers, as it was hard to show the right level of sorrow. You didn't have to be as sad as the surviving family. In fact, you didn't even need to be sad, but it's kind to show that you care. At the last part of the funeral, joyful songs would perhaps bring some relief, if not joy, into the air. After being engaged in the crying, I found them awkward.

Being a funeral cryer wasn't easy, as my income relied on dead people. These days, people were living much longer than in the past. It wasn't that I was hoping for people to die younger, but whenever someone died, it was my chance to earn some money. More deaths meant more money for me. I heard I was the best funeral cryer within twenty kilometers. There were not many cryers around anyway.

I took a nap in the afternoon. I hadn't slept well. I never slept well after a funeral. The waxed face in the coffin would appear before me for several days after the event. I always tried not to invest any emotion into funerals. I shed tears, but I didn't cry. Nevertheless, the energy required left me feeling exhausted. When I sat down at home after a funeral, sometimes I couldn't tell whether I was feeling down or simply drained.

I checked the vegetables in the backyard. There were no more garlic leaves left in the pot. I would have to wait for three or four days until they were long enough to cut again. Maybe I could go about the village to find some wild garlic. Wild garlic leaves are slightly wider and they taste more delicate.

They weren't difficult to find along village paths.

I grabbed a small plastic bag and left home.

We still have mud paths in the village. They look okay on dry days, but of course they're grubby and dirty and slippery when it is wet. Toward the entrance to the village, a couple of paths have been concreted and lead to the tarmacked main road outside the village.

"Is that you?" I heard someone's voice and turned around.

"Auntie Fattie." I greeted her and stopped.

Auntie Fattie was a thin woman, a friend of Mum's. She must have been fat before, but I didn't remember.

"What are you doing? I hardly see you."

"I'm going to look for some wild garlic."

"Wild garlic? Are you so tight for money? Nobody eats wild garlic anymore."

"I don't use it that often."

"Are you still crying for funerals for a living?" Her tone was stern.

"Yes."

"A woman from a decent family shouldn't do anything like that."

"I need to earn money."

"Yes, you do. Your husband is useless."

"He's a clever man."

"Cleverness can't feed you. Money can."

"We're fine with money, Auntie Fattie."

"I hope so. By the way, do you always wear clothes like these?" She looked at me from head to toe.

"They're my daughter's old clothes."

"They're too tight for you. Look at the blue trousers you're wearing. People can see the shape of your bottom and your legs."

I didn't say anything. There was nothing I could say.

"Don't be upset. I saw you grow up. I'm your elder."

"I know, Auntie Fattie."

"They say you'll bring us bad luck, but I don't care. People say I'm a cursed woman. I caused two husbands to die."

"You didn't do anything, Auntie Fattie."

"Don't wear those trousers," she said, ignoring what I had said.

"They're comfortable."

"Do men like them? People say you go to the barbershop too often."

"I don't. I only go when I have to."

"Nobody has to go to a barbershop."

★ ★ ★

While I was cooking dinner, I was humming some songs. Even if I wasn't a brilliant singer, I loved singing. It was like communicating with myself. I preferred to sing slow, gloomy songs. They usually made me feel less sad.

I had picked a handful of dwarf beans and thawed out some minced pork. The dish never failed when I cooked them together with some soya sauce, garlic and chili. The husband liked the dish too. When I could, I would cook something he fancied.

"The dishes smell nice." The husband picked up his bowl of rice and dug into the bean and pork dish with his chopsticks.

"Try the hot and sour potato strips." I moved another dish nearer to him.

"I made some money at mah-jongg today. I don't always lose."

"No, you don't." I was tempted to say, *If you don't play, you'll never lose*, but I didn't.

"By the way, have you replied to the daughter?" He changed the subject.

"No. I haven't decided what to say yet."

"Are you not going?" He stared at me.

"I'd like to, but what about my job?"

"Your job? You don't have a proper job."

"I cry and I get paid, so it *is* a proper job."

"You sometimes do some work. You take advantage of dead people."

"I don't take advantage of anyone."

"You're useless when no one dies." He raised his voice.

"At least I'm useful when someone dies." I also raised my voice.

"You're talking back, stupid woman." He stood up and smashed his bowl on the floor.

The china bowl shattered on the ceramic tiles. There was rice everywhere.

I looked at the mess, but didn't move.

"You wasted a bowl." He pointed at me. "I wouldn't have smashed it if you hadn't talked back."

"I didn't talk back."

"Give me another bowl of rice." He sat back down.

So, he was still hungry.

When I was clearing up the mess in the kitchen, my throat felt blocked. I wanted to shout. What would the husband do if I had smashed a bowl? I wanted to talk to someone. I wanted to shout. Would the daughter listen?

I couldn't help thinking about the daughter. I hadn't seen her for over six months. She lived in Shanghai with her boyfriend. He was a taxi driver and she was a masseuse. However, the husband thought she now worked in a supermarket. He wasn't pleased when the daughter moved to Shanghai to work in a massage parlor, since some masseuses had a reputation for selling sex. He nagged me to tell the daughter to quit her job, so the daughter and I decided to lie to him and told him she'd got a new job as a shelf stacker. I didn't think the masseuse job was a problem as I trusted the daughter. On the other hand, it was important to have a good salary if you lived in Shanghai. Masseuses made plenty of money, although the hours were long. She was pregnant now, so she wasn't really fit for her job, either as a masseuse or a shelf stacker.

The daughter had asked us to discuss her plan: I would go to Shanghai to look after her until she gave birth and bring her and the baby to our village afterward. She would stay with us for about two months, then leave the baby here when she returned to work.

I wasn't looking forward to that. I was happy to help her out, but I didn't want to keep the baby in my home. When I had to look after the baby, I wouldn't be able to work as a funeral cryer, since the daughter wouldn't let me. She never liked my job. She might think I would bring bad luck to her baby if I had contact with dead people.

When the daughter was still at school, she had been bullied because of my job. Some children told her I would shorten people's life span, so they didn't want to play with her. Her stationery would sometimes disappear, but would reappear later. Several times, she couldn't find her packed lunch. She begged me many times to stop being a funeral cryer. I wished I could, but we needed money. I wanted to speak to the teachers, but she said it would only make matters worse. It seemed the only solution to it was to give up my job.

It was easy for anyone to say that they didn't want me to be a funeral cryer, but who would make money for the family? The husband didn't have a job. I could help people in the fields or work in a shop in town, but the wages were meager. Funeral crying didn't sound like a good job, but the money wasn't bad. I had skills for crying and singing not many people had. Even now, the daughter couldn't afford to give me what I could earn. I didn't know how much she earned, but she spent more than me and also wasted a lot. She might be willing to give us some money for the extra expenses when the baby was here, but even that wasn't guaranteed.

Most importantly, the daughter needed to apply for a marriage certificate. There would be no maternity leave for her or birth certificate issued to the baby without the marriage certificate. She had said she would "do it soon" several times, and I didn't know what she meant by "soon." I had heard that word many times from her mouth in my life, but it had a different meaning from my "soon."

Sometimes, I thought maybe she didn't want to get married. While she was little, whenever the husband and I argued, I could see her nervous expressions.

★ ★ ★

"When's your next crying job?" The husband lit a cigarette after he poured some sunflower seeds from a paper bag, his feet on the coffee table in front of the sofa.

"I don't know." I shook my head.

"I hate this singing program. Their singing is as bad as yours."

"I know I don't sing as well as you, but people pay me to sing."

"They're as stupid as you. Where's the remote control? I can't stand their singing."

I said nothing, but handed the remote control to him.

"These days people are living too long. Look at those old people in our village. I don't think any of them will die soon." He lay on the sofa, frowning.

"No. Most of them are healthy."

"You should expand your business to cover a bigger area. There aren't enough people to die around here."

"Maybe I could sing at weddings."

"Nobody would want you at weddings. You're too old and too ugly. You also give people bad luck and you smell of the dead." He wiggled his legs.

The husband walked out of the living room and left cigarette ends and sunflower-seed shells everywhere. I didn't want to tidy up after him, but I knew I had to.

All right. *I am too old and too ugly. I give people bad luck and I smell of the dead.*

Did he know what he looked like and smelled of?

What did he give people?

4

There was a crying job to do in a relatively distant town, hú táng zhèn, Lake Pond Town. One of the guests at a funeral had found me through word of mouth. If I agreed to do the job, she would send a car to collect me to discuss the funeral arrangements. It would take about forty minutes to get there by car and I would be paid from the moment I left my doorstep, so I said I would go.

I was curious about the name hú táng zhèn, Lake Pond Town.

"Is there a lake or a pond in this town?" I asked the driver, a tall and dark young man.

"I've no idea. Why do you want to know?" he replied.

"Well, there's no river in my village, but its name has 'river' in it."

"My hometown's called mǎ shān"—Horse Mountain—"but we don't have any horses or mountains in our village."

The client welcomed me at the door of a large house in a Western-style villa development. It was called tài wǔ shì xiǎo zhèn, Thames Little Town. It wasn't far from sài nà xiǎo zhèn, Seine Little Town. There were two oriental stone lions guarding the entrance to the house.

The client was much younger than me.

"My husband was extremely rich, so you'll be paid well," she said, without looking at me.

"Thank you." Nobody needed to be extremely rich to pay me well.

"I'm not that sad." She fiddled with one of her rings.

"I'm sorry."

"I haven't cried since he died." She met my eyes for the first time.

"It happens sometimes. Don't worry."

"I don't know how to fake grief."

"You don't have to fake it. It's inside you."

She shook her head. "No, it's not there."

"It's not hard to cry."

"But I have to cry genuinely. People will be watching me. They'll criticize me."

"I'm sure you'll cry genuinely."

"If they don't think I'm devastated, or devastated enough, they'll gossip about me."

"Show them you're devastated, then."

"That's why I hired you. If they think I'm not sad enough, they'll make up stories about me. They'll take the money away from me."

"I'll show you how to cry." I comforted her.

Her driver brought us some tea and nuts. She smiled toward him.

"My driver's a good man. He helps with our house chores too, as there's not much driving for him to do."

"He's nice."

"Yes. More useful than my husband."

"But your husband made the money."

"Yes," she said. "We were married for nearly twenty years."

"You married young."

"Yes. We grew up in the same village. We went to Dalian to look for work when we were both nineteen."

"What did you do?"

"He learned to be a tiler and painter, and I did the cleaning."

"I used to do cleaning in Nanjing," I told her.

She nodded. "Hard work, but we saved a lot of money."

"You must have been happy."

"We loved each other. At least I always loved him."

"He must have loved you too."

"Maybe. He died in a car accident in Beijing, with a young woman in the car."

"Weren't you in Beijing at the same time?"

"No. He said he was going to a construction-materials exhibition."

"Maybe she was a client."

"They were checked into a hotel as husband and wife."

"I'm so sorry."

"I felt my heart was broken, but I didn't cry."

"Did you tell anyone in your family the truth?"

"No. Not even a ghost."

"Did the woman die?"

"No."

"Was she injured?"

"Yes, badly. She's probably still in hospital."

"Do you think she'll recover?"

"I don't want her to die."

"You're a kind woman. I'll make sure the funeral goes well."

"Make sure the funeral goers think my dead husband and I were a loving couple."

"I will." I nodded.

"Maybe we *were* a loving couple."

I knew it wouldn't be an easy job, but I would earn around 1,500 yuan. That would cover two months' housekeeping expenses for us.

I would never tell anyone the guilty pleasure I felt from time to time between funerals.

As a funeral cryer, I had met all kinds of people, including rich people. Sometimes I was a little jealous of the rich men's wives, since they didn't have to work and they had all the money they needed. I thought I would look beautiful too if I wore expensive clothes and jewelry. Although the husband said I was an old and ugly woman, I grew up hearing people say I was pretty.

However, most rich women I had met were widows. My own husband wasn't close to being rich, but at least he was alive.

I didn't have money to buy any expensive jewelry, but I could buy some new clothes for myself. I'd been wearing the daughter's old clothes for the last few years. She had too many clothes and she would throw the old ones away if I didn't take them. At the moment, I was wearing her gray sweater with the tight jeans.

When the driver brought me back after the meeting, the husband wasn't home, which was a bit unusual since it was dusk and he hardly ever returned after dark. I felt relieved, though. If he were at home, he would complain I was late and he was hungry.

I had no idea when the husband had arrived home, because I was half-asleep when I heard the bedroom door open.

He smelled of alcohol, sweat and cigarettes. He doesn't drink a lot, but I buy beer for him regularly—there are always several bottles in the kitchen cupboard. He must have been drinking with his mah-jongg friends. He drinks when he is happy or unhappy. I wouldn't ask him as I was worried he might shout at me if he was unhappy. I didn't know how to make him happy these days. Maybe I had never known.

When the husband shouted at me or threw things around, I was scared. He said there was nothing for me to be frightened of as he wouldn't hit me. He said I was lucky—in the countryside, it was common for men to slap their wives, often for no reason, all the time. They just could. Did I have to be grateful for not being hit by him?

"You woke me up." I sat up.

"I don't care." The husband threw himself on the bed.

"You're drunk."

"I'm not, you stupid woman." He raised his voice.

I turned on my side.

He pulled the duvet. "Why didn't you open the front door for me?"

"I didn't hear it. I was almost asleep."

"It was cold outside. Luckily I found my keys in my pocket."

He took his clothes off and climbed under the duvet. Within minutes, he started snoring.

I didn't want to sleep next to the husband when he stank of alcohol, but I had no choice.

To him, I didn't seem to exist in bed unless he wanted sex, and it sometimes happened after I came home with money from a funeral. Did he think he was doing me a favor? Or was it a deal? I gave him money and he provided sex? Perhaps his mood was raised by the money.

In the last ten years or so, I'd been the breadwinner in the household. When we both had to look for jobs because we couldn't make ends meet by doing our comedy duo, he didn't try very hard.

I had bought some newspapers with job adverts.

"We can move to Dalian," I suggested.

"Dalian is too expensive."

"But we can make more money. We wouldn't spend much."

"People will look down upon us."

"Which people?" I didn't mind.

"People. They have money."

"We'll have money if we work hard."

"We've worked hard, but we're still not rich."

"We're not poor. We make more money than most people in our village."

"It's not my village. It's your village."

"We'll be poor soon if we don't find any work."

"It's embarrassing to look for a job now. I'm too old."

"It'll be embarrassing when you're properly jobless." I handed the newspapers to him.

"You can go to Dalian on your own." He scrunched the papers up and threw them on the floor.

Then the brother offered to let him use one of his mopeds for free to transport people, but he turned it down.

"Does he think he's my boss?" He was annoyed.

"He's not your boss. You don't have to let him share your profits," I explained.

"So he pities me."

"He's trying to help you."

"I don't need his help. I'm not a beggar."

I was lucky enough to find a job soon, a bad one, as the husband put it. I wasn't excited about being associated with death, but I liked the financial security it provided. Although the husband didn't work, he demanded I give the money to him. He said he was looking after the money for both of us, as he was the *man* and he was in charge of the household. Back in the days when we were a comedy duo, he was the one who dealt with money matters as well.

Whenever I gave the husband money, he noted it down in an exercise book from the daughter's school years then put it in the shoebox in the drawer of his bedside table. He would go to the bank in gū shān zhèn, Solitude Mountain Town, to deposit it when the shoebox was full. He added a lock to his drawer a couple of years ago. He explained the lock was to prevent thieves, not me, but he didn't give me a key. I had thought about asking for a key, but I was worried he might accuse me of not trusting him.

He told me the money I made didn't belong to me; instead, it belonged to the family. I didn't mind who earned money or whose money it was, since I agreed that the money belonged to the family. However, I might feel a little better if I wasn't the only person who was making money. I'd be happy if he showed some responsibility. If not, some gratitude.

He liked to criticize me and made sarcastic comments about me and my work. Why didn't he look for another job himself? We lost our last jobs together, and I found a job soon after that. If he couldn't make money like a *man* who was *in charge*, he'd better shut up and stop blaming the *woman*.

The daughter had texted again, asking when I would make the trip to Shanghai. Did she assume I would go? I knew it would seem wrong if I didn't. I wouldn't say I loved crying at funerals for a living, but the money was important for the family. There wouldn't be any crying work in a modern city like Shanghai.

I couldn't really say "no" to the daughter, as I could still feel my pain from when she was bullied by her schoolmates. I was still trying to compensate for the tears she had when she was at school. Would I ever stop feeling guilty over it?

Since I started my crying job, I hadn't been to anyone's house except for my elder brother's. He lived in dà lóng zhèn, Big Dragon Town, a town about ten kilometers away. I went there several times a year to visit Mum. She used to live with us, but she moved to the brother's after Dad was sent to the care home.

The brother didn't mind my visiting, but the sister-in-law didn't like it. They had a son, and she thought he shouldn't be exposed to my deadly aura. To make her happy, I gave her vegetables from my backyard, homemade pickles and sausages. I had also given them one longevity bowl each to bless everybody and to make up for the bad luck I brought.

Apart from funerals, the place I visited most frequently was the grocery shop in the village. The husband used to do the shopping when I first started my crying job, but he soon complained that grocery shopping was too menial for him. I was happy to take over, which gave me a chance to leave the house.

I liked the fruit and vegetable section in the shop best. Everything was so colorful and I could smell the freshness of the soil and leaves. Whenever I picked up several items and put them into my basket, I could imagine their tastes on my tongue.

There were no restaurants or cafés in the village, as there was no need for them. Most of the villagers could cook well enough, and they weren't fussy about food. When there was a wedding or a funeral, some amateur chefs would be hired to cook banquets.

The only other amenity was a small barbershop on the path leading to the tarmac road. I went there regularly to have my hair done, as it was never busy. I always felt welcome, and the barber never said that I brought him bad luck or that I stank of the dead.

The barber, who was also the owner of the barbershop, was a good-looking man in his, perhaps, late forties. The shop was the front room of his house, with a wonky dining table in the far corner for his hairdressing tools.

The barber moved here several years ago when he married a widow from our village. I believed she was about my age. She'd married a man in our village when I was in Nanjing, so I'd only known her briefly. Then she and her previous husband moved away from the village for many years. When she moved back with the barber, I still barely knew her. The barber limped a little, although you wouldn't notice anything when he wasn't walking.

Sometimes when I passed the barbershop but didn't need a hairdo, I almost wanted to stop to say hello and chat to the barber, but I never did.

I remembered the conversation the barber and I had when I visited last time.

"Your hair's nice," he said. His voice was deep and gentle.

"No. It's thin and dull."

"It's fine, not too thin. Everyone's hair is different."

"I used to have much more hair."

"We all lose some hair as we get older."

"And the hair goes gray."

"That's why you have to come to my shop." He smiled.

"I hope you have more customers."

"They come and go. It's all right. I've got a new regular customer now."

"That's good."

"Do you know her? She's called Hotpot."

"No."

"She's not local. She's married to an older man in the village."

"Is she young?"

"Yes. She's got thick, long shiny hair."

"Is she pretty?"

"She's young, so I guess, yes."

I would also sometimes see Little Sister—she was several months younger than me. She was married to the elder brother of one of my friends from primary school. I had to say I didn't remember her husband's name, and Little Sister called him Dead Devil. I had heard him calling her Dead Old Woman. I occasionally saw him in the village when I was walking around, but he didn't seem to recognize me. Little Sister and I used to do shopping together in gū shān zhèn, Solitude Mountain Town, with some other young women. We sold some of our chickens to her cheaply when we stopped raising chickens at home.

Little Sister regularly gave me chicken poo to use as fertilizer. I wouldn't go into her house. She would drop a bag of chicken poo and stand under her porch, chatting with me for a little while. During the harvest season, she would tell me what produce they had, and I would buy some pumpkins or sweet corn from her.

Otherwise, I almost lived in isolation with little movement. Sometimes I was even suspicious of myself. Was I really carrying something contagious or lethal in my body? Maybe I was. I did breathe in a deadly atmosphere regularly at funerals.

I recalled the times I had enjoyed with the other women in the village, when I didn't stink of the dead. My favorite thing was scraping sweet corn from the cob. We would go to each other's houses to help in turn. There were giant bamboo trays in the front yard. We all sat down on little bamboo stools, rubbing the grains of sweet corn on washboards. There was a lot of gossip, and we all complained about our husbands and laughed.

The other activity I enjoyed was outdoor film nights. The town cinema people would come with older films, and the village committee would pay for us to watch them. That was my earliest memory of seeing men and women hugging and kissing; of course, only on the screen. I had seen young women and young men sneak away in the middle of the film when it was dark and nobody noticed. I stopped going to the films after I became a funeral cryer.

The grocery shop was quiet. An older man was sitting behind the checkout.

"We've got some fresh fish today," he said to me.

"I'll take a look." I nodded and walked to the fridge.

I tried to think who he was. It was the first time I had seen

him in the shop. He looked familiar to me, but I couldn't recognize him. Did he know me?

I put the shopping basket on the counter.

The older man read out the weight on the scales: "So, 850g
of apple, 700g of fish and 1,200g of pork. That's sixty-seven
yuan altogether."

"Thank you." I gave the money to him.

"We've got some fresh vegetables too."

"I grow my own vegetables. I don't need to buy any right
now," I said with some pride.

"We don't grow any at home. My woman doesn't like doing
it."

When I was thinking about what to cook for dinner, I felt
I was living a normal life. This was one of the very few things
I had a say in. If there was some fun in my life, it was when I
was preparing food in the kitchen. It was a time I was alone
but didn't feel lonely.

I peeled two apples and cut them into small pieces. I sprinkled a pinch of salt over the apple, shook the bowl and rinsed
it off with cooled boiled water. Mum had taught me this. The
apple wouldn't look rusty or taste soggy. I asked her why, but
she said she didn't know.

I could smell the sweetness and the freshness of the apple
in the air when I was cooking dinner. Once the husband was
home, we would share the apple.

I liked to share food. Food wouldn't taste good if you had
to eat on your own.

The best experience of sharing food was hotpot. The whole
family would sit around the hot, tasty soup, with laughter and
splashes, and it never failed to cheer you up. However, it didn't
work with two people, especially when there was no laughter.

When did I last have hotpot? When could I have hotpot
again?

The daughter had sent another text, asking me when I would go to Shanghai.

But why wouldn't she get married first? Marriage might not be great, but being on your own was lonely.

5

The husband used to be a better singer than me, although these days no one ever heard him singing.

Our secondary school was in a large town called qīng shuǐ zhèn, Clear Water Town, further than hú táng zhèn, Lake Pond Town. A lot of the students were from villages, some quite far away, like both of ours. He was from shí jǐng cūn, Stone Well Village, which was two or three kilometers from my village.

I didn't take the university entrance exams because I had to drop out in the last term to help Mum look after my sick dad. The husband achieved some good grades, but nobody would pay his tuition fees so he had to give up his university place. His parents died when he was little, and he was living with one of his uncles. His uncle didn't have money to support him. If he had been offered a place by a top university in Beijing, his village committee would have provided financial help.

Dad miraculously recovered after everyone thought he was going to die. He encouraged me to resit my exams the following year, but Mum thought it would be a waste of time and money. She thought it was more important for me to find a husband or a job.

I went to Nanjing to look for a job. Beijing, Guangzhou and Shanghai were the best places to earn money, but I didn't have the courage to go to those cities without a university degree. Besides, the living expenses would be too high.

Nanjing was about 900 kilometers from my village. For me, the main reason for going there was that I had been fed up with the cold winters in the Northeast. There was too much snow and ice, which was also the main reason why I didn't want to go to Dalian, although it was less than fifty kilometers from home. Nanjing wasn't that cold in winter and had been the capital of China during several dynasties, plus it was near Shanghai. The downside, though, was that the summers were too hot.

It was about 1,000 kilometers from Dalian to Shanghai. Going to Shanghai was like going abroad. Everything there was different, and the Shanghai dialect sounded like Korean. It was one and a half hours on the plane or an overnight boat trip from Dalian to Seoul, so Korean sounded familiar and alien at the same time. Shanghainese women were elegant and the men there were gentle and polite. Shanghainese men wouldn't dare to hit their wives. In fact, Shanghainese men wouldn't even hit each other. In the north, there was a saying about men fighting each other: as normal as three meals a day.

In Nanjing, I had odd jobs in restaurants and shops, and I also worked in rich people's households. I'd planned to open a northern dumpling bar after saving up for several years. Then I was surprised to discover Nanjing was such a gourmet city that people there wouldn't care much about dumplings.

My best experience in Nanjing was once nearly getting an admin job in a factory on the city's outskirts, but I missed out because I was unable to provide a permanent address in the city. After that, I sometimes thought about having a Nanjing-ese husband; then my child would have a permanent residence in Nanjing.

My life had a turning point when I came back to xī ní hé cūn, West Mud River Village, for Spring Festival that year. It was Chinese New Year, which was the only time of the year when there were enough days of leave for migrant workers to come home. You had a short break, then it was spring.

Mum handed me an envelope. "Here's a letter for you."

"It's from my secondary school." I opened it.

"What's it about?"

"School reunion."

"Have you missed the date?" Mum asked.

I checked the letter. "No."

"Do you want to go?"

"I don't know. I haven't spoken to any of them for so long."

"That's why you should go."

"Why?"

"To find out how they're doing."

"I'm not doing well, though."

"It doesn't matter. You're not a man. It's okay as long as you're still pretty."

"What do you mean, Mum?"

"Maybe one of your male classmates has become rich and he's still single."

"Maybe."

"Don't be picky. You're nearly twenty-five."

Mum didn't say it, but I knew I was an "old maid," according to tradition.

There was some excitement when I saw my school friends. It was odd. Although boys and girls were not familiar with each other when we were still at school, nobody seemed to be awkward with anyone now.

"You look good," we said in delighted tones to one another.

"What do you do?" was a common question.

"Are you dating?" was also a popular question.

"Are you married?" was another.

"Are you still single? No, I don't believe you." People were nosy.

After dinner at the biggest restaurant in town, we went to karaoke. I happened to sit next to the future husband and another boy. They started talking.

"What are you doing?" the other boy asked him.

"I'm working in a distant relative's company in Dalian," he said.

"It must be exciting to work in Dalian."

"But my job isn't great. It's with a delivery company."

"It's never bad to be in Dalian."

"It costs a lot to live there. What are you doing?"

"I'm helping my father-in-law in his business, near here. We sell trees, tropical trees from Thailand and Malaysia."

"You're married. I don't even have a girlfriend."

After a while, the other boy moved to talk to other people, so the future husband and I started chatting.

The noise of singing in the room was very loud, so we talked loudly.

"How is Dalian?" I asked.

"It's good. Big and busy," he answered.

"I've never been there."

"I'll show you around when you visit me." He took a sip of beer.

"Do you think I'll visit you?" I laughed.

"Do you want to?" He laughed with me.

We didn't notice we were talking to each other for so long that the others started teasing us. They said we should sing a duet, otherwise they wouldn't stop. I didn't really mind, as I liked singing, but was slightly worried about him.

To everyone's surprise, he sang well. Some of the girls asked him when and where he'd learned to sing. He said he'd never learned. Then he offered to sing a solo for everyone.

Later, he walked me to the bus stop. It was dark and I felt embarrassed standing with him waiting for the last bus. We didn't talk.

He shouted to me when I got onto the bus. "I'll write to you."

I didn't say anything to Mum about the reunion, but I hardly slept that night.

I'd never had a boyfriend. I didn't go to Nanjing to look for a husband, but I sometimes hoped I would meet a nice young man there. A man who was a bit clever and earned a bit more than me. But I never had any good luck.

Would he write to me?

He took me to a dumpling bar in the nearest town to my village, gū shān zhèn, Solitude Mountain Town.

It was a small, greasy room, but it was the only place we could sit down and talk. There were dumplings with different fillings, noodles and several cold dishes on the menu.

We ordered two plates of dumplings, one with the cabbage and prawn filling, the other with the pork and dill filling.

"Do you want to try their cold dishes?" He handed the menu to me.

"No." I didn't look at the menu. I didn't want him to spend too much money. The dumplings were already quite expensive. It cost next to nothing to make them at home.

"Try the prawn and cabbage dumpling." He picked up one dumpling with his chopsticks and placed it in my little bowl.

He made a dip with vinegar and chili sauce.

"I like dumplings." He dipped his dumpling in the sauce. "The pork and dill ones are my favorite."

"We make them at home. We grow dill."

"I don't know how to make dumplings. Can you teach me?"

"You don't need to learn. I can make them for you."

"Will you always make them for me?"

"If I have time."

"When are you going back to Nanjing?"

"I'm not. I'm staying here, looking for a job now."

"What kind of job are you looking for?"

"I don't mind. Any job."

"We can look for jobs together."

"You don't need to look for a job."

"I'm thinking about moving back."

"Why?"

"I won't be able to afford to live in Dalian if I have a family."

"But it's not easy to find a good job around here."

"People live around here, and they survive. There must be something I can do."

"I remember you were clever at school. You'll find a job easily."

"Aren't I clever anymore?"

"I'm sure you are."

"But I don't want to live in a village."

"Do you think you can find a job in qīng shuǐ zhèn? It's a large town."

"No." He shook his head. "It's too far from here."

"You can move there."

"No. I want to be near your village and my uncle's."

It was half an hour's walk from xī ní hé cūn, West Mud River Village, to shí jǐng cūn, Stone Well Village, where he used to live with his uncle's family.

It was odd when he said he wanted to be near my village when we were not familiar with each other. Maybe we *were* familiar. We had in theory known each other for over ten years. If a man asked you to go out with him, and you went out with him, that meant you agreed to develop the relationship.

After we'd met in the dumpling bar several times, I was waiting for him to say that he liked me and wanted me to be his girlfriend. But he didn't. Since it took him over two hours to come to gū shān zhèn, Solitude Mountain Town, it was hard for us to meet up. We had to write to each other to say when and where we would meet. There was also a money problem— the coach tickets weren't cheap and the dumplings were overpriced. Maybe he didn't want to be my boyfriend.

I didn't know how other young people became boyfriend and girlfriend and eventually got married. Someone had to suggest something. Who should do it? It must be the man. We'd eaten dumplings together and we'd walked in town. We'd looked in some shops too, but he'd never bought anything for me. He hadn't touched my hands, either. Did he need to ask me whether he could touch me? Did he have to ask whether I was willing to be his girlfriend first?

I wished someone had told me all about it.

Mum asked me, "How much does your boyfriend earn?"

"I don't know. And he's not my boyfriend." I felt annoyed.

"He can't be very rich if he only takes you to the dumpling bar."

"He's not."

"He's not better than the young men I found for you before."

"You told me not to be picky this time."

At that time, nobody in the village had a landline, and mobile phones were rare even in big cities. He would write to me to tell me when he would be around. I would reply as soon as I received his letter. Once, he didn't write to me for a couple of weeks or so. It was a little longer than usual. I wasn't sure whether I should write to him to ask if he wanted to break up? Or did the letter get lost in the mail? All the letters were delivered to the village committee, but I found it embarrassing to go over to ask whether there was a letter for me. Maybe he was ill.

One morning, when I was feeding the chickens in the backyard, Mum said someone was looking for me outside our house. A man, Mum said.

I was embarrassed when I saw him in front of me. I wiped my dirty hands on my apron.

Mum hesitated, then left the backyard.

"How did you manage to get here so early?" I was surprised.

"I was at my uncle's last night."

"Why did you come here?" I asked, then realized it was rude.

"I'm going back to Dalian now. Do you want to come with me? We can watch a film together." He seemed excited.

"I'll ask Mum."

"You don't have to."

"I'll ask her."

Mum let me go.

He said he hadn't written to me because he wanted to give me a surprise.

We took a bus then a coach to get to Dalian. Although it took over three hours from xī ní hé cūn, it didn't feel too long. It was a little embarrassing to be with a man in public, even if no one was taking notice of us. Neither the bus nor the coach was crowded, and I didn't see anyone I knew. He might have held my hand or put his hand on my shoulder, but he never put his hand around my waist.

He took me to a big square and a park, where I saw some Russian buildings. I had learned about them in textbooks, so I knew they were magnificent. It was only when I saw them, though, that I realized just how majestic they looked. What would it be like to be born in a city like this?

We took a look in a couple of cinemas, but didn't find anything we wanted to watch. I didn't have money to go shopping, so there was nothing to do. He had paid for the travel fares and lunch, so I didn't expect him to buy anything for me.

"Do you want to have a rest in my dorm?" he suggested.

"Okay. I *am* tired."

"I share the room with my second cousin. His dad's the boss."

As soon as he closed the door, he held me in his arms. Then he took me to his bed. He unbuttoned my shirt and undid my bra. I felt nervous, so I closed my eyes. I didn't know what he was going to do, and I could hear his heavy breathing. But nothing happened.

"I'm sorry." He sat on his bed and took out a cigarette.

I sat next to him and didn't know what to say. I felt upset, but I didn't know why. Was it because he didn't say anything nice before he hugged me? Was it because he didn't do anything after he undid my bra?

He didn't try to touch me again after the dorm incident. I revisited the situation several times in my mind, but I couldn't understand what had happened. That was the first and only time we were in a place where nobody would see us. His second cousin might have come back, but he didn't. The room was locked from the inside anyway. Why didn't he kiss me? I'd never been kissed.

I had no idea whether he wanted to be alone with me in a room again. We couldn't find a place where nobody would see us anyway. We still met at the dumpling bar. After our Dalian trip, sometimes he took the bus with me to xī ní hé cūn, West Mud River Village. We would walk straight to the bamboo grove.

When the weather was good, we would sit down and talk and sing. He told me what he had done since leaving school, and I told him about my experiences in Nanjing. We sometimes did some singing together. We would hold hands, and occasionally we hugged each other, but no more than that. I noticed he had two shallow dimples. When he was talking and singing, his dimples moved. I would fix my eyes on them.

Although we met regularly, and we had touched each other's hands and hugged, he still hadn't said he wanted to be my boyfriend. I didn't know what I wanted from him. Would I want to marry him? He was kind to me, and I could feel that he liked me and he was happy when he saw me.

Once we went to a wedding together and watched a traditional singing comedy duo at the reception. We realized we could form a comedy duo, and then we would be able to see each other more often. Comedy duos were very popular in the countryside in Northeast China. We tried out some acts at a friend's wedding, and they were well received.

He left his relative's company and rented a room in a shared apartment in gū shān zhèn, Solitude Mountain Town. I had been to his place many times to help him tidy up and cook. He would touch my breasts before I left. I felt he wanted more, but the apartment was always full of noise and other people. The worst thing was that there was no lock on his bedroom door.

We didn't always have work, but we made enough money. He negotiated deals and paid me for each job. He said we split our income in half, and I believed him. I gave some of mine to Mum and Dad, as I still ate and slept at home. I didn't have much money left each month, but I would sometimes buy food and clothes for him. Whenever I cooked for him, I let him eat most of the meat. He would buy snacks for me when he knew I was visiting.

I remembered sitting on the back of his clunky bike on some

summer evenings. The breeze blew on my cheeks gently with some heat, messing up my long hair. Mosquitoes would follow us around, but we didn't care.

He pulled me over to sit on his lap. "Let's get married."

I didn't say anything.

The door was shut, but we knew that anyone who shared the apartment with him could push the door open without knocking. His arms were around my waist. I moved my bottom a little away from him, since I could feel something warm and hard under it. I knew what that was, and I believed Mum would be cross with me if she knew I was sitting on a man. Only bad women would do something like that. But it did feel nice.

"Let's get married," he said again.

"Where can we live?"

"I don't know."

"We can live with my parents."

"I don't want to be a live-in son-in-law. People will look down on me."

"They won't if my parents don't mind. We'd save a lot of money if we lived with them."

"But do I have to change my family name?"

"I'll ask my parents. As long as our child takes my family name, it'll be fine."

"If we have a son, he must take my family name."

I said nothing. There was no point in talking about a son or daughter as we weren't even married. When he suggested we get married, it was out of the blue. Maybe I should ask him to do something for me if he wanted me to marry him. Had I agreed to marry him?

Maybe I could ask him to buy something nice for me.

No, I wouldn't ask for anything, but if he bought me something, I would accept it.

After we talked about the possibility of getting married, he carried me to his bed. He grabbed my breasts and rubbed them hard. Then he felt the zip of my trousers. I felt a little scared, so I pushed him away.

Soon after that, we got married, but he didn't buy anything for me. He became a live-in son-in-law, and he didn't need to give us any betrothal gifts or money, which meant I didn't need to prepare a dowry. It suited us both. I didn't marry well, as my parents had wished, but I was happy enough. It made me think we didn't owe each other anything when we started a new life together.

It all seemed so long ago. In fact, it was so long ago.

I didn't like to think about the past, but I remembered the husband was an attractive man when he was young. He was liked by our fellow villagers. Nobody looked down on him because he was a live-in son-in-law. He had a catchphrase— *I nearly went to university*—which earned him the nickname dà xué shēng, university student. He didn't care what people meant by the nickname, whether it was sarcasm, admiration or praise.

I had never expected to do comedy singing for a living in the long term. We didn't like the jokes we performed—they were mostly crude—but there was money in it. It was the sexual content that the audiences paid the most attention to. There were countless well-known acts we could mimic. People were never tired of the terrible jokes.

Gradually, fewer and fewer people came to our live shows. People were taking less and less interest in comedy acts, as access to other forms of entertainment was available instantly. People used their phones to watch films and play games and they spent a lot of time on social media. The younger generation had no interest in comedy acts.

We didn't have much comedy work for several years. I suggested we go to Dalian, where there were likely to be more opportunities, but the husband didn't want to. Mum said the easiest thing was to have more chickens and pigs in the backyard. Dad offered to talk to the village committee director about whether we could claim our fields back. However, we would have to promise that the fields wouldn't be neglected again, otherwise we'd have to pay a fine. The husband said that if I wanted to do it, I could work in the fields on my own. He didn't want to get involved.

Although the husband had rejected the brother's help before, when the brother's moped transport company needed some riders, the husband reluctantly accepted the offer. He gave up after two or three months. He didn't mind riding the moped if the weather wasn't bad, but he refused to go out when it was cold or wet.

I decided to use the moped myself. I didn't take passengers. Whenever we didn't have any comedy work, I rode to gū shān zhèn, Solitude Mountain Town, to do odd jobs. I would do anything available. It was like working in Nanjing again, although the pay was quite bad. If I did some work in a restaurant, I could have some free food. I thought the food was too nice for me to eat on my own, so I took it home for everyone to share.

Then one day, a funeral cryer in a nearby town was ill, and I was recommended by some people to cover for her. After that, more crying jobs reached me. I didn't want to become a professional funeral cryer, but the pay wasn't bad, and there was no other work available.

Machines and technology couldn't replace human emotions and tears. Thanks to my crying and singing skills, I wasn't abandoned by the digital era. Unfortunately, male funeral cryers weren't needed—traditionally, real men didn't cry, so a man's crying wouldn't sound genuine enough to earn money.

I soon became used to my new role. In some ways, a cryer was similar to a comedy performer, and in other ways, it was the opposite. I dressed up for performances, to make people laugh or cry. Colorful and glossy costumes for comedy acts and white gowns for funerals.

Soon my workload seemed stable enough, so the husband stopped looking for a job.

6

On my walk home from the bus stop after funeral crying, I would normally pass the barbershop. The windows were large and bright, and sometimes I could see the barber through them. I had seen his wife cracking sunflower seeds or chatting to people under their porch. She was a tall, thin woman with short hair, sometimes purple and sometimes yellow. I believe she'd waved to me, but we'd never talked.

The last time I was at the barbershop, the barber asked me whether I would like to try a new hair color.

"Do you want to try a more natural hair color?" he asked me.

"I've never thought about it. I've been having this black for a long time."

"What about chestnut?" He showed me a box of hair dye.

"Chestnut? I thought you were going to suggest yellow or purple."

"No. Chestnut looks natural and trendy."

"But why do you dye your wife's hair purple and yellow?"

"She chooses her hair colors herself."

★ ★ ★

I'd hardly dressed up or put on any makeup or done my hair in my everyday life. I bought my first lipstick and had my hair permed for the first time in my life for my wedding.

I got married over twenty years ago when countryside weddings had started adopting some city wedding rituals, such as wearing Western-style bridal dresses, having a master of ceremonies and playing fewer gross games at the reception.

The countryside bride would wear a red dress at the beginning of the ceremony, then she would get changed as many times as possible, but never into a white dress, which was a symbol of death. The number of dresses showed the wealth of the groom's family. In my case, there was no money to show off. Mum made a red dress for me; it was the only time I had worn a dress in my life. I never counted my comedy-duo and funeral-crying gowns as my own dresses.

We had some photos taken on our wedding day, and they were still in an envelope lying somewhere in the house. Those were the only photos of the husband and me together.

The husband still mocked me over my photos years after our wedding.

"You've got bright red cheeks in all your wedding photos. They look like a monkey's bottom."

"I used the lipstick as blusher. You didn't say anything at the wedding."

"I didn't notice you then."

"What were you noticing?"

"I was too busy drinking. I had no choice."

I kept my wedding dress in the wardrobe. It still looked brand-new, but it didn't fit me anymore. Even if it fitted me, I wouldn't wear it. When could I wear a dress, never mind a red one? I kept some comedy-duo dresses in the wardrobe too. They were glitzy and flimsy and were only appropriate for performing. The quality was poor, but nobody would notice when I was onstage. I had two identical white gowns to wear for funerals.

In my hometown, most women around my age or older had only worn makeup perhaps once, like me, at their own weddings. The young women in the village, including the daughter, had all gone to cities for work, renamed themselves Mary, Helen, Katherine or whatever, then applied thick makeup, dyed their hair yellow or red or purple and put on miniskirts or shorts, low-cut tops and high heels. When they returned home for the holidays, they reverted back to the bumpkins they used to be, calling themselves their old names like Big Flower or Little Red and wearing the same old clothes they wore before they left the village.

Once I asked the daughter, "Do you have an English name?"

"Of course I do."

"What are you called?"

"You won't know how to say it."

"I'll try."

"Lydia."

"Li…"

"You don't need to know."

Maybe she was right. I didn't need to know. I never had an English name. Why would I? I learned English at secondary school and always found it difficult. Now I had forgotten almost all my English. It was trendy for young people to have an English name. It showed that they were modern and part of the wider world, not just their hometown. I didn't really mind not knowing her English name. For the daughter and people like her, an English name was how they differentiated themselves from their hard-up birth family and home when they were in a big city. They didn't want their older relatives to take any interest in their lives, never mind an English name.

★ ★ ★

I used to want to give the daughter some advice on how to live and behave as a young woman. I'd given up now, after I lectured her on her relationship.

I was shocked when she told me she was living with her boyfriend.

"No, you can't live with a man." I was irritated.

"Why not?" She was looking in the mirror, plucking her eyebrow.

"People will know you sleep together."

"People think so anyway if you don't live together."

"Nobody will marry you if you're not a virgin."

"Who said that?"

"Nobody said that, but we all know."

"How many brides are virgins these days?"

"I was a virgin when I got married."

"That was because you didn't have a boyfriend before you met Dad."

"Don't speak to me like that. I'm being serious."

"So am I."

"I'm your mother."

"You're an antique, Mum."

Okay, I was an antique. At least I had my value.

To be honest, compared with the other female villagers of my age, I wasn't an antique. I wore makeup and had my hair done, although only for the funerals I cried at. I wore the daughter's fashionable clothes instead of old women's clothes. I wasn't fat or tatty.

I looked at myself in the mirror. I'd just washed my hair, so it was still damp. The gray roots were getting obvious. I combed my hair slowly.

"You go to the barbershop too often," the husband said suddenly.

"I need to go there."

"You can go. But you go there too often."

"I don't."

"You do. People say I shouldn't let you go to the barbershop on your own."

"What do you think I'll do there?"

"I don't think any man will do anything to you. You're old and ugly."

"Yes, you're right." I felt I wanted to shout, but I didn't.

"You spend too much money on your hair. You dye your hair all the time."

"It's too gray."

"Why can't you buy a black wig?"

"Why should I buy a wig?"

"You can use it forever."

"It's not natural."

"Nobody will notice it's a wig."

"But I'll know."

"You only need to wear it at funerals. Most of the time you're home. Who cares what color your hair is?"

"Don't you care?"

"Of course I don't. Your hair's also so thin. You can buy a wig with a big bun."

"I don't want to wear a wig."

"You don't even need to look nice at funerals. You're not the one in the coffin."

"People pay me to cry. I should look nice."

The husband said nothing. Instead, he cracked a sunflower seed and spat the shell out. I felt a drop of his saliva on my cheek. I wiped my cheek slowly and stared at him. He was at the other end of the sofa, sunk in the corner with his eyes drooping. The room was quiet except for his cracking and spitting noises.

★ ★ ★

When I was sitting in the barbershop, I told the barber that I would try the new hair color.

"The color will suit you. You'll look younger."

"Do I look old now?"

"No. You look young, and you'll look younger." He'd undone my bun.

"Nobody will notice my new hair color."

"I will."

"You will, yes. People wouldn't know I've got a new color."

"That's a shame."

"It's okay. I hardly see people."

"Why?"

"People don't want to have anything to do with a funeral cryer."

"That's not kind."

"I don't blame them."

"You're welcome here."

"Thank you. Maybe I'm wrong?"

"About what?"

"Maybe people in the village aren't mean to me."

"Maybe not."

When the barber was applying the hair dye in my hair, I looked in the mirror.

I didn't look young. How could I look younger?

7

I was at tài wǔ shì xiǎo zhèn, Thames Little Town, again.

The rich client looked tired.

"Thanks for agreeing to spend some time with me before the funeral," she said to me.

"No problem. It's my job."

"I'll pay you some extra."

"Thank you."

"Help me prepare my grief."

"You don't need to. It's there."

"Teach me how to show my grief, then."

"I will."

"If you do a good job, I'll give you a piece of jewelry."

I didn't say anything. I didn't need any jewelry.

"By the way, your hair looks nice," she commented.

"My barber is good."

The driver brought over a tea tray with refreshments. He sat quietly in the corner of the room, fiddling on his phone.

"I used to think I was a lucky woman. My husband was generous to me," the rich client said. "I thought he was faithful."

"He's gone now. Try not to think about it." I took a sip of tea.

"I haven't told our daughter about his death."

"Is she not coming to the funeral?"

"No. She goes to a boarding school in Beijing. I don't know what to say to her."

It was at that point she started crying.

I watched her while she was crying. It was an effective rehearsal.

As I'd wished, the funeral went well.

The funeral was held in the main parlor at the city crematorium. The parlor was decorated with white chrysanthemums and roses. My rich client held my arm tightly.

I knelt before the coffin and took a deep breath before I started to tell the life story of the man in the coffin. My rich client knelt beside me.

"Dear Boss, have you really left this world? You worked hard and you became a successful entrepreneur, but you were never arrogant or aloof. You treated your employees with kindness and you looked after your family wholeheartedly. Your beautiful and faithful wife will never forget all those precious times you spent together. She loved you so much, and she still loves you. How could she and your daughter live without you?"

I paused, as my rich client was holding me more tightly.

I continued, "Your wife and your daughter, they were the most important people in your life. You looked forward to seeing your daughter getting married at a magnificent wedding. It's so tragic. You died so young and you will never see your daughter grow up. What a cruel world."

I could feel my client was trembling.

I started crying. "Oh, Boss, how could you leave us all behind so abruptly? The sky will fall, and the earth will crack.

Your family's life will never be complete. You will be missed dearly forever. Can you hear us? Can you?"

My rich client had given all the guests some gift money upon arrival instead of receiving money, as would normally happen at funerals or weddings. Holding the envelopes containing money, the guests cried loudly, and most of them had tears in their eyes. It was hard to know whether the tears were genuine. Who could tell? As long as enough tears were shed, it was a successful funeral. I certainly cried the hardest, and I clasped my client's hands throughout the proceedings. She was quivering most of the time, but she cried all right. Her eye makeup was smudged, but she looked devastated, which was a relief to me.

My rich client sent her driver to take me home, as she was treating the funeral guests with the tofu banquet. I didn't take any food, so she gave me some extra cash.

The driver opened the door of the passenger side.

"Can I sit at the back?" I asked.

"Of course you can." He closed the door.

I was tired, so sitting at the back would avoid talking.

The car started moving as I shut my eyes. I couldn't forget the strange atmosphere at the funeral, since the funeral goers' crying was neat and almost like a chorus. Maybe it wasn't surprising, as she had gifted everyone some money. My rich client had cried loudly. She was nearly out of breath toward the end. No one would doubt her sorrow and grief. She might have been faking at the beginning of the funeral, but she was moved by her own crying. Loving or not, you had to show people there was love. Sometimes it was like telling a lie. I was the accomplice and creator of many lies.

The husband was home, lying on the sofa and smoking.

He didn't move when he saw me.

"I've eaten," he said. "How much money did you earn today?"

I gave the envelope to him. He took it and felt it.

"There's a lot of money in here." He didn't open it.

"Do you want to count it?" I asked.

"Throw the envelope away and take the money to the bedroom." He dropped the envelope on the coffee table.

"Don't forget to have a shower," he shouted.

I never forgot to have a shower after I returned home from a funeral. Although I brought money back home, I always felt like I needed to scrub away the events of the day.

I washed my hair carefully. The barber had put a lot of gel in my hair to keep my bun in place and it was hard to wash the gel out. A lot of hair fell out while I was conditioning it. The husband was right. Maybe it *was* time to buy a wig.

If I had a wig, I wouldn't need to go to the barbershop anymore. I wondered whether the barber would miss me. No, he wouldn't. I was too old for any man.

I took the money into the bedroom after my shower. The husband was watching TV in bed. It was a Chinese kung fu love story.

To my surprise, he took a quick glance at me when I handed the money to him.

"Your hair doesn't look bad. Good color." He sat up.

"I've had it for several days."

"I didn't notice it. Hotpot's hair is a similar color."

"Hotpot?"

"Butcher's wife's nickname."

"I nearly forgot he had a wife."

"He's a lucky man. She's young and pretty."

"Your wife is old and ugly," I said slowly.

"You know that."

I didn't respond to him, as I didn't want to argue with him when I was getting ready for bed. I pulled my pillow a little farther from his. He had tucked some of his side of the duvet under himself, so my side of the duvet was narrower than his. I didn't protest, as there was just enough duvet for me. The bed was a big one, so most nights the husband and I managed to sleep together without touching each other.

On the screen, a kung fu master was hit by a chopstick thrown by a beautiful young woman and fell to the ground. Those TV series were all the same, and they were repeated throughout the year. It was strange to see ancient people fall in and out of love on the screen. When there were sex scenes, I usually looked away.

Sometimes, the husband would doze off and I would turn the TV off when I woke up during the night to use the toilet. It was hard to go back to sleep afterward, as I would have random thoughts about Mum, Dad and the daughter. The husband snored, and the noise annoyed me and distracted me and tired me out until I fell asleep again.

I was curled up in my usual corner facing the wall when I felt fingers on the nape of my neck. I shivered.

"Are you okay?" the husband asked.

"I'm a little cold," I lied.

"I'll make you warm." He pulled me toward him and moved toward me.

The husband found the remote control and turned the TV off. The ceiling light wasn't working, so there was only the small lamp on my bedside table giving out some dim light.

He lay down and felt my back. It was like tickling, so it felt weird.

I knew what was going to happen and I wasn't looking forward to it. He would pull my legs apart and squeeze himself into me.

However, he wouldn't last long. Soon he would become floppy and fall asleep, leaving me in discomfort.

The husband told me to turn the small lamp off. I did.

He climbed on top of me and pulled down my panties. He thrust himself into me after he quickly took my panties off. I felt humiliated to have my top on when he was inside me. But I would feel more humiliated if I was naked. I kept my eyes open, although I could see nothing.

Then I heard him saying, "The rich widow was generous."

"She thought I was a good cryer."

"After I die, will you need to hire a funeral cryer?"

"No." I thought I'd misheard him.

"Are you going to cry at my funeral?"

"Yes."

"As a cryer or a wife?"

"Why do you ask me that?"

"I suddenly thought you might hate me. I don't mind if you hate me now, but don't hate me when I'm dead." He was moving in and out of me.

"I don't hate you."

"That's good."

He finished and took himself out straight away.

He turned onto his side, and I turned onto mine.

While I was searching in the duvet for my panties, I remembered an old saying—the water from the well and the water from the river never mix.

We'd both better mind our own business.

8

When I woke up, the husband wasn't in bed.

We didn't normally ask each other what we would do or where we would go. We would go out to do stuff, but we each did our own stuff. To be fair, there was no "out" to go to as we lived in a remote village. We didn't worry about each other. We both slept at home at night, so there was nothing to worry about. In a village like ours, the worst thing that might happen would be tripping over a stone while you were walking.

I normally got up first, and sometimes I would go out for a walk, or to the grocery shop, after breakfast. Even if I didn't buy anything, the shop was a nice place to go to. I liked to see people walking around inside with their families. When I was little, there were no shops in the village. I didn't know shops existed until I went to secondary school in town.

If I didn't go out, I would water my vegetables and do some weeding. Weeds were free and tough things: you didn't water them or fertilize them, but they grew fast and were unstoppable. If you didn't water your vegetables, they wouldn't grow. They required attention. They were useful and you couldn't get them for nothing. I'd rather be a weed. I didn't want any attention. I wanted to be free and wild. Then I could do whatever I wanted. With anyone I wanted.

If I left home later than the husband and came home earlier than him, he wouldn't know that I hadn't been home. He wouldn't know even if I was with some man. Likewise, I wouldn't know who he was with.

I checked the time on my phone. It was earlier than I'd thought. Where had he gone? Some of his mah-jongg friends wouldn't be up yet, as they'd been playing overnight.

I walked to the bus stop. I could hire a moped to take me to the bus stop, but I didn't want anyone to see me on the moped. They might gossip about me and I wouldn't have a chance to explain. The buses were infrequent, though. They came once every forty minutes, and they were usually not on time.

I wanted to see Dad. I hadn't seen him for nearly five months.

Dad had been a farm worker, like everyone else in the village, but he didn't work in the fields. He was the village accountant and cashier. He was the only person of his generation in our village who had finished secondary school. He was too clever to be a farm worker. I didn't mean any offence to farm workers, but most of them weren't able to do math as well as Dad could. He was proud of his moral goodness, since he had never stolen any money from the village funds. Normally an accountant looked after the books and the cashier took care of cash to avoid embezzlement, but the village could only afford one person to do both jobs. I was proud of him too, though for a different reason. I was proud because Dad was in charge of the village finances. Most importantly, he earned a little more than the other farm workers.

During my final year of secondary school, Dad became ill for the first time. He had a constant stomachache and could hardly eat. Mum thought it was due to his lack of manual work. He didn't go to hospital since we couldn't afford to send him. He was still technically a farm worker, and farm workers didn't have sick leave or sick pay. He was ill for several months without any income. We never knew what illness he had, and he suddenly made a miraculous recovery while Mum was preparing his funeral outfit.

When he fell ill for the second time, he was physically healthy. His mind suddenly deteriorated, and eventually he became, as Mum put it, an idiot. I didn't agree with her, so I asked the daughter to search online. She told me it was called *dementia*. I discussed Dad's conditions with Mum, and she agreed with me. Yes, but he *was* still an idiot, she said.

Fortunately, the elder brother had become one of the richest farmer entrepreneurs in the area, otherwise we wouldn't have been able to send Dad to the care home. Although I was a daughter, as a live-in daughter I contributed toward Dad's care-home expenses too. The husband had complained about it.

The elder brother had originally borrowed some money from the husband and me and bought a moped to transport people between nearby towns and villages. When he had enough customers, he recruited some men to ride mopeds for him, so he became a business owner. By the time Dad became an *idiot*, the brother was running three minibuses and fifteen mopeds.

Dad was sent to a care home called Sunset after he went missing for the best part of a day and was found in the bamboo grove. He had been ill for a couple of years by then. Immediately after that, Mum moved in with the brother and his family. He and his wife had a son who was one year older than the daughter. He was a "manager" for his father, but I believed he didn't need to do anything.

★ ★ ★

I didn't know how often Mum and the brother visited Dad. The last time I saw Dad was on a secret visit, which Mum and the brother weren't aware of. I didn't tell the husband, either. Mum and the brother didn't want me to visit Dad. They said the staff in the care home might worry about the bad luck I carried and ban the whole family from visiting Dad.

Dad had always been fond of me and thought I was a good girl. When I was young, if Mum thought I was naughty, I would have a "time-out," which included "no dinner" or some extra housework. Dad would defend me by taking my food to me and helping me do the extra housework. Mum would sometimes shout at him for defending me, but he would ignore her. When he first suffered from dementia, I was upset; then I learned to live a normal life without showing any distress. As time went by, I felt fortunate that he was still there somewhere, alive. Nothing could beat being alive.

I liked to be with Dad. When I was in the care home, I could speak freely. I would forget what I did for a living.

The manager of Sunset once caught up with me in the corridor.

"I've seen you at a funeral," she said to me.

"Are you sure it was me?"

"You were wearing makeup, but I can recognize you. You were the funeral cryer."

I kept silent.

When I visited Dad in Sunset last time, he was having lunch with the other residents in the dining room. They were having rice with cabbage and soya-sauce braised pork. Some of the elderly people were being fed by the carers, but Dad could feed himself. I offered to feed him, and he happily accepted it. He finished everything and didn't make a mess.

I had no idea whether the other residents were ill or not, but they were all extremely thin. Most of them wore a fixed expression all the time. Maybe they were too weak to move their facial muscles. It was mostly quiet, with some occasional chatter and movement, but no laughter. Nobody seemed to pay any attention to me. I wondered whether they'd realized there was a visitor in the room.

I went to Dad's room with him later and tidied up his cupboard for him.

He sat on his bed, watching.

"Who are you?" he asked.

"I'm your daughter."

"Do I have a daughter?"

"Yes. You have a son as well."

"I'm a lucky man."

"Yes. You also have a wife."

"Have I met her?"

"Yes, you have."

"When are you coming to see me again?"

This time I mainly went to Sunset to visit Dad, but I would mention the possibility of a crying contract to the manager. I felt I was taking advantage of Dad and his fellow care-home residents, but I needed more work.

Dad was a man of few words. Mum used to say he only liked to talk to me. He had hoped I would become the first university student in our family since he thought I was cleverer than the brother.

Dad didn't go to university. Finishing secondary school was a feat for him and his generation in the village. Had he even dreamt of going to university?

I'd never asked Mum and Dad what they would have liked to do in their lives. I didn't know what I would like to do, but I had a vague idea what I would like to have. A steady income, a bit more than enough money and perhaps a comfortable house.

A grandchild. Yes, I must have a grandchild before I was too old. Whatever you wanted to do when you were young, at the end of the day we all wanted the same things. What I wanted was nothing different from other older women in the village. A grandchild would bring you joy and fun, but you didn't have to take responsibility in the way you did a child. For your own child, you had to worry about their everyday life, their education and their future. But you only needed to play with your grandchild while their parents would take care of all the important matters.

Sometimes I wondered what my life would be like if I had been to university. Would my life be better? What kind of husband would I have? Would I have a son? Would he be cleverer than the daughter?

Would the husband be kinder to me if we had a son?

There would be no answers to these questions.

The bus didn't come, so I took a taxi to the care home.

I was stopped at the reception of Sunset.

"Why can't I go in?" I was surprised.

"I don't know. We have a list of people who aren't allowed in." The guard pointed to the signing-in book.

"Why?"

"The managers make the decisions. They never tell us why."

"Can you phone your manager?"

"No." He shook his head.

"I've come a long way."

"So you'd better go back now. It's getting chilly in the evenings."

The guard's tone was indifferent, almost like that of the husband. They didn't listen to you, as they didn't care about your thoughts.

★ ★ ★

There was a cold wind blowing into my face. I found the card the taxi driver had given me and phoned him. He hadn't gone far yet, so he agreed to return. I asked him to take me home. I wanted to get back as soon as possible. When I was sitting in the taxi, my heart hurt. Sunset was about fifteen kilometers away from xī ní hé cūn, West Mud River Village. I had spent altogether over fifty yuan on taxis today, but all of it had been wasted. That would buy about thirty kilos of sweet potatoes.

Was I really like the plague? When the husband played mah-jongg with his so-called friends, I wondered whether they talked about me. Did they mock him for having a funeral-cryer wife? Did he feel pressure from his friends? At mah-jongg, the person who had won the most money would normally buy snacks for the next day. Maybe I could sometimes buy snacks for the husband to take to share with his friends. If they had said anything unpleasant about me, that might stop them. There was an old saying: if you eat someone's food, your mouth becomes soft.

I heard people say the mah-jongg table was the best place to turn strangers into friends, and it was the very place where people were able to see each other's true colors and their actual intelligence. Although mah-jongg was a gambling game, experienced players hated cheats and respected winners. Some people also argued that mah-jongg was a good game, since it challenged one's attitude toward money and reflected personal qualities. That was where you determined who was trustworthy and who you could dismiss. I wondered whether the husband was regarded as a good person by his mah-jongg friends.

I might be one of the very few people in the village who had never touched a mah-jongg tile. Dad had commented that people who played mah-jongg as a hobby had very low tastes. Mum used to play with friends and relatives, and arguments between her and Dad were inevitable, even when she came home with some winning money. Mum said she only played mah-jongg because she was bored. I heard about people becoming addicted to mah-jongg and ending up heavily in debt. A lot of arguing and fighting in families was caused by mah-jongg.

The husband wasn't home. I felt relieved. He'd left home before me, but I returned home before him thanks to the taxi.

I made a few pancakes and stir-fried some pork with onions. I waited for him until our usual bedtime. I phoned him after I decided to go to bed. His phone was switched off or out of power. Since I had been waiting for him without knowing when he would be home, I didn't eat too much. I put the dinner into the fridge after I ate a pancake.

He might be winning money, so he was reluctant to leave the mah-jongg table. The village was as safe as anywhere could be, so I didn't worry at all. It wasn't a nice thing to say, but I preferred to have the whole bed to myself.

When I was lying in bed, I couldn't stop thinking: What could the husband be doing if he wasn't playing mah-jongg?

For any wife, if a husband didn't come home at the usual time and didn't tell you where he was and what he was doing, she would guess he was with another woman.

I felt humiliated.

He wasn't satisfied in bed with me, so he was looking out for fun with another woman. Whose fault was it if he wasn't happy? Was it my fault? Was I happy? I wasn't looking for another man.

I placed my hands on my breasts. The husband's hands had lingered there before, but now it seemed as if my breasts didn't exist to him. He didn't even take my top off.

Nobody had taught me anything on the subject of sex. I wondered how people would find out how to do it and I didn't know how differently people would do it. After people got married, sex was a routine and duty, and the frequency of it would change over the years. I didn't know when Mum and Dad's sex life came to an end and I never would.

One thing I wouldn't mention or discuss with anyone was that I thought men's bodies looked strange. I was scared when I saw the husband naked in bed for the first time. I also had no idea that a man's thing would swell up.

In fact, I hadn't seen the husband fully naked very often in the last twenty years. When I knew he was going to pull his underwear off, I would shut my eyes, and I turned to my corner as soon as he finished.

I turned the bedside lamp off. Although nobody would see my hands on my own breasts, I still felt intimidated with the lamp on, as if someone was watching me.

I lay there thinking about the daughter in the dark. How was she doing with her pregnancy? I hadn't heard from her for several days. Was she going to sort out her marriage registration soon?

A sudden thought occurred to me: Did the daughter feel any pain when her boyfriend was inside her? I felt ashamed straightaway: How on earth could a mother be curious about her daughter's sex life?

My fingers accidentally touched my own nipples and it brought a ticklish feeling. I squeezed them gently and felt a sensation in my body. It was a familiar but distant feeling.

I shut my eyes, with my breasts feeling restless. I was confused and nervous, but I couldn't do anything about it.

I wanted to fall asleep as soon as possible.

9

The daughter phoned.

"Mum."

"What's wrong?" I could sense something through her tone of "Mum."

"I had a miscarriage last week."

"How could that happen? Are you okay?"

"I'm fine now. I fell off a ladder while I was getting some Chinese herbs from a cupboard."

"Did you hurt yourself badly?"

"I fell on my side. It wasn't too bad, but I found myself bleeding. My colleagues called the ambulance."

"Where are you now?"

"Home. I'm on sick leave."

"Is your boyfriend looking after you?"

"He's not mean to me."

The husband came back before midday. His eyes were puffy.

"Is there any breakfast?" he said when he was walking to the sofa.

"Pancake and pork with onions?"

"Anything."

I heated up the food and took it to him.

"Where were you last night?" I asked.

"I didn't go anywhere." He picked up the pancake and took a bite. "The pancake is cold."

"It's warm. I heated it up."

"It's cold." He threw the pancake on the coffee table.

"Where were you last night?"

"I was at Butcher's, you know, playing mah-jongg."

"You've never played mah-jongg overnight before."

"That doesn't mean I can't. I'm a man. I can do whatever I want." He raised his voice.

"You should have let me know."

"Shut up now. Heat the dish up."

"It's warm."

"It's cold. Make some fresh pancakes." He lay down on the sofa.

"I will."

I went back to the kitchen. There was always so much to do there. The husband hardly set foot in the kitchen. When I was cooking dinner, he might pop in to see what dishes we were having. Most of his daytime was spent playing mah-jongg. If he started playing overnight, he would probably mostly sleep during the day.

It was common knowledge that when people were playing mah-jongg overnight, they took turns to have a nap. Although the game only required four people, whenever there was a game, some people would go and watch. If the husband had had sex with some woman in a different room, nobody would even have known while they were all absorbed in the excitement of mah-jongg.

The husband could also have been to a woman's house. The easiest and safest would be a loose woman in the village, but I couldn't think of any. Could it be one of his mah-jongg friends' wives? He didn't need to worry about being caught when the woman's husband was playing mah-jongg.

The husband looked tired when he walked toward the bedroom. If he had been playing mah-jongg all night, he would be; if he had slept with a woman, he would be too.

I retreated to the backyard and dug up a handful of pak choi. I would normally cook pak choi with a couple of cloves of garlic. I would add half a teaspoonful of oyster sauce to it if the husband wasn't being too annoying. He wouldn't get the oyster sauce today. He wouldn't notice it anyway. I liked cooking, but I hated it when he threw food away. There were only two people in this house. If I didn't cook, we would both starve.

I'd never known what type of husband I wanted to marry, or what kind of man I wanted to live with. In our village, and in a lot of places in the north, if your husband didn't hit you, that meant he was a good husband. The husband didn't hit me, if pinching me in bed wasn't counted.

As a woman, I always understood that the husband was superior to me. I grew up knowing that men were more important than women in a family, because they continued the family name. Losing the family name was an act of treachery against the family, so becoming a live-in son-in-law was most men's last choice. If the husband hadn't been an orphan, he wouldn't have agreed to marry into a woman's household. I felt I owed the husband something, as the daughter took my family name rather than his. Maybe that was why when he was bitter toward me, I didn't always defend myself.

I had learned from secondary school biology lessons that it was actually men, not women, who determined the gender of a baby. There must be enough people who knew about that theory, but nobody would mention it when a baby girl was born. Women were still blamed for not having sons.

The husband would have liked to have a son, but as an orphan, no one would nag him to have one to carry the family name. The main reason he wanted to have a son was to achieve what he hadn't achieved. A son with a university degree and a good job would give him face. But there was the national one-child policy back then. We would receive a large fine if we had a second child. The husband said if we had another daughter, we could give her away. If we were lucky to have a son, he was willing to pay the fine. It wasn't fair, as the younger generation could now have two children. However, for most people, these days it would be too expensive even to bring up one child.

To be honest, I'd also have liked to have a son. It was mainly for the sake of the husband. Having a son would raise the husband's status, perhaps, in the village. Maybe I was too sensitive. Sometimes I felt that people were watching us and gossiping about us. The husband and I didn't get on that well, but we were one unit when we faced the world outside our household. Although the husband had kept his family name when we got married, other people probably didn't believe it and you couldn't walk around telling people. Having a son would straighten his spine—that was what the husband had said.

We tried for several years, but failed.

"You're useless. You can't even get pregnant."

"It's not my fault."

"So you think it's my fault?"

"I didn't say that."

"You're too old."

I also remembered the conversation Mum had with me the night before my wedding.

"Now that you're married, I'm not responsible for you any longer."

"What does that mean?"

"From now on, you must listen to your husband. Obey him."

"Do you obey Dad?"

"You might not think so, but I do."

"Is that all?"

"One more thing. Have you slept together?"

"No."

"It's hard to believe you."

"Mum."

"You've been to his place many times."

"But there's no lock on his bedroom door."

"So you two have thought about it."

"Mum." I shook my head.

"I've never asked you. But did you have a boyfriend when you were in Nanjing?"

"No."

"So you're a virgin."

"I *am*."

Mum continued, "Remember—if your husband doesn't hit you, you're lucky. If he hits you, think what you've done wrong."

"What if I haven't done anything wrong?"

"He won't hit you if you don't do anything wrong."

"I wouldn't hit him if he did something wrong."

"He'd hit you back if you did, so don't." Mum shook her head.

"I said I wouldn't hit him."

"Now, this is the most important thing." She lowered her voice. "We shouldn't let your father hear it."

I almost knew what she was going to say, so I felt embarrassed.

"When you two are in bed, don't move. Don't do anything. Let him do whatever he wants. Only do what he tells you to. Never ask for it. Never ask for sex."

"Why not?"

"If you move or ask for it, he'll think you're experienced."

"I'll remember."

"One more thing. Look after him. Feed him good food. Don't ask him to do any housework. If he wants to help, that's okay. Keep him in good health, then when you're old, you won't have a sick and frail husband to look after."

"I *will* look after him, but not because of that."

"Listen to me. You know I'm right."

But I never told Mum that the husband didn't believe I was a virgin because I didn't bleed. I didn't know whether I should tell her. Then I remembered she wouldn't be responsible for me after I got married. I was also a little worried that Mum wouldn't believe I was a virgin.

For the first time, I started worrying about Mum. Since Dad was sent to the care home, she had been living with the brother and his family. I wouldn't say she had been extremely happy when she and Dad were both living at home, but I didn't know if she got on well with her daughter-in-law. Whenever I went to see Mum, everything seemed fine. How could I know whether everything was fine when I wasn't there? I hoped the sister-in-law didn't boss Mum around. That would upset Mum. The nephew was no harm. Mum should be happy to see him around.

Mum had been used to taking charge of things at home, so it would be hard for her now to live under someone else's roof. In theory it was her own son's roof, but in practice it was her daughter-in-law's. Would she miss Dad? Although she said he was now an *idiot*, she didn't mean it—she couldn't find a better term for him.

I hoped Mum didn't miss Dad. It was sad when you had to miss someone. I would never say it aloud, but I sometimes wished I could travel back in time to the days when the brother and I were young and we didn't need to miss anyone.

I had always liked the husband before we got married, but I wasn't sure whether I had ever loved him.

In films and novels, people said *I love you* before they kissed each other, so it looked like love was conditional. But both *I love you* and kissing seemed nice things. If the husband had told me he loved me, I might say it back. The husband kissed me briefly in the bamboo grove before we got married. The kisses were awkward. I thought our noses got in the way, but we didn't know what to do.

I didn't know whether he loved me when we were young. Did he want to marry me only because he wanted to sleep with me? He had never said I was beautiful or that he couldn't live without me.

On our wedding night, the husband was full of alcohol, like most grooms. Before we got married, I looked forward to enjoying our first night. I also believed he would be happy that at last he could do what he had wanted for a long time. Unfortunately, it wasn't what I'd expected. I was more scared than anything else. And I saw it as my humiliating failure. It must have been my fault that he didn't last. I wasn't attractive enough. He didn't kiss me, either. The worst of the worst was that I didn't bleed.

There was the Chinese nation's favorite line, which came from a Yugoslavian film: *there would be bread, and there would be everything.* Things were supposed to turn better in the future if you were optimistic. How could my life be better if the husband thought I wasn't a virgin?

The husband was hungry, so I filled his bowl with rice. It was the famous large-grain Northeast rice. Supple, fragrant and moist. People from other parts of China liked the rice too. It was our local pride.

"You're nice to me," he said when he was stabbing his chopsticks in the rice.

"Wasn't I nice to you before?"

"You were. Had I never told you that?"

I shook my head.

"You're a good woman," he said quickly.

"You don't need to say that."

"No, I don't need to. We're husband and wife."

"Why did you say it to me today?" I asked.

He didn't respond. Instead, he slurped a big mouthful of chicken soup.

"I didn't lie. I played mah-jongg all night last night." The husband lit a cigarette after he put down his bowl and chopsticks.

"You've told me."

"Don't you believe me?" He blew a smoke ring.

"What else could you have been doing?" I stacked the dirty bowls.

"Were you home last night?"

"Yes."

"You can't prove you slept at home last night, can you?"

"You're right. I can't." I shook my head.

What a strange man.

"But there's no evidence that you were home alone." He blew another smoke ring.

"I *was* home, and home alone."

"I'm joking." He laughed and then frowned.

"You should have let me know if you were going to stay up for mah-jongg."

"I didn't know I would end up playing for the whole night," he said and stretched his arms.

"Mah-jongg is so good that it keeps you awake all night."

He stared at me. "You're mocking me. You hate mah-jongg."

"Lots of people become addicted and lose all their money."

"I'm sensible."

"But do your mah-jongg partners like you?"

"Maybe. I don't cheat, so nobody hates me."

"It's good that nobody hates you. I've bought some snacks for you to share with them."

He looked surprised. "Why?"

I didn't answer his question, but opened the cupboard to show what I had bought. There were about ten colorful packs of sunflower seeds, chips, biscuits and chocolate. "Tell them I bought them."

His eyes lit up. "I will. I will."

While I was doing the washing up in the kitchen, I couldn't help imagining the husband lying in bed with a woman. I couldn't figure out what the woman looked like. Thin or fat? Old or young? Pretty?

Maybe he *was* playing mah-jongg all night.

10

"Can I borrow your mirror?" the husband asked me when I was putting out breakfast. Pancake, steamed buns and rice porridge with pickled mooli I made myself.

There was only one mirror in our house now. We used to have a table mirror, but the daughter took it with her when she moved out. The husband used to use the table mirror when he was shaving before it was packed by the daughter, but he managed without a mirror now.

I handed him my makeup mirror and he gazed attentively at his reflection before stroking his slightly stubbly chin.

"You don't look old," I said.

"I'm examining my wrinkles."

"They're not as bad as mine."

The expression on the husband's face had been unusual. It brought back a memory. He used to look in the mirror to check his makeup when we were running our comedy duo. He hadn't cared about his appearance since he stopped working. What had made him check his face, or wrinkles, again?

I hadn't had a crying job for a couple of weeks, but I didn't worry. When it was too cold or too hot, more elderly people would die. When it was wet or icy, there could be more road accidents; in summer, there were drownings. On the whole, during the change of seasons, more people would die. I never made any detailed notes, but that was what I noticed and felt.

It was heading into the depths of autumn now, and extreme cold weather was on its way. Unexpected deaths would take place, especially in poor areas in the surrounding countryside. Older people with chronic illnesses would suffer more, especially if they didn't have heating. I tried to think whether we had many old, ill people in the village.

Winter wasn't just the worst season for the elderly, it was the worst season for me and the husband, and perhaps for everyone in the village. There was still no gas in the village. The village committee had been promising that we would have either gas or natural gas since I was in my thirties. It took a long time to light a coal stove for cooking, so cooking could be a pain if the stove died out at night. On the bottom of the stove, there was a small metal sliding door. When I was little, Mum taught me how much space to leave to make sure the embers in the stove were still smoldering in the morning. The water in the kettle on the stove would be very hot after the night. I felt delighted when I mixed some hot water and cold water to wash my face.

In winter, if you kept the stove running overnight, it would make the space around it warm. I would keep the sliding door on the stove half-open and move it next to the bedroom door at night when the cold was extreme, between 15 and −5 Fahrenheit. I would get up in the early hours to put another layer of coal on, otherwise the stove would die out. Most people would dive under the duvet straight after dinner in the depths of winter. Two duvets and a hot-water bottle would make your night tolerable without a lit stove.

The village committee had also promised heating, but nobody knew when the promise would be realized. The villagers didn't blame the committee for that because the directors didn't have heating at home either. I blamed the mountains. The heating system required large-scale electricity pylon construction, but the mountains had made it difficult.

The first thing I would do on a winter morning was to boil the kettle and fill two flasks with hot water. The flasks were our wedding presents from Mum and Dad. On the body of the flasks, there were faded red and pink peonies and red double-happiness Chinese characters. They were huge and clunky. They were useful for showers. Since there was no hot water from the shower, the cold water would have to be mixed with the hot water from the flasks. We kept an enamel bowl in the bathroom. It was big enough for me to sit in, but I hardly did it. The water would flow out if I sat in it, and some of the water would be wasted. I didn't want to waste warm water, especially in winter.

I didn't know how much money we had in savings. The husband won and lost at mah-jongg and claimed that overall he made a small net profit. The bank accounts were in his name. Sometimes I was worried about what I would have to do if he died unexpectedly, since I wouldn't know how to deal with the bank cards. It wasn't that I wanted him to die, but one of us would die first. If it was me, I wouldn't need to worry about anything.

We had discussed how much money we should save up for our old age, but we never reached a conclusion. First of all, we didn't know how long we would live. Secondly, we wouldn't know the prices of things in the future. As we didn't have a city residence so were technically farm workers, neither of us had employee pensions.

If you were born into a rural residence household, you were classified as a farm worker, for most people, forever. It was the city residence that determined social status and the stability of income. Once you went to university, the rural residence would automatically be converted into a city residence. You wouldn't lose your city residence unless you couldn't find a job after graduating. If you married someone with a city residence, you could apply for a city residence yourself, and it would take many years to be offered the status.

The only way we could survive old age was to have savings, as much as possible. We didn't expect the daughter to help us out. Traditionally, only sons had a duty to offer financial support to their parents. But the sons were not guaranteed to have excess income to provide for their elderly parents, who were usually in ill-health. We didn't have health insurance since we didn't have employers. In theory, people without city residence like us could buy health insurance. The husband and I didn't buy any, though, since we were healthy enough. I didn't want to imagine how miserably ill I might become in the future.

The husband and I would be old one day. We didn't know who would die first. The one who died second would be left to live alone like Great-Great-Grandma or be sent to the care home like Dad.

One late morning, when I was about to leave the house for a walk, I heard banging on the front door.

"Who's that?"

"Me."

I opened the door and saw the husband. I was surprised, as he had gone out to play mah-jongg after breakfast. It was too soon for him to be home.

He was pale and breathless. "Butcher died."

"How?"

He shook his head. "We were playing mah-jongg in his

house. He had a big win. He was excited, then he dropped dead right there at the mah-jongg table."

"Heart attack?"

"Maybe."

"Why didn't you stay to help?"

"Somebody called the ambulance. A lot of people have gathered in their house."

I saw him shaking, so I held his hand and led him to the sofa.

"Sit down. I'll bring you some water," I said.

The husband held the cup with both hands and looked blank.

"So, Butcher died," I said.

"Hotpot's left alone now."

"I don't think I know her. Hotpot?" The name rang a bell.

"His wife. You didn't go to their wedding. You were crying at a funeral."

"Has she got long hair?" I remembered that time the barber described a young woman's thick, shiny hair.

"Yes. Shiny and smooth."

"Why is she called Hotpot?"

"She loves to eat hotpot."

So, Hotpot was called what she ate. Yes, her hair was shiny, but how could the husband know that it was *smooth*? He wasn't her barber. You had to touch someone's hair to know it was smooth. I remembered now I was crying at a funeral, so I didn't go to her wedding. The husband was right. But was I invited to the wedding? Nobody would want me at a wedding. I had a crying job at the right time, so embarrassment was avoided.

Although we'd been living in the same village, Butcher and I had hardly seen each other for many years. I doubted that I would have recognized him.

He was several years older than me and he hadn't married until recently, maybe a couple of years ago, to his distant relative's distant relative, a young woman who was a little, how to say it, *slow*. I had heard that despite the fact she was *slow*, she was pretty and obedient. I had possibly seen her briefly in the village, but I'd never spoken to her.

Butcher used to hang out with the brother and some other young men in the village, but he'd never had a proper job. He'd done some odd jobs including working as a cleaner in a butcher's shop, but most of the time he'd relied on his parents. The reason he couldn't find a wife when he was younger was mainly because he lacked a regular income.

"Do you think you could offer some free funeral crying for Butcher?" the husband asked.

"No, I can't."

"Hotpot wouldn't be able to afford it."

"But I need to earn a living. I can offer a courtesy price to her."

"What about half price?"

"No."

"You make a lot of money from each job."

"It isn't much money when you consider the periods of time I don't work."

He raised his voice. "Hotpot is poor."

"I haven't made any money recently. When was the last time someone died in the village?"

"This morning. About one hour ago." The husband stared at me, and his tone was filled with—I didn't know...maybe anger, maybe frustration.

When I was in bed texting the daughter, the husband walked into the room.

He threw himself onto the duvet and asked, "Will you offer Hotpot half price?"

"No."

"No?"

"No." I put my phone down.

He sat up. "I'll pay some for her."

"What? Your money's my money. It's the money I've earned."

"I earn money too. I earn money from playing mah-jongg."

"You say you earn money from playing mah-jongg."

"Do you not believe me?" He sat up.

"I believe you. Okay? So, you're going to spend *your* money on Hotpot instead of our food."

"I'm trying to help her. I've already told her we'll offer her half price."

"We," I repeated.

"Yes. I've got a deal for you. You can earn some money. You said you haven't made any money recently."

"And you think I should be grateful?"

"It doesn't matter if you don't want to cry for her. She probably doesn't need a funeral cryer."

"If your husband died, I imagine it wouldn't be hard to cry."

"Right. It wouldn't be difficult for you. You know how to cry." He lay back down.

Yes, he was right.

The husband took his clothes off and slid under the duvet like an eel. I had just changed the bedding, so it smelled fresh and felt crisp. His legs, unexpectedly warm and not actually too rough, accidentally touched mine when he was pulling the duvet.

I watched him move toward me and tuck his side of the corner of the duvet under his shoulder. Strangely, he hardly smelled of cigarettes. When did I last see him smoke? Yesterday? Two or three days ago? Honestly, I had no idea. I didn't pay much attention to what he did. It would be hard for him not to smoke. He had opened packets of cigarettes lying everywhere in the house. It was possible that the freshness of the bedding had masked his smell.

"I'm worried about Hotpot," the husband said.

"You're kind."

"Everyone knows she's stupid. Maybe she is. Yes, she is. She's basically an idiot."

"Why are you mentioning this to me?"

"She hasn't got any income, and Butcher didn't leave much money behind."

"Did Butcher have a job?"

"Not a real one. Sometimes he helped in the grocery shop."

"She's got a house," I said.

"But what can she do with the house? A small old house."

"It's better than ours. It's got a proper first floor."

"She doesn't need that space."

"Can't people still go to her house to play mah-jongg? People can pay her a little more rent than they did before."

"People will go somewhere else to play if she charges more. Someone needs to stand up for her."

"You can."

"I can't. People will gossip. They'll think I'm too close to her."

"Maybe you *are* too close to her."

"I'm not."

"You're already standing up for her."

"At the moment what she needs is a funeral cryer."

"I'm sure she'll be fine without a cryer."

"She might say something stupid at the funeral."

"That's none of your business."

"Butcher was my friend. He was your brother's friend too."

I nodded. "You've reminded me. I need to tell the brother Butcher's dead."

Maybe I didn't have to tell the brother. As the old saying went: good news doesn't leave the house, but bad news is spread thousands of kilometers. Someone would tell him before me. Maybe he already knew.

The husband put his hand on my thigh, but I moved my leg away.

. I didn't want him to touch me when he was thinking about Hotpot.

There might not be much so-called love between the husband and me, but I didn't feel comfortable when he showed considerable care for another woman. The husband didn't touch me again. I slowly pulled the duvet up toward my chest and tucked it under my shoulder. He pulled the duvet toward himself, then grumbled something. There was nothing under my shoulder now.

Poor Hotpot.

It must have been awful for her to see her husband die like that. It was an awkward and humiliating experience to watch your husband drop dead at the mah-jongg table in front of a crowd of people. It was such a worthless death.

I would lend Hotpot a hand. Women should help women, especially if she was a young widow.

11

Hotpot was ill.

As soon as the husband phoned me, I rushed to Hotpot's house.

The house was freezing. Hotpot was lying in bed, looking pale. Her eyes were red. The husband was sitting at the edge of her bed, looking at her.

I felt her forehead. It wasn't terribly warm.

I put the kettle on in the kitchen. While I was waiting for the water to boil, I opened the fridge and the freezer. To my surprise, there was plenty of food.

I handed the cup of hot water to the husband. "Hold the cup. I'll help her up."

I asked Hotpot, "When did you last eat?"

"I don't remember," she said in a weak voice.

"You drink this water and stay in bed. I'll cook a hot meal for you."

"Thank you."

"Don't worry about the funeral. I'll cry for you. For free."

"No, Big Sister. I'll pay. I've got money."

"You'll feel better after you've eaten something." I comforted her.

"I won't."

"You will."

"Butcher, you know, he dropped like a stone." She shook her head.

She started coughing.

I took some food out of the fridge and started cooking.

The food in the fridge was neatly organized. There were some fresh beans and onions. They looked the same as the ones in my backyard. I found some pork ribs in a plastic container in the freezer. I couldn't say the pork looked like mine, but the container looked similar to mine. Had the husband stolen our own food and brought it here? I wouldn't have minded if he had asked. But all beans and onions looked the same, and most containers looked similar.

I put Hotpot's dinner out for her on her bedside table, sweet and sour spare ribs as well as onion fried scrambled egg with rice. The husband placed a cushion behind her back attentively.

She thanked me before she picked up her bowl of rice. She asked us whether we would like to eat with her, so I filled a bowl with rice for the husband. There wasn't enough food for three people. I would eat at home.

The husband would stay while I returned home to fetch a hot-water bottle for Hotpot.

If I didn't return to Hotpot's house, I wondered when the husband would leave. He might not even come home to bed. He could say that he had fallen asleep on her chair, like someone visiting a patient in the hospital ward.

Hotpot might not be clever, but she was attractive. Since men all liked beautiful young women, I wouldn't be surprised

if he climbed into her bed. There was also a killer—she had
large breasts. If he started touching them, he wouldn't be able
to keep his hands off her.

I couldn't find the hot-water bottle. I texted the husband.
There was no reply.

When I was lying in bed, I felt my breasts gently. I wanted
them to be touched, after they had been untouched for many
years. I could ask the husband to touch them, but I didn't and
wouldn't. It would be insulting if he showed no interest.

Maybe someone else could touch my breasts. Another man. I
didn't know any men, though. Yes, I did. There was one man.
The barber was a man, and he wasn't even ugly or fat. Would
he be different in bed from the husband?

I turned the lamp off, trying not to think about my breasts
or the barber.

The husband didn't come home until the next morning.

He looked exhausted.

He explained. "You know Hotpot was unwell last night."

"Yes."

"I sat on the chair."

"Did you not sleep in her bed?"

"I didn't."

"You didn't."

"I was waiting for you to bring the hot-water bottle, but
you didn't."

"I texted you."

"My phone was out of power. What did you say?"

"*I couldn't find the hot-water bottle.* Is she okay now?"

"I think so. I won't go today."

"By the way, are you pleased I'll offer her free crying?"

"I heard you say it to her yesterday. Why did you change
your mind?"

"We should all help a widow."

"You're kind, but you don't need to do it for free."

"No? Is she *actually* short of money?" I asked casually, not expecting a reply.

I remembered Hotpot had said she could afford the funeral crying.

Butcher's funeral had been delayed for a couple days due to Hotpot's cold. Funerals were usually arranged as soon as the death certificate was issued. In the case of Butcher, it took a little longer. Although he had died at home, he was taken to the hospital to have the cause of death confirmed. The coffin would be transported to their house on the day of the funeral. The funeral would be held in the backyard, extended to the living room. The backyard was too small, and a crematorium hall would be too expensive.

In the countryside, even some rich people preferred to hold funerals at home, as it was easy for people to attend. Most friends and relatives lived nearby. Countryside funerals were usually followed by a family parade to show others their piety and grief for the deceased elderly or the sorrow for the tragically perished young.

There was a tradition of not inviting guests to the funeral. People would come voluntarily after the date and venue were revealed. There was a risk of nobody turning up at funerals apart from the family, but it wouldn't happen. People in villages were mostly very kind to each other and they were also nosy, so Hotpot didn't have to worry. At least all Butcher's mah-jongg partners would come.

I had been to many funerals in my life, mostly in recent years as a funeral cryer. It seemed nobody cared how the deceased had lived, as long as enough money was spent on their funerals. It was impossible for people to tell how well you treated your family while they were alive. However, if you didn't give your loved ones an expensive funeral, it meant that you had never cared about them. All your effort to have taken care of your family would be in vain. It sounded weird, but a funeral also needed to be lively. There was silence during parts of the funeral, but it had to be noisy toward the end, and jolly when people were eating. And the more people and more money, the better.

For example, Great-Great-Grandma had been a legend for longevity, but nobody would know whether she had got on with her family. She had lived so long, which was the most significant achievement one could make. However, nobody had ever wanted to find out about her everyday life, especially how she had felt. Whether she had been happy or not wasn't something people would be interested in. With a grand funeral to conclude, like a finale, her life was perfect.

I would say I didn't think Hotpot was *slow*. People thought she was stupid because they were told so when she was married to Butcher, to make her more matched with him, as she was much younger. According to what I had heard about her, she had the intelligence of a ten-year-old, but from my own contact with her, she seemed to be like an average adult. I had met young women like that. They might look innocent or naive from the outside, but were more complicated on the inside. I could be wrong. Who would know?

Hotpot insisted on paying for my crying.

She explained, "I don't want to send Butcher off cheaply."

"I can show you how to cry, then you don't have to pay me to cry."

She gave me a faint smile. "I know how to cry, but your crying would be better."

"You can accept some free crying from a big sister."

"But you're not my sister. I hardly knew you before."

"You know me now."

"I can afford it."

"No, you don't need to pay."

I was ironing the black belt of my funeral-crying gown with a large enamel mug of hot water when the husband came back, probably from Hotpot's house.

My iron stopped working a long time ago. I didn't need an iron very often, so I didn't buy a new one. If the top of the gown wasn't too wrinkly, it would be fine, as nobody would notice anything when I knelt down. I usually took more care of the belt and the hot water didn't do a bad job.

I used to wear a white belt over my funeral-crying gown, but the husband complained that I looked like a ghost. To be honest, looking like a ghost was appropriate for funerals. The standard funeral outfit for a next of kin was an oversized hood, a loose gown and a belt in all white linen. The white belt could be replaced with a linen rope. The sight of a group of people in white kneeling down at a funeral was harrowing. To avoid arguments with the husband, I started using a black belt, but I didn't throw away the white belt. The husband didn't know I was keeping it. He would be angry if he knew. Was I keeping it because he didn't like it, even if he didn't know it existed?

"She's fine, isn't she? I mean Hotpot." I was still concentrating on my belt.

"Not too bad."

"Strange that she doesn't want to accept free crying."

"It is."

"She's got money. More than we think."

"I don't guess how much money she has."

"I don't either. By the way, do you think she's stupid?"

"I'm not sure."

"You know her better than me, don't you?" I tried to look into the husband's eyes, but he wouldn't look at me.

"I suppose so," he said after a brief pause.

I picked up the mug and took a sip. I didn't like to waste water. "She's pretty. It's a shame she married a poor middle-aged man. No, an older man."

The husband said, "Butcher liked her."

"Did she like him?"

"It seemed she did."

"But nobody really knows how they got on."

"Nobody knows how we get on either."

"Unless we tell people."

"We might not tell the truth."

"People might not believe what they hear anyway. They might not even believe what they see," I pondered.

"What do you mean?"

"You can pretend in front of other people."

"I won't."

"Have you said anything bad about me to people?" I asked.

"No."

The husband was lying in his corner, snoring. I had been tossing in bed, unable to sleep. I didn't know what was keeping me awake—his snoring or something else. I had heard how some men snored all the time, and the wives wouldn't be able to fall sleep without the noise.

I moved toward the husband and pulled his shoulders to change his position. Now he was lying on his back and he had stopped snoring. I had done this before, and it never woke him up.

I might be wrong, but the husband smelled better now. He hadn't smelled bad before, but he had always smelled of ciga-rettes. It was difficult to say what he smelled of, but it was cer-tainly subtly softer. To be honest, I wasn't interested in his smell and he didn't care how I smelled. It wasn't that we discussed the matter, but I could sense it.

The husband rolled toward me and grabbed my arm.

He murmured, "Hotpot, Hotpot."

I hesitated before responding, "Yes. What do you want?"

"You know." He put a hand under my vest top.

I wasn't sure whether he was awake, so I held my breath and didn't move.

His fingers reached my nipples—a rare sensation made my body shiver. I felt angry, but at the same time felt too weak to push him away. *Okay, I am Hotpot.*

When the husband climbed off me, I wondered whether he knew who he had just penetrated. He and Hotpot must have slept together. At least, he was dreaming about it.

I couldn't care less about all that, though. I had felt good. I had to follow my body. It was telling me to be quiet and enjoy what was there. The only shame was that the feeling was so brief. It ended when I thought it was becoming better.

Strangely, this time it didn't hurt.

I wouldn't say a word. I wouldn't.

12

Butcher's funeral was a little awkward, as there weren't many attendees. A couple of Butcher's distant relatives turned up, but nobody from Hotpot's family came. I had no idea whether she had informed her family about Butcher's death. I saw the brother. We only nodded to each other, but didn't talk, and he left before me. I didn't count, but there couldn't have been many more than twenty guests. The atmosphere at the wake later was more cheerful. It was understandable, in a way, for people were celebrating a new life. Hotpot was pregnant.

The husband and some of Butcher's mah-jongg partners cooked the tofu banquet in order to save money for Hotpot. The food at wakes was usually nearly as abundant as at weddings and it cost a fortune in restaurants or to hire local chefs to cook at home. I didn't stay for the food. I thought perhaps people would prefer not to have me there. Most of them knew me, so it would be awkward if they didn't want to be near me or talk to me. They probably wouldn't notice when I wasn't

there. I also didn't want to be there with the husband, as I didn't
know how to speak to him when other people were around.

After Butcher's funeral, Hotpot and I became friends. Well,
maybe we weren't quite friends, but she was the first person
outside my family I was able to be physically near to for a long
time. She never said anything about bad luck or my deadly smell.
Neither did she say that I couldn't be near her. She could ask
the husband to pass on a message to me if she didn't want to
see me. Possibly she was too stupid to understand the nature of
my job, but I'd rather believe she wasn't stupid but didn't mind.

I did speak to the barber, but it was mainly about hair and it
was associated with my funeral-crying job. When I visited Hotpot, it made me feel I was a normal person and I didn't worry
too much whether I was carrying any ill fate.

Since early pregnancy could be difficult and the shock and
grief could lead to a miscarriage, I went to Hotpot's house regularly to check on her. I helped her tidy up the house, throw
unwanted things away and work out what needed to be bought.

"How are you feeling?"

"I'm not bad."

"Do you have morning sickness?" I asked.

"No."

"That's good."

It was good that she was well enough. It was also good that
there was no need to check on her every day.

Hotpot and I also made some reusable nappies from old
T-shirts and bedsheets. In the city, rich people would use dis-
posable nappies, but they were too expensive and wasteful for
poor people living in the countryside. I also checked the house.
It was okay, but maybe a fresh coat of paint on the internal walls
would be nice. The baby deserved a nice place to be born into,
even if there would be no father.

★ ★ ★

I was knitting a blue baby sweater when I asked Hotpot, "How long have you been pregnant?"

"I don't know. It hardly shows." She stroked her belly.

"When did you have your last period?"

"I don't remember."

"You need to go to the hospital to find out how long you've been pregnant," I suggested.

"I was going to, but then he died."

"You'd told Butcher?"

"Yes. He was happy." She nodded.

"Poor man. He'll never see his son."

"Do you think I'm going to have a son?" she asked.

"That's what people would say. Always, a son."

"Do you want to have a son?"

"I used to. It's impossible now."

"It's good to have a son to carry on the family name."

"Luckily, both of my parents-in-law are dead. I mean, I didn't have any pressure."

"I'm the same." She had a faint smile.

"I'm a live-in daughter, so my son would have my family name if we had one."

"Men don't like that."

I changed the subject. "What are you going to do after the baby is born?"

She shook her head. "I don't know."

"Can you sing?" An idea came to my mind.

"I like singing, but I can't sing in tune."

"As long as you're not too shy to sing in front of people, you'll be fine."

"I'll be fine for what?"

"You can be a funeral cryer, like me."

"No. I'm bad at singing."

"It doesn't matter whether you're good or not."

"Why not?"

"Singing isn't important. You're good at crying. Your crying sounded genuine at Butcher's funeral."

"I *was* sad."

"Sorry. I meant you were sad."

"Maybe I wasn't so sad, but when I saw tears in your eyes and heard your lovely crying, I couldn't help crying myself."

"Thank you. I never thought my crying was lovely."

"It was. Your crying made people believe your own husband was dead."

"I don't think he wants to hear that."

She blushed. "You know what I mean. I say stupid things. I'm not clever."

"You're not stupid," I said quickly.

"I am."

"As long as your singing is loud and clear, that's all that matters."

"It's embarrassing to sing loudly in front of people."

"You can practice."

"I'll think about it."

"By the way, you need to eat well and rest well."

She nodded. Her eyes were moist with tears.

The husband hadn't played mah-jongg since Butcher's funeral. I might be wrong, but there was something glowing in his eyes. It hadn't been there before, or at least, I hadn't seen it for years. Was it there before we got married? He didn't lie in bed playing on his phone as much now, and he was talking about buying a wall mirror.

Although I suspected he was having an affair with Hotpot, I had sympathy for her—a pregnant young widow. Whenever I made dumplings, I would ask the husband to take some to her. If they were together, I wouldn't be able to do anything to stop them anyway.

However, I couldn't forget that old saying: if you assume your neighbor has stolen your axe, the more you look at them, the more they look like a thief.

One day, I received a letter.

I was surprised when I opened it. It was from the rich woman I cried for at her husband's funeral:

Dear Cryer,

How are you? It has been quite a while since I received your service. I hope your business is going well, not that I hope a lot of people have died.

Death is the most frightening and devastating thing for all of us, and no one would want to talk about it until it has happened, when it is too late. It is so awkward when death meets your loved ones. I wish I could be the deceased, not needing to grieve, which is unbearable, which could go wrong.

I would like to thank you formally in this letter and tell you how grateful I was to you for the funeral crying you provided. When my husband died, the shock was beyond everything else, so I didn't have a chance to grieve until you helped me pull myself together. The atmosphere at the funeral was exceptional. Your pre-singing and pre-crying prepared me for my tears, and they also allowed me space to cry genuinely. I felt my tears were real and I was able to bid a proper farewell to the husband I had mistrusted.

I also want to tell you one regret I have. My husband and I had an argument before he left home. I didn't say goodbye to him. I had always suspected he had a lover. If I had known he would die soon, I wouldn't have argued with him. All would be forgiven if he could come back to life.

My daughter and I are going to move abroad. We have not decided when or where yet. I have hired an education agent to look for schools for my daughter in different countries. Once we have chosen a suitable school, we will move to the country where the school is accordingly. Our driver will also go with us. He has been a loyal employee and he will be very helpful when we are abroad. He wants to look after me.

I want to live in a place where nobody knows me and nobody knows about my past. Hopefully we will start afresh. My daughter is excited about the prospect of being able to see me every day. I have been lying to her. I have told her that her father is abroad, looking for schools for her and a house for us. I will tell her everything once we have settled into the new place.

No, I will not tell her everything; I cannot tell her about her father's love affair.

I visited the woman after the funeral. She had been in ICU for some time, but eventually she survived. She was still recovering, but she would be fine, the doctors said. I left her some money. She had been the husband's responsibility, so he would have approved of my decision. I can live without any guilt or regret, and I would like to wish her better luck with men. Although I was furious about their relationship at first, I now hope they had loved each other. By the time I arrive in a new country, she will probably have forgotten about my late husband. At least I hope so.

The reason I am writing to you is that I need to talk about my story and do not want anyone to do anything about it, so you are the safest choice for me. Your experience and experiences must have prepared you for all the strange and awful situations you might not like to witness and deal with.

While I am writing to you, one thing occurs to me—your job must be extremely hard, as there is no joy in it. I have no idea whether you like your job or not, but I would like you to know that your job is important and I hope you always find some satisfaction or pride in it and you receive gratitude like mine.

Although we have only seen each other briefly and we will most likely not see each other again, I feel close to you.

I wish you a very happy life, whatever it is like right now.

Best wishes from a strange friend.

A strange friend—strange as in odd, strange as in unusual and strange as in unfamiliar. However, it was from someone who regarded me as a friend, who did not worry that I might bring her bad luck and I might smell of the dead.

She called me a "friend." If she didn't go abroad, maybe we could become friends. I folded the letter carefully back up along its original creases. I should keep it in the drawer of my bedside table. I had been keeping all my letters there since I was a young woman.

I hadn't received many letters in my life. I received a few from Dad when I was in Nanjing. Dad's letters were long, and he wrote to me on behalf of the family. He would start with current affairs in detail before he asked me how I was. The letters usually finished with a question in which he asked me whether I was short of money and told me he could post me money if I needed any. I had to laugh, as I went to Nanjing to earn money, not to spend it.

Before we got married, the husband would write to me about when and where to meet up, since there was no other means of communication available to us. He could use his work telephone, but he could only call our village committee to pass on a message to me. Of course we wouldn't want to do that. At that time, mobiles looked like thick bricks, and they were only owned by wealthy people. He once said one of his ambitions was to own a mobile phone.

I had never expected written praise like this from anyone. I made sure the funerals didn't go wrong and I readily accepted payments. At the end of the day, it was business, and it wasn't appropriate if you became too sentimental. I didn't have enough energy for all that grief. If you did feel the sadness, the best thing to do was to ignore it, bury it and forget about it. For me, it was mostly about making a living. I couldn't pretend that I didn't care about money.

There was a golden necklace enclosed in the envelope. The

chain wasn't that thick, but it was shiny, with small diamonds, and it felt solid. It looked nearly new. It looked expensive and beautiful, but I wouldn't wear it. People would think I had lost my mind if I wore a shiny necklace. I could give it to the daughter, or sell it. Then I remembered a French short story we read at secondary school: a woman borrowed a diamond necklace from a rich friend but lost it; she spent many years earning money to pay for it, but at last found out the diamonds were fake when she had lost all her youth and beauty.

So you couldn't trust rich people.

The rich woman also said in the letter their driver wanted to "look after" her? What did she mean? Maybe the driver liked her? Or did she like him?

The husband had been talking about getting a job in town. I didn't make any comments. I used to ask him to look for a job, but he said there were no jobs around and he was too old.

In a way, I was glad he wanted to work, but it would have been more helpful if he had tried when he was a little younger. I hated to say it, but I wasn't too optimistic about his chances of finding new employment. Who would give him a job? What kind of job could he do? He had no skills, and he was lazy.

Occasionally I thought about the allocated fields we had lost—there was still pain inside me. The brother and I used to help Mum grow wheat, rice and sweet corn in our fields after school. We did well, so we never needed to buy flour or rice after we handed in our quota of crops to the village. The brother moved to town after he left school, but he still helped Mum in the fields whenever he could.

Farm workers were only given allocated fields in the early 1980s, when China started its reform and open policy. Before then, all the adult villagers had to work full-time in the fields.

After the revolution in 1949, landlords' fields were confiscated by the government to be used by the villages. Villagers went to work in the fields to earn labor points that would be calculated into cash and crops at the end of the year. The points were not determined by hours of work, but by age and gender. Young men were worth the most points as they were potentially the most productive laborers. For this reason, teenage and adult sons were important. I remembered playing with the brother by the ditches near the fields while Mum was working in the fields. It didn't occur to me then, but when I was older I realized Mum was the only laborer in our household for a significant period of time.

With the allocated fields, the harder you worked, the more you harvested, whatever your gender or age. I didn't like to work in the fields, but I never said so as I didn't want anyone to think I was lazy. The brother said he hated it, but he worked hard in the fields. As a teenage countryside girl, my ambition was to go to university so I could earn a salary. I didn't want my income to be affected by weather or insects. I wanted to be paid regularly, but I never had a salary.

However unwilling I was, there always seemed to be no escape for me from the fields and the countryside. After I got married, it was my responsibility with the husband to work in the fields with Mum. Although we were busy with our comedy duo, we still had time to work in our allocated fields if we wanted to help.

The husband showed no interest in growing anything. Since our comedy-duo income was good enough, we decided to buy flour and rice from our fellow villagers instead. Eventually the fields were neglected and the committee took them off us and let them to other villagers. Now I was regretting our neglect.

If the husband wanted to help earn money, he didn't need to find a job. We could raise several pigs in the backyard. The chicken run was still there too. It would be smelly and dirty, but the money we could make wouldn't be smelly or dirty. However, the husband would never do it. As his nickname suggested, he was a clever "university student" and there was no way to persuade him to deal with pig poo and chicken poo.

I couldn't help imagining what the husband and Hotpot were doing together. He could be the father of her baby.

Hotpot didn't have a reputation for being clever, but who cared whether she was clever or not? You didn't need to be clever to be able to attract men. Twenty years before, I was as slim as her, and my hair was also shiny and smooth. No men would be interested in me now, because I was old and ugly. I didn't have large breasts either. They had never been large.

The husband would jump into Hotpot's bed—if she allowed him.

My guess could be wrong, but I felt a little jealous, and the thought of being cheated on made me frustrated. The best solution was perhaps to find some more crying work to do, to distract myself with some other engagements.

Maybe I was right. The reason why Hotpot didn't want to accept free crying could have been that she felt guilty for already having the husband "for free." That was her sympathy for me.

When I was planning my work, I felt sad.

Why should I work so hard?

Why wasn't anyone there to take care of the financial side of my life?

Then I remembered I had a daughter.

Life couldn't be the worst if you had offspring, even if I only had a daughter. I was ready to work hard for her, as I had no choice. At least the daughter had my family name. This was the so-called biggest benefit of being a live-in daughter.

The husband had wanted a son desperately. To be honest, it was more important for me to just become a mother, so it was for the husband's benefit I hoped to have a son too. As a live-in son-in-law, having a son would really give him some face. When the daughter was born, he was cross with me, as if it was all my fault. I felt some guilt over the husband's anger, and I naturally had some sympathy for the daughter. The feeling of being in the same boat made me want to give all my care and love to the daughter.

The husband got over the pain of not having a son when the daughter started talking. He thought she was cute and almost as clever as a boy. We both hoped the daughter would go to university and have city residence. Her schoolwork was fine until she went to secondary school. She started hanging out with the other girls, doing nothing, and stopped listening to me. I was disappointed.

Maybe it was my fault that she hated school in the end. I'd wanted her to live the life I'd dreamt of when I was young, but she made her own choice, which was no choice. Would things have been different if I wasn't a funeral cryer? She might have liked school and done well.

Whatever, the daughter would have all my life savings. When I was old, hopefully she would take care of me. After I died, she would send me off properly. Would there be a funeral cryer for me? Would she be as good as me? A funeral cryer crying for a funeral cryer sounded comic.

The daughter would use my money to pay for my funeral costs. I wouldn't owe her anything. She would even have quite a lot of my money to herself after I was gone.

When things didn't go well, money would talk.

13

The husband had looked up his address book and found some useful contacts, most of whom were our old school friends. I was sometimes curious about what my old friends from secondary school were doing and how they were doing. Nobody would be living a life like mine. I didn't want them to know I was a funeral cryer still living in a smelly village.

"Are you sure you want your friends to give you a job? Isn't it like begging?"

"I don't care as long as they give me a job."

"You're too old. You said that several years back."

"When they offer you a job, they don't say you're too old."

"Why do you want to look for a job now?"

"I'm just thinking...if I died suddenly like Butcher, I wouldn't leave any money behind to you."

"Maybe it's the other way round. If I died suddenly, you wouldn't have any money."

I was expecting him to be mad at me, but he wasn't.

I sensed some tension in the silence.

★ ★ ★

Unfortunately, the husband didn't find a job he wanted after talking to some of our old school friends. There had been jobs available, mostly working in shops or restaurants. He had thought about accepting a kitchen job in gū shān zhèn, Solitude Mountain Town, as a sous-chef, no previous experience required. The pay wasn't bad, with free food and accommodation. However, he said he preferred to come home every day, which meant arriving home around midnight. I didn't see any problem in that. He would be fine if he didn't see me every day, and I wouldn't mind. That was probably his excuse for not accepting the job, though. Everybody knew kitchen work was tedious and exhausting.

The husband moaned about his misfortune for several days after he gave up looking for jobs. He'd discovered that a couple of his friends were rich now. He thought it wasn't fair, as he was cleverer than them.

He shook his head. "I shouldn't have left Dalian in the first place."

"That was because we were getting married. You said Dalian was too expensive."

"I didn't know I would end up with no job and no money. This ugly village has killed me."

"If you want to make money, we could raise pigs and chickens," I suggested.

"They stink."

"Nobody likes the smell, but it brings money."

"It's disgusting to have to deal with pig shit and chicken shit."

"Nobody likes it, but that's life."

"Life's better without shit."

"Life would be better if you were a real 'university student.'"

He stared at me, but didn't say anything.

The mah-jongg gang had been quieter since Butcher died. Perhaps they were all worried they might die suddenly at the mah-jongg table too. They were usually forgetful, though. We all were, weren't we? After a while they would be the same again. At the moment, they were probably mourning for themselves silently—as if it could have been them instead of Butcher.

I couldn't help imagining the husband and Hotpot naked in bed. They probably wouldn't sleep together during the day in her house. In our village, people might come to your house without any warning. They came to say hello, they came to ask you what you were doing, and they came into your house for any reason or for no reason. If your dinner was ready, they would sit down and eat with you. Many people still didn't lock their doors during the day. I had been to Hotpot's house and noticed her door was always open. Of course, she could lock the door and ignore any knocks when she was with a man.

He might well be there genuinely helping her with some housework or keeping her company. He used to be a kind man when he was young. He used to fetch water from the village well for our older neighbors before there was tap water.

I didn't stop the husband from going to Hotpot's, nor did I encourage him.

There wasn't much to do in the village. If he didn't go out, he would be at home with me. He would be lying on the sofa watching TV, cracking sunflower seeds and smoking most of the time. When he was home at lunchtime, he wanted a proper hot meal too, otherwise he would say I was a lazy woman.

I admired our ancestors, whoever had invented mah-jongg. How could people kill their time if there was no mah-jongg to play?

The daughter had asked me to go to Shanghai again. She was back at work and planning to get pregnant again. She was worried she might have another miscarriage, so if I stayed with her, it would give her some peace of mind.

I would go to the post office to send some money to the

daughter instead. She could eat better with some extra money. I had been keeping some cash in my pillowcase, and the husband didn't know anything about it. I didn't have to save secret money, since I didn't have anything secret to spend it on. The husband would be angry if he knew. Perhaps that was why I was doing it.

Money could provide some peace of mind for the daughter. My main reason for not going was that nobody knew how long it would take her to fall pregnant again. As much as I would like to be useful to the daughter, there was more freedom in my own house. Although having children before getting married wasn't a good idea, I didn't want to say anything to stop the daughter. These days, many young people wanted to be childless. As a mother, I should feel grateful that she wasn't one of them.

Then I thought about Mum, my own mother. I had been distracted by Butcher's funeral and Hotpot's pregnancy, so I had forgotten to visit her. She wouldn't mind as long as she knew I was fine. I'd spoken to her on the mobile phone—in fact, on the brother's phone. She seemed cheerful enough.

What about Dad? Since I wasn't allowed to visit the care home, I felt it was inappropriate for me to ask either Mum or the brother whether they had visited Dad recently. Sometimes it was difficult for me to say how much I'd like to see him. Since he was unable to recognize me, my disappointment and pity had accelerated and nearly exceeded my affection for him. Sadly, the bond between a father and a daughter was gradually fading, but I never felt myself unworthy in his company.

I heard someone behind me greeting me while I was choosing some pork in the grocery shop. I turned around. It was the barber. He was holding a couple of large empty crates.

"Hey, how are you?" he asked.

"Fine. How are you?"

"Good. How are you?" he repeated.

"I'm okay. I'm not busy at the moment, so I don't need to have my hair done." I pulled a strand of hair around my ear.

"I went to Butcher's funeral, but you didn't see me."

"Sorry."

"That's all right. You were busy, and you left early."

I apologized, "It was my fault. I should've seen you. It wasn't a big funeral."

"It wasn't your fault at all. By the way, your singing was good."

"Thank you. But I didn't like those songs."

"Why not?"

"I feel like a clown singing joyful songs at funerals."

"That's what people want. Don't worry."

"I'd rather not."

"Your hair looked nice. I'll have no work if you start doing your hair yourself."

"I didn't think about my hair, as the funeral was in our own village."

"I was only joking. I can't really make a living as a barber anyway."

I was curious and pointed to the crates. "Are you working here?"

"Sort of. I co-own this shop."

"I didn't know that."

"Not many people do." He shook his head.

"It's a nice shop."

"I usually come here in the morning to sort out the deliveries and check the stock."

"Hard work, isn't it?"

"It's not too bad." He rolled his sleeves up and looked around.

"You don't look like a barber today."

"What do I look like?"

"You look like… I don't know."

"I like to spend my time in the barbershop."

"Why?"

"It's quiet there."

"It is."

"By the way, I saw you walking in the bamboo grove," he said when he was walking up to the counter with me.

"I like to have a walk."

"Me too."

Yes, I knew that. I'd seen him in the grove, but I didn't know he'd seen me.

When I was making my way out of the shop, the barber caught up with me. He was holding a little basket. "Try these eggs."

"I've got eggs at home."

"These are special. I bought them off our fellow villagers. Free range and fresh right from the chicken runs."

"How much are they?"

"They're free from me."

While I was searching my bag for the wallet, he had gone. I turned around. He was walking to the back of the shop, limping a little. I felt sad. When he asked me what he looked like, what I was thinking was he looked handsome. He would have been happy if I had said that. But how could I say something like that to a man?

I spent the rest of the day tidying up the house and cooking. I looked at the eggs from the barber. They were slightly smaller than normal ones. I knew what they tasted like and I liked the bouncy orange yolks. I used to pick up fresh eggs laid by our own chickens; sometimes the eggs were still warm.

I used three eggs to cook an egg and tomato dish. I bought the tomatoes in the shop, bright red and ripe. The husband took half of the dish to Hotpot's, and I filled a small container with the soya-sauce braised pork for her. I learned to cook the pork

Shanghai style when I worked as a nanny in Nanjing. It was sweeter than the Northeast style.

When I was eating dinner alone, again, I started imagining what the husband and Hotpot might be doing. Hotpot's tummy was showing, so hopefully they wouldn't have sex now. I hated my thought, but couldn't help it.

While I was eating the egg from the barber, he popped into my head. I'd never spoken to him outside his barbershop before our brief encounter today, although I had seen him here and there in the village. It seemed absurd, as if we were in the wrong place. Nobody in the village knew him well, since he was a newcomer. No, he wasn't that new anymore, but he was still seen as a newcomer. When a man didn't have friends he had grown up with where he was living, he would always feel like a newcomer.

I tried to work out how long the barber had been here, but I couldn't. Three years? Or more? I couldn't remember when and where I saw him for the first time, either. He was the first barber in xī ní hé cūn, West Mud River Village. I used to do my hair myself until he arrived.

When I saw the barber in the bamboo grove, I was surprised. I had never seen anyone there before. For most people, there was nothing in it. For me, there was memory. The husband and I used to spend some happy times there together. We talked about our future plans and sometimes the atmosphere was almost romantic. It was in the bamboo grove where we had some awkward kisses. Recently, I recalled the husband's gentle smiles and dimples when I walked in the bamboo grove on my own.

I forgot who I was and what I did for a living when I was in the bamboo grove.

After my walk in the bamboo grove one morning, I dropped by Hotpot's house. I had brought some homegrown vegetables as well as a baby hat I had knitted.

The house door wasn't locked, so I knocked and pushed it open.

Hotpot was sitting at the dining table, sewing some baby clothes.

"You're good at sewing."

"No, I'm not good at anything."

"Yes, you are."

I sat down and picked up a piece of cloth.

She felt the baby hat. "You're so kind."

"I'm doing what a big sister should do."

"Nobody's done anything for me in my life before." She shook her head.

"I'm sorry."

"It's okay. I didn't do anything for others myself."

"I'm sure you did."

"No. I was lazy and selfish. I never worked."

"I think you can become a good funeral cryer in the future."

"I've told you I can't sing."

"You can cry."

"But it's hard when you have to pretend."

"It's not quite pretending. You always feel sad," I explained.

"I guess if people pay you to cry, it's not too bad."

I didn't agree with her, but I didn't want to discuss it.

I looked around and asked, "Is there anything I can do for you?"

"If you're not in a hurry to go, you can fold my clean washing." Hotpot pointed to the chair next to me.

"I've got time." There was only a small pile.

It was mostly her underwear, including a pair of long johns and a thermal top. Then I picked up a pair of panties—no, they were men's underwear.

"Are these...?" I didn't know what to ask.

"They were Butcher's." Hotpot grabbed the underwear.

"But he's dead."

"I'm wearing them because I need something loose to wear." She stroked her tummy.

"But you can buy large panties."

"Large underwear are the same. And free." She put the underwear on the pile I had just folded.

"It's good to have free things." I stood up. It was time for me to go home.

I didn't walk straight back home. I wanted to find the husband. I didn't know where he was playing mah-jongg. They went to different people's houses to play. I didn't want to phone him. There was a fury inside me. I wanted to ask him to his face why his underwear were in Hotpot's house.

But were they his underwear? They were gray with some loose threads. The husband did have similar underwear. Did men's underwear all look similar, though? Hotpot said they were Butcher's underwear. Why couldn't I just believe her?

I unlocked the door. The house was cold.

The husband wasn't home yet. These days he was coming back home later and later. He didn't explain and I didn't ask. I didn't care much, as I didn't mind being on my own.

Since I was home alone, I took out my makeup mirror to look at myself.

There were several light lines on my forehead, and the wrinkles around my eyes were deeper. My hair was frizzy and needed trimming, but the worst was the gray roots. If I wanted to look young, I had to have my hair dyed once every three months. Was it worth doing it?

Did I want to look nice for the husband or myself?

My phone rang.

It was the daughter. "Mum, are you coming to stay with me?"

"Not now."

"When?"

"When you're heavily pregnant."

"Is Dad home?"

"No."

"He's playing mah-jongg?"

"Yes."

"Has he been nice to you?"

"We're fine."

"Don't argue with him."

"We don't really argue."

I put the phone down on the bedside table next to an old light bulb. It was from the ceiling lamp. It went about a year ago, and the husband said he would change it. Of course nothing happened. I'd recently changed it myself, but he hadn't noticed.

I used to think it didn't matter whether I had a husband or not. I'd never said it to anyone, but I considered the husband a nuisance and a burden. Since Butcher died, I'd been thinking about the benefits of having a husband. In theory, the husband should be able to fix things, carry heavy things or reach things that were too high for me. Although I had to do all these things myself, at least there was someone I could talk to, and someone I could eat with.

But if the husband kept his underwear in another woman's house, he'd better stay where his underwear were. Hotpot said those were the underwear she was wearing. Odd. I would never wear men's underwear, old tatty men's underwear.

The room was quiet. It was so quiet that I wished the night would be over soon. I wanted the morning to arrive so I could get up.

As I was on my own, I thought about Dad, who was also alone. I wondered what he would be thinking in his box room at night when he was unable to fall asleep. I wasn't allowed to go to the care home any longer because I was a funeral cryer.

What if I told them I had stopped being a funeral cryer? A lie wasn't a proper lie if there was no damage done to others.

Visiting Dad would make me feel like a good daughter. It was a matter of feeling good. It might not be important to other people, but it was important for myself. He wouldn't know whether he saw me or not, but I would know.

Then I thought I should have my hair done before I visited Dad. These days, I only had my hair done for funeral crying. Why shouldn't I have my hair done on an ordinary day?

Dad and my hair: they were so unrelated to each other, but they seemed to be tightly connected with my idea of *feeling good*.

I could also see the barber an extra time.

14

The husband hurried back home soon after he went to Hotpot's.

"Hotpot's crying," he said as soon as he saw me.

"Crying? Did you make her cry?"

"No, I didn't. She was crying when I arrived."

"Did she tell you why she was crying?"

He shook his head. "I asked her, but she wouldn't say anything."

"Do you think she'll tell me?"

"You're both women."

"But I can't lend her large underwear."

"What are you talking about?"

"Underwear."

I shut the door behind me.

The front door was ajar. Hotpot was eating dinner. She wasn't crying, but her eyes were puffy.

"How are you?" I greeted her.

"Fine."

"Are you sure?"

"Yes."

"Were you crying earlier?"

"Yes. I sometimes cry. Crying makes me feel better."

"Do you want to talk to me?" I sat opposite her.

"I do, but I don't."

"Why?"

"Nobody can understand me."

"Maybe I can."

"But you can't make things better."

"Perhaps I can make you *feel* better," I insisted.

"No, you won't make me feel better, but I don't mind telling you. It's a secret."

"If it's a secret, you don't have to tell me."

She pointed to her bump and said, "This baby. I don't know who the father is."

I sat up.

She continued, "I thought I knew, but now I'm not sure."

I still didn't say anything.

She sighed. "It doesn't matter, does it?"

"I think it matters."

"I've slept with other men."

"I imagine so."

"Do you want to know who those men are?"

"I don't mind if you don't tell me." I felt my heart was in my throat. Was the husband one of them?

"They've asked me not to tell anyone. They all have wives."

"Don't tell me, then."

"They were nice to me. They made me feel comfortable." Her face glowed.

"You made them feel comfortable too."

"Yes, they told me that." She nodded.

"You had a husband."

"But he was… He wasn't a strong man."

"How did you start with those men?"

"At first they came to say hello when Butcher wasn't home."

"So you let them visit you again."

"I didn't invite them."

"They touched you, and you let them?"

"They gave me money."

"That was prostitution."

"And presents."

"What kind of presents?"

"Usually snacks. Also shampoo and once a fake gold necklace."

"They weren't very generous, were they?"

"I know, but I wasn't worth that much."

"So they didn't give you a lot of money either?"

"They didn't have a lot of money. They tried their best."

"Did they force you to sleep with them?"

"No."

"Did Butcher know?"

"I told Butcher. He said if I didn't mind, he wouldn't mind."

"Did he actually say that?"

"We were poor."

"Do you think Butcher set it all up?" I was furious.

"I don't know. I don't mind."

"But you were crying because you didn't know who fathered the baby."

"I cried, but I wasn't angry. I was sad."

"If Butcher wasn't the father, that means your baby will have a father, still alive," I said.

"You're right." She nodded.

I asked, "How many men?"

"Only three."

"Only three," I repeated. "It's easy to find out, then."

"How?"

"Hospitals do tests."

"I won't do it." She shook her head. "They don't want their wives to know."

If the husband was one of those men, there would be a one in four chance of him being the baby's father—three customers and Butcher. How could I find out whether he was one of them? I suspected they were all Butcher's mah-jongg friends.

On the other hand, if all three men thought they were the father, Hotpot would be given money by all of them. She would be better off if she didn't know who her baby's father was.

As I was walking on the mud path near home, preoccupied, thinking about Hotpot and her mysterious men, I nearly bumped into someone.

"Sorry." I stopped. It was the barber.

"It's okay." He smiled.

"I nearly knocked you over."

"You didn't," he said. He was carrying a large brown paper bag.

"Are you going home?" I looked in the direction of the barbershop.

"Not yet. I'm taking some food to a customer. She bought some sweet-corn cobs and potatoes, but they were too heavy for her to carry."

"You're nice."

"I can deliver for you next time."

"I'm okay, but thank you."

"See you soon in the barbershop."

He waved to me when he walked away. I stood and watched him disappear in the dusk.

Could he be one of those three men?

Once I was home, I stepped into the kitchen. The husband had left an empty chip bag and a chocolate bar wrapper on the worktop. I'd asked him many times to throw rubbish in the rubbish bin, but he never bothered. I scrunched the waste plastic up and threw it into the bin behind me.

There were dumplings in the freezer, so I took them out and shallow fried them.

When the husband was cooling down his dumplings, I made a dip with chili oil and vinegar.

"Pork and dill." The husband took a big bite.

"Your favorite."

"I don't mind."

"Do you remember the dumplings we ate at the dumpling bar?"

"When was that? We never eat out."

"A long time ago. We weren't married then."

"I remember now." He nodded.

"The same dumplings."

"No, different."

I wasn't very happy. "Of course. I'm not a professional dumpling maker."

"These are better. More pork."

"I've got a crying job the day after tomorrow. It's a big one, for a rich family," I told the husband when we were in bed.

"How much are they paying you?"

"1,299 yuan."

"That's good. You're a good funeral cryer."

"I'm not bad."

"Nobody's paid more than Great-Great-Grandma's family."

"Nobody else has lived for over a hundred years."

The husband put his hand under my top and touched my nipples. "Do you like it?"

I kept silent.

"You like it. All women do." He then murmured to himself, "I like it too."

I stayed still.

"I want to hear you groan." He pulled my top off and dropped it on the floor.

I felt humiliated.

He pulled my legs apart. "Don't pretend you don't want it."

The next morning, the husband and I didn't speak to each other. He had failed, he had failed in bed when he was full of energy and confidence. He was annoyed with himself, so he grabbed me and pinched me in silence. He twisted my arms too. It wasn't the first time he had failed and not the first time he had pinched me, but he had never hurt me so much before.

My arms were still in pain, but I had to ignore it. I had housework to do and I needed to remember my funeral script, which was a long one. Rich families had big funerals and long scripts. This one was for the ex-wife of a rich man. Rich men usually had stories, and the wives' stories were almost always stereotypical: they married the men when they were poor, believed in them and supported them wholeheartedly; when the men became rich they didn't love the wives anymore, but they wouldn't dump the wives; no matter how many lovers those rich men might have, most of them would come back to the wives eventually.

This woman, the rich man's ex-wife, had fought some kind of cancer for several years, but didn't pull through. The name of the cancer wasn't mentioned, as the focus was on the determination of the woman. She had fought hard for life—for herself and for her children, and for her husband, people she was reluctant to say goodbye to. All your problems suddenly seemed trivial when you were fighting for life.

This ex-wife was a different sort of ex. She wasn't abandoned by the husband, but made herself a former wife when she was ill. She made the decision in order to protect the family wealth. I didn't know what that meant, but nobody told me and of course I wouldn't ask. I had the impression that people thought she was an amazing, selfless woman.

I also noticed the age of the woman. She was two years younger than me, so death could be right around the corner ahead of me.

Sister, I will do a good job for you, I said to the woman in my head.

When the husband and I sat down to eat lunch, I decided to break the silence.

"I had a chat with Hotpot yesterday."

He stirred his chopsticks in the rice. "I forgot to ask you about her last night."

"We were remembering our dumplings in the past."

"We were young once."

"I'm old and ugly now."

He took a glance at me, but said nothing.

"Hotpot was fine. A pregnant widow got emotional," I said.

"Was that all?" he asked, then poked some rice into his mouth.

"She was worried about the baby."

"The baby will be fine."

"She doesn't know who made her pregnant."

"How could that be?"

"She's slept with other men."

The husband didn't show much interest in the mystery of the baby's father. It was a little bit odd. I was waiting for him to ask some questions, then I could tell him more details. I wanted to see his reaction.

He was lying on the sofa, having a snooze. Maybe this was how he was trying to avoid talking to me. I had something more important to do. I needed to have my hair done for a major crying job.

There was a customer in the barbershop, so I pulled out a chair from under the dressing table by the door for myself.

The customer looked like someone I used to know, but couldn't recall.

It seemed I had to wait for a long time, but I didn't mind. I liked to watch the barber's fingers move skillfully to curl the woman's hair with curlers. I had never seen his hands so clearly, since I could hardly see them while he was doing my hair. His fingers were long.

The woman suddenly turned around to me. "Hey, it's you. I know you. How are you?"

She turned out to be the mother of one of the daughter's school friends. Several years ago, the family moved to Dalian.

"I'm decorating our old family house. It's been empty for years."

"Why do you want to decorate an empty house?"

"They're all dead, and we won't come back to live in the village. We're going to let it out."

"Who will rent it?"

"Some city people. They come here to stay for the weekend."

"I didn't know that."

"There aren't many of them yet."

"Why do they come here?"

"They like it here."

"They like it here?"

"You wouldn't understand. They think it's beautiful here."

"Beautiful?"

"They come to walk in the mountains."

"There's nothing there."

"That's what they like."

"That's odd. Are you enjoying living in Dalian?"

"Well, you have to be rich to enjoy living there. My future son-in-law is an entrepreneur, so we're okay. How's your daughter doing?"

"She's in Shanghai."

"What's she doing there?"

"She runs a decoration company with her boyfriend. End-
less work," I said proudly. I hated lying, but I couldn't tell her
the truth.

When it was my turn, the woman got up and said to me,
"Please visit us in Dalian."

Then she picked up her shiny handbag and walked off in her
high heels.

I thought to myself: *I would like to visit you, but I haven't got
your address.*

While the barber was giving me a head massage, I was half-
lying on the reclined chair.

My eyes were closed, and I felt I could fall asleep any second.

The barber's fingers were quite strong, so sometimes it hurt
a little when he was massaging my head. I never complained,
because soon I would feel fine and comfortable. I always asked
him to do it quickly, as I didn't want to make his fingers too
tired. The massage was free with a hairdo, so I would feel
guilty if it took too long. I didn't want to take advantage of
anyone. He would ignore what I said and spend as long as he
wanted to.

Today, it was a bit unusual. I felt slightly embarrassed. After
I'd chatted to the barber in the grocery shop and on my way
back home, I felt there was something wrong between him
and me, or rather, something different. I'd seen him outside
the barbershop before, but now it seemed he was everywhere.

We weren't talking. I was too tired to talk. I hadn't slept
much the night before, speculating on the mystery of Hotpot's
baby's father. And the bedroom incident hadn't helped. Then
suddenly, the massage stopped—or I thought it had stopped,

but no, it didn't stop. His fingers were still in my hair, but it wasn't massaging anymore: it felt more like caressing. His touch made me feel something I had never experienced in the barbershop before.

When he was dyeing my hair, the barber suggested I only have the outside layers done, which would do less damage to my hair.

He said, "Your hair looks good. You don't have a lot of gray hair. I wouldn't recommend having your hair dyed if you didn't go out to do funeral crying. You're paid to look how people expect, aren't you?"

"Not really. *I* want to look good."

"You looked very nice at Butcher's funeral. You looked like a film star."

My cheeks felt warm. "Thank you."

"By the way, I noticed that you bought a bag of rice in the shop. Don't you and your husband grow rice in your fields?"

"No. We don't have any fields."

"We don't either. You know the rice in the shop is bought from the villagers. I'll let you know whenever we have some new rice."

"Thank you. I used to buy rice from them as well, but they don't sell to me anymore."

"Why not?"

"I'm a funeral cryer."

"I'm sorry."

"I don't mind." I shook my head. "Maybe they genuinely don't have much left."

"If you need anything, let me know. Here's my mobile number."

"Thank you."

"Can I have your number too?"

★ ★ ★

The barber had written his number on a shop receipt. The ink was light, so it took me a while to make out the digits and save them on my phone. I threw the receipt in the kitchen bin and picked up the funeral script to practice, but I was preoccupied. I was remembering the barber's fingers in my hair.

I was looking at the barber's number on my phone when the husband came into the kitchen. I quickly put the phone in my pocket.

"What's for dinner? I'm hungry." The husband looked around the kitchen.

"I need to learn this script first. You can have some snacks."

He opened the cupboard. "Do you want me to help you learn your script?"

I handed the script over to him. "You're good at helping people these days."

"What do you mean?" the husband asked.

"You know."

The husband looked at me in silence, holding the script up in the air.

15

This was perhaps the grandest and most formal funeral I had cried at.

A pretty young woman was waiting for me at the funeral parlor. She was introduced as the wife of the very rich man. The very rich man wasn't in the hall yet. As he was the most important person for the funeral, he would arrive at the last minute.

I could be mistaken, but I didn't feel the sorrowful atmosphere I had anticipated. Everything was neat and in great order. There was a huge framed color photo of a smiling woman at the front. A pretty woman.

Perhaps seeing my confused expression, the wife said, "It's Big Sister's wish. She didn't want to have a black-and-white photo. She didn't want us to cry, either."

"What shall I do?"

"Do what you would normally do. We'll still cry for her. We'll show our love and grief. He wants to send her off in style."

He must be the very rich man.

The background music was soft and soothing, a little depressing. It wasn't the loud and heavy traditional funeral music I was familiar with.

I began my crying. "Big Sister, how are you? We know you must be watching over us. You must be smiling. We all love your smile. We are crying, though. You don't want to see us crying, but we must, Big Sister. How can we not cry now that we won't see you again? No, we will see you again one day. We will reunite with you one day over there.

"You are a role model for women. You're selfless, dedicated, hardworking and tolerant. You helped Big Brother set up a company and led it with him. You didn't give up working even after you fell ill. Your last three years in hospital have shown what a great character could achieve. You encouraged and reassured Big Brother and you found an excellent assistant for him. The business has expanded since then.

"Both of your sons are doing well in their father's business. They and their father will miss you forever. Your father and your mother are not here today since their hearts are already broken and they cannot bear to witness the farewell to you. Please don't worry—they will be looked after lovingly by your family and friends. Our happiness in the future will not be the same because of your absence, but we will endure to lead a successful and prosperous life as you wished. Big Brother will name the new high-rise he is building after you, so you will be immortalized forever.

"Be there. Wait for us. We will never forget you."

The very rich man gave me a white envelope in the corner of the hall after the funeral. He praised me for my crying and said he wished me good luck.

"My late wife…you know she was my ex-wife. We got divorced after she was admitted to hospital. She said it would be easier if she helped me sort out financial matters while she was still alive. She found a distant cousin of hers to be my wife, as she wanted our money to be in safe hands. She was wise, and I'm grateful."

I had no idea why he was telling me all this.

He continued, "I've never told anyone else this, but I'll tell you. I hate her at the same time. I had had a lover for several years. She was very pretty. She left me when I married my new wife."

"Do you miss your lover?"

"Not anymore. My new wife is also very pretty."

"Yes, she is. But why are you telling me all this?"

"Because I need to tell someone, and I won't see you again. I didn't want to upset my ex-wife when she was dying, so I married the woman she'd chosen for me."

"Did she know you had a lover?"

"I don't know."

"Whether she knew it or not, she chose a good woman for you."

"Yes."

"I won't tell anyone. Did you love your late ex-wife?"

He nodded. "I think I did."

"That was why you gave her a grand finale."

"She was my wife, so she deserved it. I'm doing it for our sons as well."

"She will rest in peace."

"I hope she does. By the way, have we met before?"

"No, I don't think so."

"You look familiar, and sound familiar too."

"Do I? Maybe I just look ordinary."

"I didn't mean to offend you."

"No, you didn't."

On my way back home on the coach, I was trying to think whether I had seen the very rich man before. He looked and sounded familiar to me too. I had his new wife's name as my client, so I didn't know his name. From the script I had been given before the funeral, I learned his late ex-wife was the daughter of the director of a village. Without her father's help, the very rich man wouldn't have become very rich.

I remembered at the reunion of our school friends, one of them talked about his love story. We were all in our mid-twenties, and he was one of the few boys who was married with a child.

He told us his story in a lighthearted way:

"It's a forced marriage. One day, many years ago, when I walked past one of my neighbors' houses, I asked the girl at the door if we could walk to school together. Her father looked me up and down from head to toe and nodded his head. He also said I would have to protect her if I wanted to walk to school with her. I suddenly thought I was a hero and I promised I would. Since then, I've been protecting her. You might have seen her around school, two years below us. How old was I then? Ten? Father-in-law is the director of the village committee. I didn't know about it then, though. A forced and arranged, but happy and promising marriage..."

I must have seen the very rich man's sons at the funeral, but I didn't pay much attention. His sons must resemble their father when he was young.

He might be my school friend, but he might not.

I did some shopping after I got off the coach in gū shān zhèn, Solitude Mountain Town. I just missed the bus home when I came out of the shop. Now I had to wait for forty minutes for the next bus to come. It would be a long way to walk back home, but it would be too cold to stand at the bus stop for more than half an hour. However, it wasn't too dark. Perhaps I could start walking back home to keep myself warm and hail a moped when I saw one.

On the same pavement, I saw a man loading his bike with

some boxes. I might be mistaken from the back, but I sped up to him.

"Hey. Is that you?" I asked. I didn't know his name.

The man turned around. "Oh, it's you."

It *was* the barber, and he didn't know my name either.

He smiled and pointed to the boxes. "I've bought some new hair products."

"I'll try them."

"Yes, you should."

"I've just done a funeral today in a faraway town," I told him. "A woman. Similar age to me."

"Very sad."

"Yes. The bus won't be here for a long time. I might start walking home."

"We can walk together. I've got too many boxes, otherwise you could sit on the back of my bike."

"I'm too heavy. I might cause a flat tire if I sat on your bike."

"No, you're not heavy. You don't look heavy."

"I am."

"Let me lift you up to see whether you're too heavy."

"No, no. I'm not heavy, then."

"But I can tie your shopping bag to my bike."

"I can carry it. My bag isn't heavy."

"It'll feel heavy later." He took my shopping bag.

"Thank you."

"It's nothing. What about your handbag? It looks full."

"It's only my funeral-crying gown. It's light."

Then I noticed a hospital carrier bag. "Have you been to the hospital?"

"Yes."

"Are you ill?"

He shook his head. "Nothing serious. The medicine helps."

"I hope it doesn't trouble you."

"I don't feel unwell. By the way, what have you bought?"

"A chopping board, two pairs of slippers and some pot noodles. They were out of stock in your shop."

"Sorry. You should have let me know. You've got my number."

"Thank you, but it's a lot of trouble for you."

"Not at all."

Walking next to a man seemed surreal. I had hardly walked with the husband since I started funeral crying. We used to be together a lot, but that was because we were working together. We had never walked hand in hand either.

I hoped the barber would hold my hand while we were walking together. Maybe all I was thinking about and imagining was walking like that with a man, a man I liked very much or a man maybe I loved. I didn't know how *love* felt, but I heard it was good. It must be good, otherwise there wouldn't be so many books and films about love.

I didn't know the barber well, but walking with him seemed to be nice. I knew how good he was at cutting hair and washing hair and dyeing hair, and of course his head massages were good too. I didn't know how he and his wife would walk together. Did they hold hands? Or did he hold her waist? He wasn't doing anything special to me, but he was good company while I was walking. So, it was all nice, even if it was getting dark. It was kind of nicer when it was getting darker…

After some silence, the barber said, "How long have you lived in the village?"

"All my life."

"All your life? I thought it was your husband's home village."

"He was an orphan, so he moved in when we got married."

"Your parents?"

"Mum lives with the elder brother in dà lóng zhèn"—Big Dragon Town—"Dad's in Sunset, a care home."

"I'm sorry about your father."

"It's fine. I thought everyone in the village knew. There are no secrets in the village."

"You see, I'm a newcomer. I'm not that new anymore, but I don't know many people in the village."

"Do you like it? The village?"

"It's nice and quiet. I like the bamboo grove." He paused.

I liked the bamboo grove too, but I didn't say.

"Did you use to live in a village?" I was curious.

"No, in a city, a small one, only a little bigger than a big town. I ran a supermarket."

"Was it big?"

"It wasn't small. I gave it to my son before I moved here. My son's mother left me when he was little."

"But you know how to cut hair."

"I was a barber before I opened the supermarket. Standing up all day, too tired."

"But you're a barber again now." I was surprised.

"I don't like standing up all day, but I like doing people's hair."

"Your wife…"

"She's not my wife. We didn't register. We live together."

"I didn't know that."

"Nobody knows. People assume we're married. I always say she's my wife."

"Where did you meet her?"

"She was a cleaner in my supermarket."

"I haven't seen her recently. Is she in the village now?" I couldn't help being nosy.

"No. She's visiting her son."

"Is it far?"

"Not near."

"You're home alone at the moment." When I realized I shouldn't have said it, it was too late.

"Yes. You can come over for a cup of tea. I've got a nice room upstairs."

The barber wanted to drop my shopping bag in my house for me, but I insisted on carrying it home myself. The husband wouldn't be happy to see me with the barber; not because it was the barber, but because he wouldn't be happy to see me with any man. I also didn't want anyone to see me with the barber.

However, the husband wasn't home. I felt relieved. I wanted to be on my own for a little while, thinking about something. I wasn't sure what that something was, but I could feel there was something in my head.

Did the barber invite me to his house? Was he only being polite? It sounded strange, but it was true—if I went to his place for a hairdo, it was his barbershop; if I went there for a cup of tea, it was his house.

Would he hold my hand if I went? Would he do something else? Would I let him?

He was only an ordinary man, perhaps a little taller than the husband. He would look better if he weren't lame.

If he weren't lame, he wouldn't be living with a widow. That wasn't to say anything against the widow, but he would certainly have more options if he weren't lame.

While I was lying in bed, I couldn't get the barber's girlfriend off my mind. I had never been anyone's proper girlfriend in my life. When the husband and I became more than friends, we never referred to each other as boyfriend or girlfriend. Then we worked together before we got married.

It was nice to be a girlfriend. I was slightly jealous of the barber's *girlfriend*. It was nice that there was still a man who would like you to be his girlfriend when you were not young or beautiful.

One odd thing was that most people had a wife or husband without having a friend of the opposite sex previously. For example, I didn't know much about men before I got married. The husband was the first and only man I became close to. How could I know he was the right man for me to live with all my life? On the husband's side, it seemed he didn't know much about women.

How many women had the barber had in his life? Did he know much about women?

I shouldn't be close to a man. I shouldn't go to the barber's place for anything other than my hair, never mind the upstairs room.

If I wanted to be touched by a man, there was one at home.

If I wanted to drink tea, there was plenty at home.

I repeated to myself: *I shouldn't go to the barber's place for anything other than my hair.*

16

The husband and his friends had chosen to play mah-jongg at Hotpot's house most days of the week. They took snacks and drinks there to share with her as well as a small amount of money for the rent of the mah-jongg venue. In this way, they kept Hotpot company and she could have some regular income.

It didn't take long for people to forget about Butcher's death. After all, there was no point in doing nothing but wait for something bad to happen. Probably nobody in the village would drop dead like Butcher for many years.

I had sent the daughter some money, and she wasn't asking me to go to Shanghai right now. She had been in Shanghai for about three years. She wanted to leave school when she was sixteen, but I insisted that she go to senior middle school and take university exams. She didn't get good enough marks in the exams to go to university, which was what I'd expected. She said I'd wasted three years of her life doing nothing at school.

Living in Shanghai was a dream for most people who lived elsewhere. The daughter and her boyfriend weren't really living in Shanghai, though. During the day they went out somewhere in Shanghai to make some money, and they slept somewhere in Shanghai at night. They would leave Shanghai one day, when they had saved enough money or when they had had enough of Shanghai. They were not experiencing Shanghai, not being Shanghainese. They were newcomers and would be outsiders forever. They could never say they were *from* Shanghai, since they didn't have permanent Shanghai residence.

I didn't want to be part of Shanghai. I preferred to be an obscure visitor in Shanghai with nobody noticing me. I was fascinated by its noise and the *people mountain, people sea*. I loved all the things you could buy in the shops. Most of them were luxuries I couldn't afford, but I didn't mind. There were so many people walking on the streets, and I wondered how many of them were *from* Shanghai.

Sometimes I felt guilty about not having been born in a big city like Shanghai myself, otherwise the daughter would have city residence. When the daughter went to Shanghai for work, I almost knew she wouldn't be able to get Shanghai residence, but she had an outside chance of marrying someone from Shanghai. Then even if she didn't have city residence, her children would. That would be a breakthrough for our family. However, she didn't seem to have had any chance to date a local Shanghainese man, and she didn't care.

She probably didn't feel at home in Shanghai, so meeting a Shanghainese man wasn't that appealing. I could understand how the daughter felt. Shanghai was too grand to be my home. So was Nanjing. I didn't blame anyone. I blamed myself for not having the knowledge and skills for a permanent job in a big city. My home was in a small village, a smelly village called xī ní hé cūn, West Mud River Village. No matter how unattractive it was, it was my home. I didn't like it, but it was the destination I returned to. Wherever I went and however long I stayed there, I had to come back here.

At the moment, there was some hope for the village. The woman I'd seen in the barbershop, who was the daughter's friend's mum, had said our village would be sold to some property developers.

Would I leave this smelly village for somewhere nice?

There had been rumors about something like this for over ten years. The village committee had nearly sold our village after years of negotiation with some property developers from Dalian. Several years ago, the committee had asked for half a billion yuan, but the highest bidder was only willing to pay 300 million yuan so the deal fell through. There hadn't been any solid interest from any developers since then.

So, the village was on the table again. I asked the woman about the source of the information, and she said it was confidential. According to the woman, rich people would like to buy villas, and our village was perfect for villas. The mountains, the bamboo grove and the reservoir would attract buyers. Although the reservoir was empty now, it would be easy to fill it with water. The villagers would be paid to move somewhere else, but some apartments would be built for the villagers who would like to return. There would be a big development, she said.

It would be a good idea to ask the daughter what she would like to have, an apartment in the village or somewhere else. Whatever we owned would eventually become the daughter's, so it would be easier if we let her choose. I didn't mind where, as long as we could live in an apartment. Apartments were easier to maintain than houses, as they were neat and not dusty, and they would be away from the smell of pig poo and chicken poo. The only downside was that I wouldn't be able to grow vegetables. Maybe I could. The apartment would almost certainly have a balcony.

★ ★ ★

Hotpot had had a checkup in the hospital recently. Everything was fine, and the baby was big and healthy. It seemed she had been pregnant for longer than I thought.

One day when I was in her house sewing some bibs for the baby, she suddenly burst into tears. I was silent until she stopped. If she felt better after crying, I didn't want to disturb her.

"I killed Butcher." Hotpot rubbed her eyes.

"What?"

"After he knew I was pregnant, he said I shouldn't sleep with those men anymore."

"He was right."

"He also found some work to do. He said he wanted to be a responsible father."

"Where did he work?"

"He worked in the village grocery shop."

"What did he do there?"

"He unloaded the deliveries in the early hours. Sometimes, he went there during the day too."

"But how did you kill him? I thought he died from playing mah-jongg."

"That was what people saw."

"How did you kill him?"

"He finished work earlier than usual. I was in bed with a man when he arrived home."

"So you didn't stop sleeping with those men."

"They argued. Then he collapsed."

"He didn't die straightaway?"

"No. That man helped Butcher up and promised he wouldn't sleep with me again."

"Was he Butcher's mah-jongg mate?"

"Yes. He stayed for mah-jongg."

"That was crazy."

"People were coming. They didn't want people to know what had happened."

"So you all pretended nothing had happened."

"We had to." She nodded. "Then Butcher won a big game and died."

"Why are you telling me this?" I couldn't tell whether I believed Hotpot or not.

"If he hadn't seen me with that man in bed, he wouldn't have died."

"Do you think that man who was caught by Butcher is the father?"

"I don't know."

"You should find out."

"But I'll lose the house and money. Butcher's parents left him some money. It's mine now."

"So you don't want to find out who the real father is?"

"No. Butcher will still have a child to sweep his tomb and I won't have a bad reputation."

"It's up to you. If you want the father to be responsible, you should find out."

"I don't think any of them wants to take the responsibility."

"When they slept with you, they knew what they were doing. Did you not protect yourself?"

"How?"

"Did you take pills?"

"No. I couldn't find any in the village shop."

"Did they not wear condoms?"

"No. They said I would feel more comfortable if they didn't wear them."

"To make you feel more comfortable? Not for themselves?"

"That was what they said."

"But they should know they might make you pregnant."

"They said it didn't matter if I got pregnant."

"Why?"

"They said I was married, so it would be normal if I was pregnant. Nobody would gossip."

"You might have caught something from them."

"I didn't."

After a pause, I asked, "Have you slept with them again since Butcher died?"

"Why do you want to know?"

"You don't have to tell me."

"Butcher's dead now, so I'm a free woman."

"You *are* still sleeping with them?"

"Yes."

"Even now?" I pointed to her bump.

"They don't mind."

The daring for sex is as great as the sky—this is a Chinese saying. When I was young, Mum also told me that some men would do anything for sex, so I should keep myself away from them. I thought she was exaggerating, as I had never been in danger from men. I didn't need to worry about it at all now, since I was old and ugly and no men would be interested in me.

I imagined the husband lying in bed with Hotpot, but I didn't feel angry. I could well be wrong, since there was no proof. Why did I send him to take food to Hotpot? Was I subconsciously hoping something would happen? Why? Was I wanting him to feel guilty? Was I also hoping he'd be nice to me when he was feeling guilty?

Was the husband that man who was caught naked by Butcher? Hotpot didn't say who that man was. Was she waiting for me to ask her? Would I believe her if she said that man was the husband? I tried to remember whether the husband left home for mah-jongg early on the day Butcher died. I couldn't recall.

What kind of husband was a good husband? I used to think the husband wasn't bad, but he had pinched me in bed. I didn't know whether pinching was the same as hitting. The standard was low, but sadly, it was also the reality. When women were being judged, "not hitting the husband" wasn't part of the criteria.

I had no idea whether the husband thought I was a good wife or a good person. We were just two people living together, and we happened to be a man and a woman.

These days, nobody called me by my own name. Perhaps people had forgotten it, or some people had never known it. I was *that woman who cries at funerals*. The husband and I hadn't called each other anything for years, and it didn't bother me. Names were only important when people were born, when they got married and when they died.

When I was crying at funerals, I had to call out the names of the deceased at the beginning and the end, and I sometimes also read out the names of the mourning family if required. When the names of the deceased were heard in the hall or the courtyard, there was an atmosphere of awe. It was like the announcement of their leaving.

Dad and Mum never called my name gently. There was no need. Everyone talked loudly in the village. A lot of people gave their children random names. The most common pet name for a boy in the countryside was Dog Egg or Pig Baby, and Girl Egg or Little Flower for a girl. I would be embarrassed if Mum and Dad called me anything like that. It was worse than no name.

In a way, I was glad that I wasn't identified by my name. I hated myself when I was waiting for people to die. But who would care? Who would care about a woman with no name? A woman with no name hardly existed.

But now I would like the barber to know my name, and I wanted to know his name.

17

I didn't know when the husband would be back home.

The duvet was thick and warm enough. I held both of my breasts with my hands. The breasts felt floppy and dry, and they were empty inside.

I felt pathetic. How long had they been as soft as this? Had they dropped a size? Did I ever know my size? I suddenly felt stupid, not knowing about my own breasts.

I tried to think about the bras I was using. Had the bras been too loose? Then I felt rather ashamed of myself, as I hadn't bought any bras for years. I never knew my bra size. It was too complicated for me to understand the sizing and I found it too embarrassing to try bras on in the shop. I would estimate my size and buy the plain ones. At the moment, all my bras were worn out and I hadn't cared about them. I had no idea how many bras I had. Two or three? I would grab a bra when I went out for a funeral. If I remembered, I would wear one when I went to the barbershop.

I squeezed my breasts slowly and gently. They grew a little fuller and they were less floppy afterward. The nipples felt hard and slightly big too.

Feeling anxious, I placed my hands on my tummy. It wasn't too big, but not flat either, and it was soft too—with fat. I could easily pull a handful of my belly. I felt upset. How long had it been like this?

My hands slid down to my panties. I knew my panties were clean, but old, as old as my bras. Wrapped up in them, were my bottom and… I didn't know what I looked like under my worn, ripped panties.

When would the husband come back? Was he playing mah-jongg or lying in Hotpot's bed? He wouldn't be caught by Butcher anymore.

I woke up late in the morning, feeling exhausted.

The husband wasn't home. Had he come back at night and left again before I woke up? No, I could tell he hadn't come back at night. There was no dent on his pillow and the side of his duvet was flat.

After breakfast, I prepared a lunchbox for myself—eight dumplings and an apple. I then placed the lunch box in the bottom of my bag carefully. It was a nice leatherlike black bag with a metal chain. I had "inherited" it from the daughter.

It took me much longer than I had thought it would to travel to Sunset. I had decided to try my luck. Even if I was stopped again, I wouldn't give in and leave. I would try my best to get into the building.

I took a bus to gū shān zhèn, Solitude Mountain Town. It would be a while before another bus came, so I entered a small shop near the bus stop.

It was a shop for everything. In one corner, some underwear caught my eye. There were some colorful lace bras and panties.

I browsed the panties and felt embarrassed. They were so thin and narrow they would only cover half of my bottom. The bras were padded, so they might be able to lift my sagging breasts up.

I quietly put everything back where they had been after I checked the prices. They were not that expensive, but they weren't cheap. My old underwear was comfortable despite its shabbiness. The new underwear might look nicer, but nobody would see it and appreciate it—not good value, then. My money could be spent better on more useful things.

When I got back to the bus stop, everyone who had been waiting had gone. I looked into the distance and saw the bus disappearing. I had missed it.

I felt annoyed but could do nothing but stand at the bus stop. I wouldn't take a taxi this time, in case I wasn't allowed into the care home again. I didn't want to spend money in vain.

Nobody stopped me at the reception of Sunset.

When I saw the manager, I knew why. The previous manager had left.

The manager's office was small but tidy.

"Don't worry about your father. He's got a temperature, but he'll be fine. He's asleep now. If you wake him up, he won't go back to sleep easily." She waved her arms.

"I won't wake him up. I'll be quiet."

"Elderly people are light sleepers. You don't need to see him. I've told you he's fine."

"Of course I would like to see him. It took me a long time to get here."

"Perhaps we can open the door, and you can take a look at him."

"I can wait. I'll wait until he wakes up. I want to talk to him," I said.

"It's up to you. I understand you want to see your father, but he won't recognize you. You know he's still alive. That's all you need to know."

I didn't say anything.

She pulled one of her drawers. "I know you're a funeral cryer."

"But I don't carry any bad luck." I was nervous and sat up on the chair.

"I'm not superstitious. You can be our funeral cryer."

"Thank you." I sat back.

"This is the data of our patients. I mean, our residents. I used to be a professional nurse, a professional nurse in a specialist hospital. I'm used to saying 'patients.' Sorry."

"This is a large care home, isn't it?"

She smiled. "Yes. It's not small."

"You must have a lot of residents."

"Just over two hundred. I plan to start organizing activities for them like ballroom dancing, mah-jongg and film nights."

"My dad would like to watch films."

"Films would suit most people here. They can just sit there."

"Some of them are quite old."

"I would like them to live long, but everyone dies. Let me take a look here. One...two...three...four...the record shows that in the last three months, we've had five deaths. All the funerals have taken place." She closed the folder.

"Do you think the families of your residents would want the care home to organize funerals for them?"

Her eyebrows jumped up. "Very much so. Yes, I think so. Too much for the family in many ways."

"I'm happy to work with you."

"So you want to sign a contract with us?"

"How does it work?"

"Basically, our deaths here would be your priority. We would inform you whenever there is a death and let you know the budget. We understand you might not be available all the time. I don't mind who the cryer is. As long as you arrange it, that's fine."

"I haven't got anyone to work for me right now," I said.

"It's not urgent. It looks like we aren't expecting any deaths soon." She stood up.

"Do you think we can go to my dad's room now?"

The manager knocked on the door of Dad's room. There was no response. She knocked again before she pushed the door open.

Dad was lying on his bed. Half of his body was on the edge of the bed, with one arm nearly touching the floor.

I knelt down in front of his bed and tried to move his body farther up toward the wall. His body was stiff and cold.

The manager apologized repeatedly, "I'm terribly sorry. Really sorry. We thought your father was asleep all that time. You know old people doze off all the time."

"When was the last time anyone checked on him?" I asked, shaking.

"There should be a record. I'll ask them to find out."

The manager called for help.

A nurse came. She had no idea how long Dad had been dead.

I fixed my eyes on Dad's face. He didn't look too old and he didn't look ill either. I didn't want to think about how long it had been since I last saw him. His eyes were closed. It looked as if he were asleep.

I was taken to the manager's office. She asked me to sit on her chair. She moved the box of tissues toward me. I took a tissue, but I had no tears.

"I need to tell my mum. And my brother." I was quivering.

"We'll inform them for you."

"I killed my dad."

"No, you didn't."

"Nobody wanted him."

"We were taking good care of him."

"He's dead. But you said you were taking good care of him."
I shook my head.

"I'll do whatever we can to comfort you and your family."

The husband was lying on the sofa smoking when I arrived
home.

He sat up as I closed the door.

He shouted, "Where have you been? Why didn't you answer
the phone? Do you know what time it is? I'm hungry."

"Dad's dead."

The husband followed me into the bedroom.

"What happened?" he asked.

I didn't say anything. I didn't want to say anything. He
wouldn't understand. He had hardly had a father.

"Tell me."

"I want to lie down. I'm tired."

My body was tired, but my mind wasn't. Lying in bed, I
couldn't keep my eyes open, but I couldn't fall asleep.

I didn't know when the husband had slid under the duvet.

His body was close to mine, and I could hear his breathing.
He smelled of cigarettes and something else. I couldn't tell what
that something else was. It might be my imagination.

The husband drew me into his arms slowly. "Don't cry."

I wasn't crying. I hadn't cried at all.

I heard him again in the dark. "Maybe you should cry. Don't
stop crying."

I kept silent.

He continued, "Your dad was a good man. He was nice to
me."

"He was nice to everyone."

"We used to drink beer together."

"We shouldn't have sent him to the care home."

When I woke up in the morning, I saw the husband sitting on the floor next to the bed.

"Shall we phone the daughter?" he asked.

I shook my head. "No. I'll text her."

"Your dad liked her very much when she was little."

"She liked him too."

"How did your mum take the news?"

"She was very sad."

"She must be shocked. They had been husband and wife for a long time."

"She blamed herself. She said she should have visited him more often."

"He would still have died even if she had visited him more often."

"I didn't visit him often enough either."

"How was your brother?"

"I'm not sure. He seemed calm, but he said our family had started disintegrating."

"Maybe he was right. When there's no father, families are different."

"I have no father now, just like you."

"You still have a mother."

"But I hardly see Mum."

"What are you going to do now?"

"I'll arrange a funeral. We're going to say goodbye to Dad properly."

I wanted to visit Mum before the funeral, but in the meantime I was too nervous to see her. The brother said I didn't have to, as there was nothing I could do at the moment. I felt useless and helpless. Dad had gone, and whatever I did, I wouldn't be able to bring him back.

Maybe I did carry bad luck around. My visit to Dad had cost him his life.

Was Mum blaming me for Dad's death? She didn't say that, but it didn't mean she didn't think so.

18

"Everyone is an orphan," the husband said.

"You sound like a philosopher."

"You will be an orphan too, unless you die before your mother."

The brother and I went to the hospital to see Dad's body one last time. Then he would be moved to the crematorium for the funeral.

When I saw the brother, I was shaking.

He patted me on the shoulder. "It wasn't your fault."

"It was. I didn't go to his room as soon as I arrived."

"Even if it hadn't happened this time, it might happen another time."

"It might not happen."

"One day it would. At least you were there this time."

"We deserted him."

"Yes, we did. We're all responsible for his death."

"But I'm more responsible than anyone else."

"We all die on our own, in pain, even if we're surrounded by people who care about us. No one will accompany us to the land of death."

Dad had choked on a piece of sticky rice ball. The care home admitted neglect, even though he would have died anyway if someone had been with him. The fact that he was alone when he died meant the care home was automatically liable for his death.

The care home offered to pay us a good sum of money—100,000 yuan—on condition that we didn't sue them, as they didn't want any bad press. At some point, I would have liked them to officially admit their wrongdoing, since that would show I didn't carry a lethal atmosphere, but a simple check seemed to be a better option. Even if we sued them, what could we gain apart from money, which would definitely be less than we'd been offered?

"What are you going to do with the money?" the husband asked.

"The money is Mum's."

"She doesn't need it."

"It's still hers."

"She'll give it to your brother."

"That's possible. I'm the daughter." I didn't mind.

"She should write a will."

"How could I ask Mum to do that? It's like saying 'You're dying soon' to her."

"It's a lot of money," he mumbled to himself.

The husband took his top off and asked me to turn the lamp off.

He took my clothes off in the dark and buried his head between my breasts. "What do you want?"

I was surprised and embarrassed. I didn't know what I

wanted, and I wouldn't tell him what I wanted even if I knew. Throughout the many years we'd been husband and wife, he'd never asked me what I wanted, and I'd never asked him what he wanted.

What did he want?

I didn't reply to him, and I didn't move either. He covered my breasts with his hands as if my silence had encouraged him. I suddenly felt ashamed of my sagging breasts.

He didn't mind. His fingers were touching them. As my eyes were closed, my mind was far away. I had no idea what was happening or why it was happening.

When he was trying to squeeze himself into me, my body suddenly became stiff. At the same time, I felt dry inside. I quickly turned onto one side.

I thought I should apologize, but I didn't.

The husband had started snoring, and I didn't know whether he was pretending to be asleep. Maybe I should have opened my legs wide and welcomed him.

It had somehow scared me when he touched my breasts. Something must have gone wrong. What was that?

When I woke up in the morning, the husband had already gone out. I smelled food, then I saw a plate on my bedside table—several slices of apple, a deep-fried dough stick and a glass of water.

My heart tinkled. The husband had never done this for me. But why?

I stroked my belly slowly. I should have let him, maybe. I was almost looking forward to what was going to happen before I turned away from him. Even if he didn't last long, or even if he failed again, it didn't matter—he was trying to be nice to me.

But why?

He wanted me to get money from Mum. That must be it. He liked money, not me.

★ ★ ★

I'd never expected to inherit money from my parents. I knew
they had saved up some money and had spent most of it when
the brother got married. Mum and Dad had let the husband and
me stay in their house with them. We had been responsible for
Mum and Dad's expenses, so it had all sounded fair until Dad
was taken to the care home and Mum moved into the brother's.

I had given most of my savings from Nanjing to Mum and
Dad before I got married. Some of the money had been spent
on our wedding, and I didn't know how much money there
was left. The house had been repaired and Mum and Dad had
also bought some furniture, including the first sofa in the house,
which we were still using at the moment. I had no idea whether
any of my money had been given to the brother.

It was a son's responsibility to look after his parents in their
old age, so the parents would leave everything behind to the
sons. I had never thought about getting my savings back from
Mum and Dad, but the money from the care home was a different matter. I wouldn't have thought about getting any of it,
though, if the husband hadn't mentioned it.

The house I was living in wouldn't have any market value
until the village was sold to property developers. It was built on
Mum and Dad's allocated land by the village committee, so in
theory it was owned by the committee. It was called a house,
but it only had one floor, plus a bit more. Mum and Dad started
building an upstairs when the brother and I were teenagers. It
took several years to build three walls upstairs, then construction stopped. My memory of that period was having to eat
plain rice mixed with soya sauce and spicy garlic sauce instead
of proper dishes from time to time. The brother didn't want to
stay at home, so there was no urgent need to build more rooms
for him to get married.

Now the downstairs ceiling was sealed where the stairs joined, but the staircase was still there, and it was taking up some space downstairs. I was using the steps as shelves for dried food, such as bags of dried mushrooms and black fungus. I hoped that one day the stairs would be used as stairs and I would have some upstairs rooms.

We were not the only people who had an unfinished upstairs floor. It was normal in the village, so I never thought there was anything wrong. The brother and I used to share a bedroom until I was about thirteen, then I slept on a small bed in the corner of the living room. It wasn't a proper living room, as we hardly went there. We stored hay and sweet-corn stalks there for the stove. The room was messy, but I had one tidy corner. Mum and Dad let me have a small chest of drawers to put my clothes and personal belongings in. I was quite content in my little world. I never thought there was anything wrong that the brother had his own room, while I didn't.

The daughter slept on the sofa in the living room for quite a few years before she left for Shanghai. We didn't put hay or sweet-corn stalks there, as we built a shed when I got married. The living room was a proper living room. I felt sorry that I didn't manage to provide a bedroom for her. She didn't mind, since most of her friends didn't have their own bedrooms. Some had to sleep on the floor.

Although there was no official information, rumors were spreading. The husband had heard his mah-jongg friends talking about offers from developers. According to the size of the land our house and the backyard was covering, we would hopefully be compensated with three two-bedroom or two three-bedroom apartments. If you didn't want the apartments, you could take money instead, but it would be less than the value of the apartments. People in the village were all calculating what they would gain with some excitement, when there were no signs of any developers yet.

I wasn't greedy. I would ask to keep one apartment. I had lived in the house all my life—I should have the right to share some value, since I had maintained it. The brother would keep two, if we had three, and I didn't mind.

The apartments didn't exist, though.

Then I had a thought. If I hadn't been in the care home talking to the manager, we wouldn't have known how Dad had died, so there wouldn't be any compensation. It wasn't the brother who had earned the fortune—it was me, together with Dad. I wouldn't say I was the hero of the family, but it would be fair for me to share the money even if I was only the daughter. I hoped the brother would be reasonable. We got on well enough.

But I wasn't sure about the sister-in-law. She had a son, so she would try to get the money for him—as much as possible. There was nothing wrong. If I had a son, I would do the same.

When the husband first nagged about getting my share of the compensation money, I genuinely didn't mind not getting any. Now that I had worked out I was actually the co-earner of the money, I wanted some of it. I knew I wouldn't get all or even half, but I wanted enough of it, a fair amount.

But how could I get it? If Mum suggested I receive some, it would be easier, but I doubted she would. I thought of the famous old Chinese saying laying out the relationship between a mother and an adult son: follow your husband when he is alive; follow your son after your husband has died.

I didn't want to fall out with the brother. He had protected me when I was little, so I was never bullied at school or in the village.

There should be a way out, but there was no one I could discuss the matter with. The husband would be keen, but I didn't want to discuss it with him. I didn't know how to start a proper conversation with him anymore. These days he wanted me to listen to him, but he didn't always let me finish what I was saying.

It didn't use to be too bad when we were young. We discussed our marriage arrangements, our comedy-duo jobs, the daughter's school choices and I even asked him for advice about my funeral crying. We discussed the range of pricings I would accept for jobs. In fact, my funeral-crying hairstyle and the style of the gown was a result of discussion. But something had changed over time. It was the atmosphere between us. There was tension, and I didn't know when it started.

I sighed; I wished *someone* would give me some advice on how to persuade Mum to give me some money. I wasn't expecting all of it. Dad would probably like me to share some with the brother.

Would Dad be glad that, at last, he had been a *useful* idiot for the family?

19

I'd been in the funeral parlor for nearly an hour, waiting to see Mum.

I hadn't seen Mum as much as I would have liked since I started working as a funeral cryer. Whatever other people might have said about me, I'd never heard Mum saying anything against my job. Even mothers of funeral cryers had to keep in touch with their families, didn't they? What about people who worked in crematoria, hospitals or police, where they also had contact with dead people?

When Dad became an *idiot*, people might have thought I'd brought bad luck to him, though nobody said that to my face.

I was nervous, very nervous.

When the brother and I were discussing funeral plans, it wasn't difficult. We both agreed that I would obviously be the best candidate for the funeral cryer. We didn't need one, in a way, he said, as we were a loving family and we would all cry genuinely. However, Dad had been a decent man, so he was worth a professional send-off. It was also for the family's good reputation.

We had chosen to have the funeral in the crematorium instead of at home. I was offered a small discount by the manager. Their crematorium was the one my clients used a lot, so I knew the manager. The price was still high, but it would be worth it. The more money we spent, the more respect and love for the deceased was shown. In Dad's case, compared with the compensation money he had earned, the price wasn't a big deal.

Mum was devastated that she hadn't prepared a death outfit for Dad to wear. There was no time for her to sew one, so she paid a small fortune to have one made by a tailor. It made her feel guilty too. She kept blaming herself for not being a good wife.

Mum had told me to turn down the discount from the manager, but I accepted it, as courtesy wasn't given to me very often. If the manager hadn't offered the discount, I wouldn't have asked, since asking for a discount would be seen as disrespectful toward your deceased loved ones. The same thinking applied to makers of coffins; there were no discounts for them either. I had been asked by some coffin makers to help sell coffins. Although the commissions were tempting, I had never done it. Earning money from dead people through funeral crying was bad enough, but selling coffins for profit would make me feel disgusted with myself.

I had talked to Mum on the brother's phone a couple of times before we started preparing for Dad's funeral. She sounded upset but controlled; she didn't say Dad's death was my fault, and I believed she would never say it. There were many things in her life she would never say anything about. Being a woman, now old, her opinions were never important. She was one of the lucky women of her generation who had never been hit by her husband and who was being looked after by a son. Well, as for her not having been hit by her husband, that was my assumption since I had never seen Dad hitting her. The brother had never mentioned anything like that. But how could we know whether Dad had hit her before the brother and I were born?

I still regularly gave small amounts of money to Mum, but it didn't count much as I was the daughter. Only a good son was a blessing when you were old. Being a daughter and a woman, I knew I was not valued that much because I had a brother and I didn't have a son. Anyway, I hoped Mum appreciated my filial piety.

Dad had almost favored me when I was young, but I knew it only seemed that way. It did no harm to seemingly favor a daughter when you also had a son. The son was important enough without needing to do anything. On the other hand, Mum had shown more affection toward the brother.

I would cry for my father, as a daughter and as a professional cryer. It was all free, and it would save the brother some money.

Mum entered the hall with the brother's son holding her arm. I hadn't seen her for about three months. She had aged. She looked all pale and frail in her white mourning gown. Her face seemed dry, but with some subtle beauty from her youth remaining in her eyes. It was difficult to tell how she felt.

I quickly walked to Mum and gave her a hug. She didn't say anything to me, but I felt a firm press on the back. My tears welled up immediately.

The brother approached to lead Mum away to her seat, while I walked to the front of the hall. I tightened up my white belt, the belt I kept after I stopped using it. I wondered whether the husband thought I looked like a ghost.

The second I heard the squeaky noise of a suona, I danced my steps toward the coffin...

The brother booked an abundant tofu banquet in a restaurant near the crematorium. Some of our old fellow villagers talked about Dad enthusiastically, remembering him as an intelligent and honest accountant and cashier who had never stolen the village's money.

There were over thirty guests. I had seen some of the faces at Butcher's funeral. Although we lived in the same village, I hadn't spoken to these people for a long time. I was familiar with most of the faces, but couldn't recognize everyone.

The brother was walking between tables to talk to people. He was holding a glass of water. At the tofu banquet, sons of the deceased were not allowed to drink alcohol. The brother prepared some fine liquor for male guests, but it wouldn't matter if there was no alcohol. People would appreciate it, as the liquor could be very expensive and strong. Nobody would drink too much. Half a tiny cup would be enough for most people. It wouldn't be a respectful scene if you were drunk at a tofu banquet.

I wasn't sitting with Mum and the brother's family. The guests took turns to pay their condolences to Mum, but nobody came to speak to me. I sat quietly with the husband. I had been overwhelmed with sadness by my singing happy and noisy songs. Although I understood it was fair for the funeral goers to want to go home in a lighter mood, it made me feel I was a bad daughter without filial piety.

Then I caught a glimpse of the barber. He was talking to some people who were sitting at the same table before he turned in my direction. Our eyes met. Neither of us looked away for several seconds. Nobody noticed us. The husband was busy eating. He was making the loudest noise when he was slurping the soup.

The sister-in-law collected and kept all the money we received from the funeral goers. I didn't know how much there was, and the money would belong to them. It wasn't that I wanted the money—I was only sad that the sister-in-law was considered a more important part of the family than I was. She belonged to my family because she was married to the son of my family, and I didn't belong to my family anymore because I was married. I wasn't even allowed to sit with Mum at Dad's funeral.

I was an outsider.

I had asked the husband to have a walk with me in the bamboo grove, but he said he didn't want to. It wasn't that he didn't want to have a walk with *me*, he simply didn't want to go for a walk.

The husband and I had never had a walk together since we got married. I had never seen any other husband and wife walk together in our village just for the purpose of walking. People didn't do it. I had hardly seen a husband and wife talking to each other gently, either. They would normally shout at each other and blame each other.

I needed to have some fresh air in the bamboo grove. The reason why I had invited the husband was that I had realized we were a family, and we should do things together. Having a walk was a starting point.

I was hoping that he remembered the happy moments we had had in the bamboo grove so many years before. I was also hoping that the little memory would be able to soften our hard relationship.

The bamboo grove was quiet as usual. Bamboo wasn't native in the north, so the grove in our village was unusual and almost seemed exotic. Nobody knew how the bamboo came here and how long it had been around. You could buy bamboo plants everywhere, but bamboo groves were rare in Northeast China. The bamboo grove was a selling point to the property developers. I was glad they valued it.

I saw some bamboo shoots bursting out from the ground. Since the grove belonged to nobody, the bamboo shoots were free for everyone. They were delicious in soup or braised with soya sauce and sugar. I would bring a knife next time I came.

When I was walking into the depths of the grove, I saw someone walking out toward me. Although I couldn't see the face, I knew it was the barber. He was lame. I had seen him in the grove, but only from afar, not like today.

"You're having a walk? On your own?" the barber asked.

"Yes, I'm on my own."

"Sorry your father died."

"At least he didn't suffer."

"Are you all right?"

I nodded, then started crying.

He put his hand on my shoulder. After his fingers had lingered for a while, he hugged me.

I tried to push him away, but he didn't take his arms off me.

"People will see us." I struggled.

"No. Nobody comes here."

"I'm going home now," I said.

He stepped back. "I thought you might come to speak to me."

"When?"

"At your father's tofu banquet."

"There were too many people."

"You were sitting with your husband, but you weren't talking to each other."

"I didn't notice that."

"He's nice to you?"

"Yes."

"I'll be nice too." His voice croaked.

"I'm going home now," I repeated.

"I'll be nice too," he repeated.

I turned around quickly and started walking as fast as possible. When I thought the barber couldn't see me, I began running. As my house came into my sight, I slowed down.

The husband opened the door after I banged on it several times.

"Have you not got a key?" he said as he disappeared down the hallway.

I didn't check, but I knew I had all my keys in my handbag.

There were some clothes on the sofa. They were the clean washing I hadn't had time to put away, but the clothes were wrinkled now. The husband must have sat on the clothes without looking.

There was a mess in the kitchen. The sink was full of unwashed bowls and plates and several plastic carrier bags were lying on the floor.

I took a deep breath and I rolled my sleeves up.

The kitchen was quiet. In fact, the whole house was quiet, like the saying: you could hear a pin drop. I didn't know what the husband was doing. Most of the time, he had nothing to do at home if he wasn't watching TV or smoking or cracking sunflower seeds. Strictly speaking, smoking wasn't doing something. Sometimes I was worried he might doze off while smoking; then he would burn the house down and kill himself, and possibly me.

If he died before me, I would send him off in style. I would do a brilliant job for him. I would cry hard and shed genuine tears, for him, for myself, and for the lost and wasted years. In some ways, I would like to die before him. I wanted him to regret how he hadn't looked after me. He probably wouldn't regret that, though. Perhaps he would miss the days when he was taken care of by me, and the times I gave him the money I had earned.

If I died before him, he wouldn't be able to receive money without doing anything. He would miss me because of that. Meanwhile, nobody would cook, clean and wash for him. He would also cry hard and shed genuine tears.

So it would be better if he died first—otherwise he would live a miserable life without my money or my care. Would he live like a tramp if I died first?

Death was unpredictable.

When we were both alive, I would be nice to him. I didn't want to regret anything.

As I was chopping the pork into mince, the daughter came to my mind.

She didn't go to her grandpa's funeral, which was my decision. Although I was going to, I didn't tell her about his death. She had been trying to get pregnant, so she might well already be pregnant by now. Heartbreak could lead to a miscarriage, and long train journeys were hard for a pregnant woman. It might be cruel to say it, but the younger generation was more important than the older one. If she had another miscarriage, she might not be able to fall pregnant again, which would be a disaster and nobody would ever want to marry her. I was still a little cross with her. I couldn't understand why she wanted to have a baby before getting married first. Maybe her boyfriend didn't want to get married?

She might be cross with me for not letting her know that her grandpa had died. If she hadn't been able to see him when he was dying, though, there was no difference when she would find out about his death.

I poured the minced pork into a wooden bowl and mixed it with dill, soya sauce, sesame oil and a pinch of salt to make filling for dumplings. I loved dumplings, but nobody had made them specially for me. When I was little, we often had them. Everybody sat at the table and prepared everything together. Mum would prepare all the ingredients. She never asked anyone what fillings they would like to have, as she knew what was the best.

"Is dinner ready? I'm hungry," the husband shouted from the living room.

I was hungry too.

"Only dumplings. Won't be long," I replied.

"What filling are you making?"

"Pork and dill, your favorite."

"Again? I don't mind."

I knew he minded, and I knew he didn't like just anything. He knew I was nice to him, and he knew I wouldn't cook him just any food, but he was reluctant to admit it.

As I was boiling the dumplings, I washed everything in the sink and dried up. It was his home, and it was also my home. I didn't expect him to help. I tidied the kitchen for myself, not for him.

"Delicious," the husband said as he chomped and nodded.

I stirred the dip slowly with the tips of my chopsticks and tasted it.

"The dip's too spicy. I've put too much chili sauce in it," I said.

"Not for me." He shook his head.

"Does it taste the same as the dip you made when we ate at the dumpling bar?"

"Did I make the dip?"

"Yes."

"I don't remember." He shook his head.

"The dip you made was nice. By the way, I've put some dumplings in a container for Hotpot."

"You're kind."

"She's due soon, isn't she?"

"Yes."

"I wonder who can take her to the hospital."

"I don't know."

"I wouldn't mind taking her, but I might not be at home," I said.

"I can if you don't mind."

"I don't. She's a widow. The whole village should help her."

★ ★ ★

After the husband left, I sat at the front window.

It wasn't dark yet, so I could see everything outside clearly. The husband walked briskly, as if he couldn't wait. He didn't know I was watching. Would he walk a bit more slowly if he knew there was a pair of eyes on his back?

Then I caught a glimpse of a shadow. It was too far to tell who it was. The shadow kept still for a little while before disappearing.

I wondered whether the shadow was the barber. It wasn't close enough to tell whether the walker was limping.

My heart thumped.

I felt strangely nervous, and there was a pain in my stomach.

20

I was texting the daughter when the husband walked into the bedroom.

"You're back."

"Hotpot liked the dumplings," the husband said as he was taking his socks off.

"Don't leave your socks here." I raised my voice.

"I won't."

The door was open, so the socks flew through the door frame.

"Who are you texting?"

"Who do you think?"

"How's the daughter?" the husband asked.

"Still sad."

"You should have told her and let her go to the funeral."

"I was worried she might be pregnant."

"Is she?"

"Probably not. I didn't ask."

"If she can't get pregnant, she can adopt Hotpot's son."

"Is Hotpot having a son?"

"I don't know. I meant if she couldn't get pregnant and Hotpot had a son…"

"I'm sure she'll get pregnant. Nothing compares to your own child."

"I don't really want to become a grandpa. It makes me feel old."

"If we're going to be grandparents anyway, I think it's better before we're properly old."

"But she's not married."

"That's today's young people."

Then the husband mentioned the money issue, the money from the care home.

"I'll speak to Mum," I suggested.

"You said you wouldn't," the husband said.

"I will now."

"How are you going to do that?"

"I don't know yet."

The husband took his clothes off and moved toward me.

He tugged at my panties. I pulled my waistband up.

"I'm the husband." He tugged at my panties again.

"What do you want to do?" I sat up.

"Nothing," he said.

I clambered into bed and closed my eyes. I stretched my arms and kept them on top of the duvet. I didn't want to be touched, and my pose kept the husband away without offending him too much.

I felt dry again. My skin and the inside of my body. I learned at school that human body was 70 percent water, but I didn't understand it. After so many years, I was more confused. How could I feel so dry if I was mainly water? Ultimately, being dry or wet didn't matter, as we would all be dry in the end, and we would decay and fade into nothing.

★ ★ ★

The barber was digging the bamboo shoots with his scissors. He put his scissors down when he saw me. I gave him my knife. It would be much easier to dig with a knife. He asked me to throw away the knife. He rubbed the mud off his hands onto his trousers and put his arms around my shoulders. Then he cupped my face with his hands. His lips were moving toward me. I pushed him away and started crying.

Somebody was shaking my arm. "What's wrong?"

I opened my eyes, but it was dark.

I heard the husband. "Why are you crying?"

"A nightmare. I had a nightmare." I stopped crying.

"What happened in your nightmare?" he asked.

"I don't remember."

"You woke me up." He turned back to his corner.

I remembered the dream. Of course I did. And it wasn't a nightmare.

In the morning, I had a headache. My body told me to stay in bed, but my mind had an urge to find that knife, the knife I was holding in my dream.

I searched all the drawers in the kitchen, but I couldn't find the knife I had seen in my dream.

"What are you looking for?" the husband asked.

"Nothing."

"You can't look for nothing."

"I'm not looking for anything. I'm tidying up. By the way, are you playing mah-jongg today?"

"Perhaps I can go there to take a look. I haven't played for a couple of days."

"You went there yesterday."

"I didn't play. I was watching."

"Does the barber play mah-jongg?"

"Why do you ask?"

"I'm curious. You know he's not that busy in his barbershop."

"I've seen him at Butcher's house, but he doesn't play that much."

"So he sometimes watches people play?"

"I don't notice. I guess so."

"If you want to play today, go and find your friends, then." I wanted to be on my own.

I couldn't find my knife, the knife in my dream. Maybe I didn't have a knife like that.

Life was so unexciting. I had nothing important to do, so I was searching the kitchen for a knife from my dream. Why should I spend time looking for an unknown knife, a knife I had only seen in my dream? I must be mad.

The weather had been dry, almost as dry as me, so the bamboo shoots wouldn't grow fast. I wondered whether they felt dry like me. Unfortunately, nobody would water them, apart from the rain. The only trouble was you wouldn't know when rain would arrive, and when it came, it might not be the right amount. Although the bamboo shoots didn't know what amount they were expecting, when it was right, they knew.

Then I realized that I was the same as the bamboo shoots: I didn't know what I would like to have, but when I had it, I would know. I felt some empathy for the bamboo shoots now. Maybe I shouldn't dig them up and eat them.

I had just been to the backyard to check on my vegetables, which were also dry and a bit thin. They were normally luckier than the bamboo shoots, since they were watered by me as well as the rain. It was my fault that they were dry. I hadn't remembered to water them since Dad died. I'd had the time, but not the mind.

After giving my vegetables a big drink of water, I left for the grocery shop. There were always fresh vegetables there, nearly as good as mine. Of course, the barber might be there.

★ ★ ★

I stopped in front of Little Sister's house and called her name loudly. I wouldn't knock on her door. She didn't have a mobile phone. She never left the village, so there was no point in having a mobile.

Little Sister opened the door and stood there.

"Have you got any chicken poo?" I waved to her.

"Yes. I'll get some for you now."

"I'm going to the shop. I'll come and collect it later."

"No problem."

"Thank you." I started to make a move.

"Don't go yet. I've got something to warn you about."

"What?" I was surprised.

"There's some gossip about you."

"Gossip about me?" I couldn't believe my ears.

"People saw you and the barber."

"What?"

"You and the barber were in town. You were holding hands and he put his arm around your waist."

"No. They were lying."

"I don't know."

"Don't you believe me?"

"You need to be careful with the barber."

"What do you mean?"

"Do you know how he became lame?"

"Was he born that way?"

"No. He was caught in bed with someone's wife, and he was beaten up by the woman's husband."

"Who told you that?"

"People." She shrugged.

"Did you believe them?"

"I don't care." She shook her head.

When I saw the knife on a corner shelf in the shop, I felt that I was in my dream again. I picked up the package. The blade was half the length of my hand with a wooden handle and a pointy end. It wasn't shiny. It looked dull and cold, and it didn't look like it could dig the bamboo shoots out easily. I didn't know whether I had seen the knife before, except in the dream. The knife might have been lying there for a long time and been seen by many customers, including me.

It wasn't until I checked the price that I realized it was more expensive than I had expected for a small knife. I hesitated for a while before I carefully placed it into my shopping basket.

Before I went to the checkout, I walked along all the aisles in the shop. I was disappointed, as the barber wasn't there.

I passed Hotpot's house on the way home. The village wasn't big and there were no dead ends, so I could take any route. Her house looked narrower than ours, but it had a proper upstairs floor. It looked tatty from outside. It would still cost a lot of money to restore a small house like this. There was hardly any construction or decoration going on in the village, since everyone was waiting to own the new apartments, either in the village or somewhere else.

Why should I worry about her house? My house didn't look better than hers.

Some noise came out of the house with the door half-open. Mostly it was the noise of mah-jongg tiles. The noise wasn't loud, almost soothing, like the sound of dry-frying peanuts. After constant touching and rubbing from the players' fingers, the mah-jongg tiles would become smooth and shiny, but never dry.

Playing mah-jongg was known as "Building the Great Wall," because the tiles resembled walls when they stood up in straight lines in front of the players; and it required team effort, dedication and, of course, money.

Although the new knife looked dull, it was surprisingly sharp. I cut some potatoes with it, and it didn't slip at all. I would have no problem digging up the bamboo shoots with it.

There were some dumplings left from the night before. I would shallow fry them for the husband when he was back. And for myself, I would cook the potato I had cut with the new knife together with some eggs. I didn't want to spend too much time in the kitchen.

Then I realized that I had forgotten to collect the chicken poo from Little Sister on my way back. I couldn't believe that people had made things up about the barber and me. I didn't even know how to defend myself. If I had admitted to Little Sister that I was walking with the barber, it would be like confirming what people had said. To be honest, I wished we had been holding hands and he had put his arm around my waist.

But could it have been true that the barber was caught with someone else's wife in bed before he moved here? Was he sleeping with someone else's wife in the village now? But the same "people" invented a story about me. Why should I believe what they had said about the barber? Then I remembered Hotpot said that the presents she received from the three men she slept with included some shampoo. Who would give someone shampoo as a present? Who would have spare shampoo to give away? The barber. And the barber had offered Butcher a job… On the other hand, anyone could buy shampoo for people as it was a cheap present.

Was the barber trying to lure me into sleeping with him? He told me he had a nice room upstairs. He had also said he would be nice to me too.

The brother phoned.

"Mum wants to have a chat with you," he said.

"Okay. I'll speak to her now."

"No. She doesn't want to talk to you over the phone."

"Shall I come over?"

"I suggested you two meet up in a restaurant near my house. You could have some nice food together."

"That sounds good."

"But she wants to go to your place."

"That's fine."

"I'll bring her over." He hung up.

I didn't ask the brother what Mum wanted to talk about. He probably didn't know anyway. If Mum didn't want to say something, no one could make her say it.

I was lucky that Mum was going to visit me while I was considering talking to her about money. Of course, I would like to meet her in my house, not in a restaurant. We could go to a restaurant for some nice food, but we didn't need to find a place only to talk. At the same time, this was still her house, so she was going to see me in her own house.

Mum and Dad's bedroom remained the same as before, although covered in a thin layer of dust. I would clean the room thoroughly before she arrived. She might want to take a look at her old room. There were still many of her personal belongings in the room, and Dad's too. I had thought about sorting them out, but decided I would do it when I had time; then it seemed I never "had time."

Whatever Mum wanted to discuss with me, I would take the chance to raise the money issue, the compensation money Dad and *I* had earned. Anyone could blame me for Dad's death, but without me, there would have been no money. Nothing could bring Dad back now, so why couldn't they let me take some credit for the income?

Mum might want to make some arrangements for her own funeral. Dad's recent death must make her think about her own situation. I knew Mum couldn't overcome the fact that Dad didn't have his last outfit ready when he was alive and she'd had to have one made by a tailor.

I wouldn't suggest Mum have her outfit made well in advance, since it was even worse than asking her to write a will. Any suggestion like that would be interpreted as *You're going to die soon, so make sure you've got some nice clothes to wear when it happens.* It was believed that if you made the last outfit for your parents, they would be blessed with longevity. However, it would be better if Mum raised the topic.

The brother bought some fine fabric several years ago when Dad was diagnosed with dementia. He was the son, so it was his responsibility. It was my duty, together with the sister-in-law, to sew the outfit. These days, most people would pay a tailor to do it, and you could also buy ready-made ones. However, you would show you cared about your mother or father if you made the outfit for them yourself. They would be blessed in the other world, and they would bless you and your children with longevity.

I felt guilty about Dad's last outfit too. We had forgotten about preparing one for him since we sent him to the care home. We didn't think about it as we didn't see him around. We were also concentrating on his mental state, not his future death. No, we didn't think about his death, or at least I didn't. So we had dumped him well before he died.

Before I received Mum, I wouldn't know what she wanted to discuss. I decided I should stop guessing and start planning what I wanted to talk to her about at my end.

I wanted some money from Mum.

21

Mum arrived in the brother's car with a suitcase. She didn't just want to meet me in my house, her own house, but she also wanted to stay for some days. She told the brother she would let him know when she would like to go back.

Mum sat on the sofa, looking around her. "It's still the same."

"Yes, but not as tidy as before." I was embarrassed.

The brother didn't give me enough notice, so I didn't have a chance to tidy up the living room.

"It doesn't matter. This is your mess, not mine."

"I've cleaned your room. I haven't changed anything there."

"Good."

I helped Mum unpack her suitcase. It was the old suitcase I took with me when I went to Nanjing. There were clothes, toiletries, towels and a wash bag. At the bottom of the suitcase, there were several bags of dried food and plastic bags full of random items. The contents of the suitcase looked like the luggage you would take for a holiday.

Mum dug into a corner of the suitcase and took out a sweater with something wrapped inside it.

She carefully placed the sweater on the bed and pulled something out from inside the sweater. It was a dark brown wooden box, half the size of a shoebox. I thought I knew what it was, but I didn't dare ask.

"It's your father."

I didn't know what to say.

"I haven't found a graveyard for him yet. Most graves are too expensive."

"They are."

"Before I find an affordable grave, I'll have to keep the box at home. Your brother's wife said the box would bring us foul luck."

"How could she say that?"

"I told her to shut up."

"Did you argue?"

"I didn't."

"What else did she say?"

"Not much. She said I should be grateful that she was feeding me."

"What did you say to that?"

"I told her to shut up."

"What did the brother say?" I asked.

"Nothing."

"He should have taken your side. You're his mother."

"I don't care. I'm not going to return to his house. Do you mind if I live here? I'm going to die here."

"Of course I don't mind. This is your house, your home, always yours."

"I won't live here for too long. I'm old. I might die soon." She shook her head.

"You aren't old, Mum."

"That's nice of you, but you don't need to comfort me."

"These days people live for many, many years, you know."

"I don't want to live for too many years."

"Mum."

"It costs too much either to live or to die."

"Mum, you've got me."

"Don't worry. I've got money. The check from the hospital."

Mum was tired, so she wanted to have an early night. However, we couldn't stop talking to each other.

The husband looked surprised to see Mum lying on the sofa when he came back home from his mah-jongg session. In fact, he was more intimidated than surprised. He hurried to our bedroom after greeting her.

When we were young, he used to tell me he was scared of Mum. Although she had always been nice to him, he often held back. As a man, it was awkward to live with the parents-in-law. He was somehow relaxed when he was with Dad. They didn't talk too much, but they would sit in the backyard smoking cigarettes and drinking beer together.

During the first few years of our marriage, the husband and I were relatively intimate. Unfortunately, the sound-insulation of the walls wasn't good, so we had to be as quiet as possible at night. Some days, when we got up in the morning and saw my parents, I felt embarrassed, since I was worried they might have heard something the night before. That was still a mystery to me.

"I didn't know your mum was coming," the husband said.

"I thought I had told you." I shook my pillow.

"How long is she going to be here for?"

"I don't know. It's her home, so she can stay for as long as she would like to."

"Has she said anything to you? Did she mention the money?"

"No," I lied.

"You should have asked her."

"Let her have a rest first."

"We're not rich. If she stays here for a long time, we can't afford it." He warned me.

"You shouldn't say that if you want her money."

"You want her money too."

"She's my mother. I'll have her anyhow."

"Does her money not make a difference to you?"

"Of course not."

I didn't want to argue with the husband, especially while Mum was here.

He said I was useless when I was with Mum. I said nothing as there was no point. He didn't have parents, so he wouldn't understand that your mother was always your mother, and you were always that ignorant child in her presence.

He took my hand in the dark. "You're a clever woman. You'll persuade your mother to give you money, won't you?"

"Can we not talk about money?"

"What shall we talk about?" He moved closer to me.

"Nothing." I turned my back to him.

"What did you say?"

"I don't want to talk about anything."

"Why not? I'm your husband."

He pulled me toward him, but I pushed him away.

He mumbled something. He must have been swearing.

Suddenly I was a "clever woman," not "stupid," since I was useful when I was needed to ask Mum for money. Did the husband think he could decide whether I was clever or not?

Mum seemed to be in a good mood in the morning. We watered the vegetables in the backyard together.

She asked, "Where's my trowel? There are many weeds here."

"I don't know."

"The trowel is useful. You can also dig the bamboo shoots out with it."

"I've got a small knife for bamboo shoots."

"You have to be very careful when you use a knife. The bamboo skin and roots are tough and slippery. It could cut you badly if you're careless."

"I'll try to find the trowel."

"It'll take a while for the bamboo shoots to grow mature enough. It's been too dry. We need some proper rain."

I was slightly overwhelmed. Mum had asked me about where some of her things were, including the trowel. I didn't remember seeing the trowel for a long time. Did she take the trowel with her to the brother's? She also wanted to make cushions. She said she had left the cushion fabric in her wardrobe, and at least a couple of things in the kitchen cupboard were missing— a biscuit tin and a bone china bowl.

She was cross with me when I showed my ignorance of the whereabouts of her items. In the end, she concluded that I had thrown them away. I said *no* several times, but she said she didn't want to argue with me.

Mum was in her room when the husband came back.

He was carrying a paper bag. "I won some money today. Look what I've bought from the grocery shop."

I opened the paper bag and found some barbecue pork.

"Your mum likes barbecue pork," he said.

"You remember that."

"I went to the barbershop and spent the rest of the money I'd won."

"Nice haircut."

"The barber isn't too bad."

"I'd told you before."

"It seems his wife has left him."

"How could you know?"

"We chatted."

"What did he say?"

"He said he was on his own, so he was going to have pot noodles for dinner."

"The wife isn't home, then. It doesn't mean she's left him," I pondered.

"I don't know and don't care."

I didn't say that she was the barber's girlfriend, not his wife.

After dinner, Mum told me to go to her bedroom with her. She pointed to the bed. "I'll make my own last outfit."

I saw some fabric lying on the bed. "Mum." It was the fabric the brother had bought for Dad.

"Don't be sad. Everyone dies."

"Shall I make it for you?"

"No. I'm not superstitious. It doesn't matter who makes it."

"I can help you."

"You don't have to. I hope you don't mind having me here."

"I'm glad you're staying with us."

"But I won't stay for too long."

"You said you weren't going back to the brother's."

"I say that, but he's my son. I must live with him until I die."

After a brief hesitation, Mum asked, "You and your husband still aren't getting on well, are you?"

"There are worse couples, Mum."

"He's not a bad man, but he's rather useless."

"It's difficult for him to find a job."

"Why can't he raise some pigs and chickens in the backyard?"

"He doesn't know how."

"Feed them. He's just lazy."

I kept quiet.

"Don't be cross with me. Ignore what I say if you don't like it."

"I'm not cross."

"Most husbands are useless at home."

"Dad was a good husband."

"He was quite useless too."

"He was a good father."

"He was."

The husband sat in bed, smoking.

"Stop smoking in bed."

"I won't burn the house down."

"It's not good for your health."

"Smoking in bed?" He laughed.

"Smoking anywhere."

"Don't you think smoking is manly?"

"No."

"Hotpot does."

"Does she?"

"Yes. Most women do."

"So you and Hotpot like each other?"

He stared at me for a second and stubbed the cigarette out in the ashtray. "I've never slept with her."

"What are you talking about?"

"Hotpot. She wants to, but I don't."

I switched the bedside lamp off.

He switched it back on. "Can you say something?"

I shook my head.

"Are you angry with me?" he said.

"No."

"Can you say something?"

"Yes. I want to have a haircut."

"What?" He looked confused.

"You told me to say something."

I switched the lamp off again. This time, he didn't switch it back on.

I heard him murmur in the dark, "I've given her some money, so she wants to thank me."

"Did she not force you?"

I pulled the duvet and tucked it under my shoulder.

"I can sleep with her for free, but I don't," he said to himself.

"What a good man."

You've given her money, so she's not free. I'm free, I thought to myself.

22

The door of the barbershop was open, so I walked in, but didn't see the barber.

I hesitated before sitting down to wait on a chair near the mirror by the door.

I heard the barber talking to someone in the back room. I held my breath.

"I've told you. There's nothing between her and me."

"I know what you're like." It was a woman's voice.

"Believe me. I've never touched her."

"Has she not seduced you? Look at her jeans. They're so tight."

Then I heard a bang, like furniture falling over. The woman screamed and swore.

I got to my feet and dashed out of the barbershop.

Were they talking about me? It could be any woman. But my jeans *were* tight. Was that his girlfriend? Was she home now? Maybe she was back now, or maybe she had always been home.

It could be any woman. If the girlfriend wasn't home, and he had a lover...

I went for a walk in the bamboo grove before returning to the barbershop.

The barber asked, "Are you sure you just want to have your hair washed?"

"Yes. It's too cold to wash hair at home."

"I'll use my best salon shampoo."

"Thank you."

It was the first time I'd had my hair washed in the barbershop. I had always thought it wasteful to pay someone to wash your hair, but I wanted to see the barber.

I lay down on my back on the long shampoo bed and closed my eyes. I felt strangely awkward when the barber's fingers were in my hair. His fingers were touching and massaging my skin gently; although only my scalp, it was still my skin. Several times, his fingers touched my ears, and he would take his fingers away quickly. I had been to the barbershop many times to have my hair trimmed and rinsed, so the touching of his fingers was familiar to me. However, this was the first time those fingers were stroking my hair, as if forever.

It was so comfortable I nearly fell asleep.

"Your mum's here, isn't she?" the barber asked me when he was applying conditioner to my hair.

"Yes. How did you know?"

"Your husband told me."

"Yes, she's staying."

"I can cut her hair. I'll cut her hair for free."

"Why?"

"You're my regular customer, my most regular customer."

"Thank you, but she cuts her own hair. You know most people here do."

"I know. That's why I appreciate your visits."

"You do good buns for me. Thank you."

"Your hair's nice. I can only do good buns with nice hair."

"You're very kind."

"What do you want to do with your hair now?" he asked me while he was drying my hair with a towel.

"Nothing."

"I'll blow-dry it for you," he offered.

"It'll dry itself quickly."

"You'll catch a cold in the wind with wet hair. It's chilly outside."

"I'll be fine."

"Let me blow-dry your hair," he insisted.

He turned on the hair dryer and said something. It was so noisy that I couldn't hear him, but I didn't ask. We were both silent while he was blow-drying my hair. I felt so warm.

Mum was washing vegetables in the kitchen when I entered the house. "I've checked the mooli in the backyard. I think it's ripe enough to dig out. We need the trowel."

"I'll try to find it. We can use my new knife."

She shook her head. "The knife's too sharp. It'll bruise the mooli easily."

"So the knife's no good for either bamboo or mooli."

"I'm afraid not."

"I'll buy a new trowel."

"You must have thrown my old trowel away."

I hadn't thrown the trowel away. I hadn't thrown any of Mum's things away. But how could I prove that I hadn't thrown anything away?

I didn't want to insist that I hadn't done it. There was no point. Hopefully the missing items would turn up.

The husband was counting the money in bed. It was the cash I brought home from my funeral crying, left over after the husband took most of it to the bank. Over the years, there was quite a bit of cash. Perhaps there was some from his mah-jongg winnings. Although he said he earned more than he lost at mah-jongg, he had never shown me any proof. I tried my best to believe he was telling the truth.

"Do you know how much cash we've got here?"

I shook my head.

"Do you want to know?"

I shrugged. "I don't care."

"There's also a lot of money in our savings account," the husband said.

"How much is a lot?"

"Our total money and the money from your dad's death would nearly be enough for us to buy an apartment in town, somewhere like gū shān zhèn."

"We won't get all the money."

"Once we've got our share of your dad's money, we can borrow some money from your mum or your brother."

"Mum doesn't have much money. I don't want to borrow money from the brother."

"It doesn't matter. We helped your brother when he started his business."

"But he let us get married in this house."

"When I moved in, he wasn't living here. We looked after your parents for him."

"But why do you want to buy an apartment in town?"

"Buying a property is the best investment when you have money."

"We don't know anyone in town," I said.

"That's why I want to move there."

"Why?"

"We know people in the village, but it's like not knowing anyone."

"You're right. Nobody likes me."

"It's not you, it's what you do for a living."

"It's the same. You've got some friends in the village, though."

"They're not friends. They're my mah-jongg friends." He shook his head.

"What can you do in town?"

"Maybe we can open a shop." He sounded enthusiastic.

"Would I still cry at funerals?"

"You can if you want to. Nobody would know you're a funeral cryer."

"Are you sure you want to move?"

"It's boring here, dirty and smelly."

"What shall we do with our house?"

"Nothing."

"Why?"

"It's not ours. It's your mum's."

"What about the new apartments in the village?"

"Where are they?"

The husband soon fell asleep and started snoring.

The bedside lamp was still on, so I could see his face clearly. He had a double chin and there were lines on his forehead and in the corners of his eyes. I felt sad, for him and for myself. I could imagine how awful and old I looked. We had been married and spent many years together, but neither of us knew how many years there were left for us.

There were two different characters with the same meaning, "marrying," in Chinese. One was for women, and the other was for men. When a woman got married, it was jià (嫁), meaning "a woman going to a man's home"; when a man got married, it was qǔ (娶), "fetching a woman." Your son's children belonged to your family, but your daughter's children belonged to the son-in-law's family.

In the husband's case, although he was a man, his getting married wasn't "fetching a woman," like most men, but was

"going to a woman's home." He had never had his own terri-
tory. He had been a person without a home since he became
an orphan.

How old was he when he became an orphan? Has he ever told me?

If we moved to town, I wouldn't see my fellow villagers anymore. I didn't mind. I wouldn't be able to take a walk in the
bamboo grove, though. I would miss my homegrown vegetables in the backyard. What about the barber? He was a good
barber and I needed a good barber. There was also something
else about him. I missed his hug, the only hug he gave me in
the bamboo grove. I hoped nobody had seen us. I wanted to
find out whether he liked me.

The husband wouldn't see Hotpot. I did suspect he was having an affair with her. I would probably never know the truth.

Perhaps I should have some sympathy for the husband. If he
had been to university, he might have got a job working in a
big company in Dalian. If we hadn't set up a comedy duo, he
would have found a job somewhere. At least he wouldn't be
stuck in the village. When we did our comedy duo, although we
lived in the countryside, we didn't do any work in the fields. I
used to feel proud that we didn't have to work like farm laborers. Not many people wanted to work in the fields for a living
if there was a choice.

We could be better off in the village if he raised pigs and
chickens. He could still play some mah-jongg. Mum said he was
lazy. Maybe she was right. I knew it was smelly and dirty and
hard work, but if one day nobody paid me to cry at funerals, I
wouldn't mind having pigs and chickens in the backyard. If the
backyard was smelly, the house would be smelly, then I would
get used to the smell, so I wouldn't think the village was smelly.

I wondered whether things would be different if we had a son.
Although the husband had got over the idea of having a son and
had said he didn't mind having a daughter, he had also said he
would do anything for a son. He had encouraged the daughter

to work hard at school, but she found schoolwork difficult and uninteresting. Would he have tried harder to find a job if she had had the ability to go to university? As a proud dad, would he have been motivated to earn some money for the daughter's higher education?

Would he do anything for a grandson if the daughter had a son?

23

Mum wanted to go to the grocery shop with me. We decided to walk to the bamboo grove to take a look at the bamboo shoots.

It looked like nobody had dug up any bamboo shoots.

"It's too cold to be outside digging," Mum said.

"The shoots are too small and thin. We need some rain to help the bamboo grow."

"Yes, the soil will be loosened. Easy to dig." She nodded.

"Hopefully it will rain soon."

I searched the shelf in the shop where I found the small knife, but there were no garden tools.

Maybe I could ask the barber to order a trowel for me. I didn't know why he gave me his number. I didn't need it. If I wanted something, I could tell him when I had my hair done, unless I needed something urgent. No, I never needed anything urgent. He had my number too, but I doubted he would call me or text me.

But if he liked me, he would like me to text him and we could arrange to see each other when I wasn't having my hair done. He could also text me. When would I receive his messages?

Mum and I bought some chicken wings and eggs from the grocery shop. I didn't see the barber in the shop.

Mum would like to eat dumplings, so she had prepared some dough before we went to the shop.

I made a pot of green tea, then we sat down to make dumplings.

"Does he go out to play mah-jongg every day?"

"Almost."

"He doesn't have a job, so he should do some housework."

"He does when I work," I lied.

Mum shook her head. "No, he doesn't."

Mum and I didn't have any further exchanges until I stood up to boil some dumplings.

"You're married, so I shouldn't get involved," Mum said.

"You're my mum, you can say anything you want."

"I don't want to, but maybe I have to if I give you money."

My eyelids twitched.

I placed two plates of dumplings on the table.

"I'm going to give most of the money to you," Mum said.

"What money?" I knew, but I still asked.

"The money your dad earned from the care home."

"No. I'm the daughter. Even half is more than enough for me."

"It's your dad's money. You're his daughter."

"The brother is his son. He should get more."

"He's not your dad's son."

I dropped my dumpling.

"Did Dad know?"

"Yes."

"Who's the brother's father?"

"He's dead."

"Did I know him?"

"Yes. Don't ask me who he was."

I wouldn't ask.

"What did he look like?" I tried to filter all the older men I had known in my life.

"Similar to your dad."

Hearing what Mum said, I couldn't help laughing.

"Why are you laughing?"

"Mum, at least you've had two men. I've only had one man in my life."

"You still have chances to have more men."

"That's not possible. There are no men in the village."

"If you want to find a man, you'll suddenly see lots of men."

"I'm too old and ugly for another chance."

"No, you're not."

"You're biased. I'm your daughter."

"You're a pretty girl. But I don't think you should have another man as you've got a husband."

"I won't, Mum. You're pretty, Mum."

"No, I'm not. I was pretty when I was young."

"Did you have many suitors?" I was curious.

"A few. Your dad was the clever one, so I chose him."

"It sounded like a clever choice."

"Maybe. By the way, am I eating too much?" Mum put down her chopsticks.

"No, of course not. You can eat as much as you like."

"No, I can't. Your brother's wife thinks I eat too much."

"Did you tell the brother?"

"He was there when she said it."

"Didn't he say anything?"

"No. She said it was healthier to eat less."

I stood up. "I'll boil some more dumplings for us."

★ ★ ★

When Mum was taking a nap in her room, I filled the stove with some new coal. I would leave the stove open and running for a couple of more hours before I sealed it.

Mum said it was for the family, for Dad's family, that she had slept with another man. She couldn't get pregnant for several years, and they didn't know why. Dad's family desperately wanted a boy, just like any other family.

Mum and Dad were frustrated and disappointed. They were both healthy and they also had sex as often as possible to make it easy for Mum to fall pregnant. Then they gave up. At first, they were going to find a woman to be a surrogate, but that would be obviously scandalous. When Dad decided that Mum would try with another man, it was almost seen as heroic by Mum. He chose the man for her, and the man was paid to keep the secret. Mum became pregnant after sleeping with the other man several times.

Surprisingly, Mum fell pregnant again three years later. I was unexpected.

But…was I Dad's daughter? According to Mum, I was. Had Dad been as convinced as Mum? I didn't want to say I didn't believe what Mum had told me, but Mum was the only person who could be convinced. Did she sleep with the other man secretly after the brother was born? Did they become lovers when the man was sleeping with Mum for money?

If I were Dad's daughter, the brother could well be Dad's son. Therefore, who had fathered the brother, or me, could remain an unsolved mystery.

Why did Mum believe the brother was the other man's, unless she didn't sleep with Dad while she was sleeping with the other man? There was no reason why she should stop sleeping with Dad when she was trying to get pregnant with the other man. I wouldn't ask her. She might not even remember, or might not tell me the truth. It wasn't an appropriate question for a daughter to ask anyway.

On the one hand, I was pleased that Mum would give most of the money to me. But how was she going to break this news to the brother? How could she prove that the brother wasn't the father's son? The brother wouldn't be happy at all, and the sister-in-law would be mad at me. If she spread the news, that would humiliate my old mother. However, there were a couple of other possibilities: the brother already knew who his father was, or it could just be a story invented by Mum because she wanted to give money to me.

I heard that once people reached a certain age, they didn't care what they did as there wasn't much damage they could do to themselves or other people. And people wouldn't become annoyed with them for anything. People weren't bothered. Mum was far beyond that certain age, so maybe she wouldn't be embarrassed to say that she had a child with a man other than her husband.

The husband would be as shocked as me. What would he say about Mum?

To be fair, the husband used to have higher standards in life. He used to read books at night before he took up mah-jongg. We didn't have many books at home, but I'd been keeping the daughter's textbooks. There were literary extracts in her Chinese textbooks that the husband enjoyed reading, and he sometimes even read the science books. Dad would borrow magazines and newspapers from the village committee for him. But he had never bought a book to read. A pile of paper, a waste of money, he said.

He first started as a backup for Mum's mah-jongg circle, as the game required four players and there were occasions when one of them was unavailable. Since he soon became good at it, more and more people began inviting him. He used to play once or twice a week when he was still working.

Now he was as ordinary as any other man in the village, if not worse.

★ ★ ★

"How long is your mother going to be here?" the husband asked in the dark.

"I've told you, I don't know."

"It's our home."

"It's her house."

"There is no freedom when she's here."

"We used to live with Mum and Dad, but you never said anything."

"I had no choice then."

"What kind of freedom do you want?"

"We're husband and wife. I don't want anyone else to live with us."

I was almost touched, but I didn't know what to say.

The husband tugged at my panties.

I froze. Was he going to pull them off? But he grumbled, "I'm tired."

He rolled over to his side.

I closed my eyes, and rolled over toward my corner.

When I was about to fall asleep, I felt something under my panties. It was the husband's fingers.

He pulled me over and quickly climbed on top of me. My legs felt his thing, warm but floppy. He removed my panties and adjusted his body to the middle of my body. He rubbed against me slowly until he wasn't floppy.

He was slow and quiet, then he suddenly stopped.

He complained, "You didn't move."

I didn't know what he meant.

"You were lying there like a dead fish. It's no fun if you don't move," he said.

I didn't respond.

"You were silent too. You ruined my night, stupid woman."

Yes. I ruined his night.

I felt sorry for him. I felt sorry for myself, too.

24

I had a crying job in a nearby village called zhēn zhū hé cūn, Pearl River Village.

Several of my secondary-school friends were from the village, but I had never been there. It was bigger than my village and it was closer to gū shān zhèn, Solitude Mountain Town, which made a huge difference. There was more movement between zhēn zhū hé cūn and the town than xī ní hé cūn, West Mud River Village. And zhēn zhū hé cūn seemed to have more energy. I saw children playing along the paths, and there were apple trees and pear trees outside people's houses.

I didn't see any mud paths in the village. I didn't smell any pig poo or chicken poo, either. There were dogs and cats running around.

I wondered whether any of my friends were still living in the village. Would I bump into any one of them? Would they speak to me? They might not recognize me, though.

"Hey, you're walking into that pear tree." I heard someone shouting.

I stopped walking and looked up to where the sound was from. I was almost facing the tree. I saw a man standing near me.

"Are you...?" he asked me, or kind of asked me.

"Do you know me? Who are you?" I asked him. He was a man about the husband's age, so also my age.

"Sorry, I didn't know you," the man said. "I mistook you for a school friend."

"That's okay."

When I was told the name and the age of the deceased, I was shaken. It was a girl I knew from my secondary school. I felt a chill on my back. I remembered the very rich man's late ex-wife as well. It was really our turn to die now.

Nobody told me how she had died. Illness or accident? The bereaved families didn't always tell me the cause of death, but through the chats we had while preparing for the funeral, I would normally have an idea.

How would I cry for a long-lost friend at the funeral? We hadn't seen each other since we finished school, and I didn't know what she would look like now.

She wasn't a close friend of mine, but almost everyone knew about her at school. She had been called to be spoken to by the headmaster several times for inappropriate behavior. She was the only girl I knew who wasn't shy about her breasts, unlike most of us, who wore loose clothes and almost hunched while we were walking. I recalled the boys' eyes on her. She was criticized by some teachers for *luring bees and attracting butterflies*. She was nicknamed "Bubble Tea" by the boys.

I sat in Bubble Tea's parents' living room with a couple of her female relatives. It seemed there wouldn't be enough guests for the funeral. She didn't have a husband or any children, and none of her siblings were close to her. Her parents were frail, especially her mother. I had only caught a glimpse of her parents when I first arrived. They were both resting in their bedroom. The two female relatives were her uncles' wives, who lived in the same village.

One of the female relatives said maybe no funeral was needed, as nobody really cared, and the crying was quite expensive...

"I can cry for free." I thought I shouldn't pretend I had never known her.

"Why?" They were surprised.

"I was her best friend at school," I lied.

So they told me what had happened to Bubble Tea. She became a "Damaged Shoe" after she was dumped by her fiancé in her twenties. A Damaged Shoe was used to describe a loose woman, every man's lover. In the past, prostitutes would hang an embroidered shoe as a symbol under the gutter to attract clients. Over time, the shoe became weathered in the wind and rain and sun, so it faded and was damaged. A Damaged Shoe was the most humiliating nickname for a woman.

People believed she had slept with many men, some as lovers and some as clients. They had all given her food or money or presents. Mothers would warn their daughters not to go near her. Her dad used to hit her with a bamboo stick, but he had to rely on her income when he became old. She had lived peacefully at home with her parents for the last ten years or so.

Bubble Tea was killed in an accident. Her body was damaged and so was her face. She was being reshaped in the crematorium, and it cost a fortune.

What accident? There was silence. They wouldn't tell me. I didn't need to know anyway.

Did the police get involved? There was still silence.

I promised the funeral would be a proper one, although small, and I wouldn't charge any fees.

★ ★ ★

"Can I go to Bubble Tea's funeral?" the husband asked when we were eating dinner.

"You don't need to ask. You know you don't need an invitation to go to a funeral," Mum said.

"It'll be good if you go. There won't be many people at the funeral." I shook my head.

"I'll inform some school friends."

I told them Bubble Tea's story.

"Can her parents afford to pay you? You should give them a discount," the husband suggested.

"I've offered to cry for free."

Mum nodded. "You should. Losing a child is the worst thing that could happen to parents, especially elderly parents."

"She must have been killed by someone," the husband said.

"Maybe," I said.

"By a woman," he added.

"Why?" I put my chopsticks down.

"Who would have damaged her face? A jealous woman."

"Bubble Tea wasn't as bad as her reputation," the husband said when we were in the bedroom.

"I never thought she was bad."

"It was true that she let some of the boys touch her breasts, but she never slept with any of them."

"How do you know?"

"I don't know for sure, but I never heard any of the boys boast about sleeping with her."

"What about some of the male teachers? There were rumors."

"She let them touch her, and they let her pass the exams."

"That wasn't what teachers should have done," I said.

"Maybe they *were* rumors."

"I hope they were."

★ ★ ★

I found it hard to fall asleep, since my mind was full of Bubble Tea.

How did she die? Why wouldn't anybody tell me? Did she kill herself?

How badly had her body and face been damaged?

If she had killed herself, she would only have managed to damage her body, say, with a knife, but wouldn't have been able to damage her face at the same time. If she had died in an accident, what kind of accident would have damaged her body as well as her face at the same time?

Was she killed by someone, someone who had hated her so much? Who would have hated her so much? Had her breasts been damaged? She must have suffered. How much had she suffered? She must have been scared when she realized she was going to die. How scared had she been?

The husband said Bubble Tea must have been killed by *a jealous woman*. A wife of a man Bubble Tea had slept with killed her by accident after quarrelling. It wasn't impossible.

A hand placed under my top and reached my breasts, but moved down quickly. The cold fingers stayed on my belly.

What was the husband thinking about? Had he ever touched Bubble Tea's breasts?

The hand didn't linger for long.

The husband wasn't in the bedroom when I woke up. It was late morning. I had no idea when I'd fallen asleep. My eyes were heavy and my head hurt.

I remembered the man I saw in zhēn zhū hé cūn, Pearl River Village. Who was that man? He said he mistook me for his school friend. Was he one of my school friends? I couldn't recognize him. I didn't know how much I had changed since I left school. Maybe he recognized me but decided he didn't want to talk to me because I was a funeral cryer? The husband was still in touch with some of his friends, so I could ask him whether he had contact with people in zhēn zhū hé cūn.

Mum was sitting on the sofa, doing some sewing. I had filled my hot-water bottle. I placed it on Mum's lap.

"I've started making my last outfit." Mum held the hot-water bottle in her arms.

"Mum." I sat down next to her. I wanted to hug her, but I was too embarrassed to do it.

"Everyone dies. I only hope I won't die miserably."

"You'll live for a long time yet, Mum."

"I hope so, but you never know. We never know when we'll die."

"I'll look after you, Mum," I said quietly.

"I don't want to trouble you. Your father's death was a good one."

"Mum."

"He didn't suffer and he even earned money from his death."

"Sorry. It was my fault."

"No. You can't stop death, and you can't postpone it. It's life."

"I'll look after you," I repeated.

"Don't worry about me. I might die tomorrow. I might live for one hundred years."

I didn't want to discuss death with Mum, so I didn't respond. Death was what I dealt with for a living, and there was enough for me. I tried not to have anything to do with it in my everyday life. Mum's death was something I would have to think about, but not discuss.

"Have you looked for my bone china bowl?" Mum asked while we were having lunch.

"I have, but I couldn't find it."

"Do you think it's been stolen?"

"Who could have stolen it?"

"It's not a cheap bowl. Your dad bought two when we got married."

"Where's the other one?"

"It was broken a long time ago."

"I'll keep looking."

I wrapped some shredded pork and spring onion in a pancake for Mum. She unwrapped it and sprinkled some chili powder over the pancake.

She took a bite and nodded. "I want to talk to you about something more important."

"What's that, Mum?"

"You know what. Money."

"Don't give me too much money, Mum. I'm only a daughter."

"I don't mind giving your brother money, but not his wife."

"The brother's money is hers too," I said.

"It's not hers if they get divorced."

"You can't make them divorce."

"I believe she's seeing another man."

"Why do you think so?"

"I don't know how. I just know."

"I know she's said something unkind to you, but…"

"She's stupid. Don't you think she should be nice to me if she wants my money?"

"She should be nice to you even if you didn't have money."

"She assumed I'd give my money to your brother, so she didn't care what she said to me."

"But do you think they'll get divorced?"

"I don't know. Maybe your brother is seeing another woman."

"Why do you say that, Mum?"

"I don't think he likes his wife that much."

"People don't always get divorced if they don't like each other, Mum."

"I think I know more than you on that subject."

"I'm sure you do. Does the brother tell you he doesn't like his wife?"

"Your brother. I tell him everything, but he doesn't tell me everything."

"Have you told him he isn't Dad's son?"

Mum didn't answer my question.

She stood up. "Your pancakes weren't bad, but too thick."

Mum walked back to her bedroom to carry on making her last outfit, so I decided to have my hair done. I wanted to pay respect to Bubble Tea. Her hairstyle always looked good.

I felt stiff, so I also needed a massage, a full-body massage.

25

I could see the barber moving around holding a long broom through the windows. I watched for a little while before I knocked on the door.

The place seemed different. I looked around and thought the barbershop looked more spacious. The dinner table wasn't there any longer, and the windows were spotlessly clean.

"I was sweeping the floor. Hardly anyone comes when it's cold." He leaned the broom against one of the dressing tables.

"It's clean and bright."

"It's not bad. I haven't got anything to do."

"Is your wife—no, girlfriend—home?"

"She was back, but she's gone again."

"Why does she always go away?" I asked quietly.

"She's bored in the village."

"But why did she move back here?"

"I wanted to live in a village."

"Not many people want to live in the countryside."

"It's better for my injured leg. The air is fresher in the countryside and I don't need to hurry."

"Your leg?"

"I was hit by a car while I was riding a bike."

"Did the car run over you?"

"No. It ran over my bike. My leg was stuck under the bike."

"Does it still hurt?"

"No. Do I look awful when I limp?"

"No. You don't limp."

I sat on the swivel chair. I could see myself in the large mirror in front of me, an ugly, old woman.

The barber put a bib around my neck and asked, "Have you washed your hair yourself?"

"No. I'm not going to wash my hair myself anymore." I didn't know why I had said it.

"I'll make sure your hair is shiny and fragrant."

"Can you give me a massage first?"

"Of course."

"A proper one, not just a head massage. I'm tired."

"No problem."

I looked at myself in the mirror.

"Are you okay?" he asked.

"Look. I'm so old and ugly." I pointed to myself in the mirror.

"No, you're not. You look lovely," he said gently.

"A school friend of mine died," I told the barber.

"Still so young." He adjusted the hairdressing chair.

"She died in an accident."

"What kind of accident?"

"I don't know. She might have been killed by someone."

"Why do you think so?" he asked. His fingers started rubbing my shoulders.

"Her family didn't tell me everything."

"Everyone has something they don't want to tell others." His hands paused on me.

"You're right."

Although the head massage was free, you would have to pay for a proper massage. I had never had one before, as I thought it was a waste of money. I wanted to stay in the barbershop for a little longer, so having a massage was a good idea.

The back of the hairdressing chair had been lowered, so it was comfortable to sit back. I half closed my eyes. Something caught my eye in the far corner of the room where I wouldn't have been able to see if I wasn't leaning back. It was a bag under a stack of chairs, a lady's small cross-body bag. I could see the thin and long strap. It must be the barber's girlfriend's bag. But why was it on the floor? It looked like the bag had been pushed and squeezed between the legs of the chair.

Should I ask the barber to pick the bag up? Were they looking for it?

No. It had nothing to do with me. We all had things lying around at home in the wrong places.

The massage lasted forever. It was comfortable, and I shut my eyes. I was half-asleep most of the time. I could easily have dozed off, but I tried my best to keep myself awake. I wasn't sure what I would look like when I was asleep, so it would be best not to fall asleep. I didn't want him to see me drooling.

It might have been a dream. I felt the barber was rubbing my breasts while he was giving me a massage. I opened my eyes and nearly jumped up.

When he did my hair, we didn't talk. He moved his hands more slowly, but I could hear his breathing. I tried to stay still.

I didn't ask how much I needed to pay. I left some money on the dressing table and hurried home.

It was cold and windy outside with a drizzle, and I didn't have my scarf. I might have left it in the barbershop. I didn't remember whether I had taken it with me when I left home.

★ ★ ★

I felt my hair after I arrived home. It was messy and wet thanks to the wind and rain. It was the worst thing when my hairdo was ruined before a crying job.

I was combing my hair sadly when I received a text message: "There will be no funeral as Bubble Tea will be cremated soon due to the difficulty of restoring her face."

I had to admit I felt a sense of relief, but I was devastated at the news. What did Bubble Tea's face look like now? She had been the same age as me, so I wouldn't imagine her being as beautiful as when she was young. She might have been ugly and old like me, but at least I was still alive.

I also felt furious. Nobody respected her when she was alive, and nobody cared about her when she was dead. Everybody deserved a decent send-off. Her ashes could be present; her photo could be present. A funeral was a farewell party. I wanted to wave goodbye to her with my genuine crying.

Then I realized her parents might not be able to pay for the restoration of her face, so they had to cancel everything.

So long, Bubble Tea.

I was on the verge of tears, but I didn't cry. Mum was here. When you were living with someone old, it was bad luck for them if you cried. I needed to cry, since the tears I accumulated for Bubble Tea needed to be released.

I would make a phone call to the manager of Sunset. There were many elderly people there, and some of them must be dying now. Their bodies and minds were too vulnerable for severe weather conditions.

It wasn't that I wanted them to die. They died, and there would be a funeral, and someone would have to cry for them. I would be their funeral cryer and I would do a good job. I didn't cause their death, so I shouldn't feel guilty.

I rang Sunset, but there was no answer and the call went to voice mail, which gave me a different number. I dialed the num-

ber, but it wasn't a care home. Instead, it was a hotel. I asked
them about the care home, but the operator said it was a new
hotel, and she knew nothing about Sunset.

Should I pay a visit to the care home or the new hotel?

Where was the care home now? Even if the care home had
been closed down, they would have made some arrangements
for the old people. Where had they been relocated to?

Then I was overwhelmed by a sense of self-loathing. The
husband was right. I was useless when nobody died.

The husband seemed upset when he learned Bubble Tea's funeral had been canceled.

"I've never heard of anything like that. You can cancel anything, but you can't cancel a funeral."

"Maybe it's better like this. You probably wouldn't be able
to recognize her now." I comforted him.

"I'm sure I would."

"No, you wouldn't. Her face is damaged."

"Do you know when they're going to cremate her? Can we
see her before she's cremated?" he asked.

"I don't know."

"Do you want to see her?"

"I don't think it's a good idea. Let's remember what she
looked like when she was young."

"I remember what she looked like," he said.

I also remembered her curvy figure, and I imagined the husband remembered that too.

"By the way, Hotpot's just given birth to a baby boy," the
husband said when we were in bed.

"Today?"

"Yes, although she was taken to hospital yesterday."

"Who took her?"

"Not me."

"Was everything okay?"

"Yes, but the baby was premature."

"Was the baby healthy?" I asked.

"I think so. Just a little smaller."

"Babies grow fast."

The husband soon started snoring. I didn't ask him too much about Hotpot and her son. He must be glad both Hotpot and her son were doing well. He could even be the father, so he might be over the moon.

I used to feel annoyed when the husband snored, but now I didn't care as it might not last for too long. One day, all his snoring would disappear for good, and the smell of cigarettes or sweat, which I hated, would cease to exist.

If the husband died before me, I would make arrangements for a decent funeral, and I would cry for him. If I died first, who would cry for me? When I died, Mum might still be alive, you never knew, so she would cry for me.

If I could decide, I didn't want a funeral. They could just burn me into ashes and spread them in my backyard to help the vegetables grow. By then, if Mum had gone, the daughter would be the only person who would cry for me genuinely.

Thinking about the daughter, I realized I hadn't received any messages from her for... I didn't know how long. To be honest, she wasn't the best daughter, and I didn't miss her badly. She had been an average child. She passed exams at school, but she wasn't very beautiful. It was mean to say it, but as a woman, you had to be beautiful if you weren't that bright. She didn't do much housework for me either. However, she was my only child, and I would leave all my money to her. I would like to know whether she was pregnant or not. I would be more willing to give my money to her if she had a child. I wanted to be a grandma.

If I had a grandson, I would have something meaningful

to do. The husband and I might get on a bit better. When the daughter was little, the three of us had some happy times.

I should phone her. It sounded more real.

When I woke up in the morning, I couldn't keep the daughter out of my head. I sat up. The husband had taken up most of the space in the bed, and his head was also under the duvet.

I picked up my phone from the bedside table. There were some cracks on the screen. It was an old phone from the daughter. I had had it for at least three years.

She didn't answer the phone, but she called back a couple of hours later.

"Sorry, Mum, I was on my shift, preparing the herbs for a foot massage."

"Are you still doing long hours?"

"I'm fine. I can manage. The manager has promised she'll let me work on reception once I'm pregnant."

"So you're not pregnant now?"

"No, I'm not."

"Take it easy."

The line was cut off before the daughter replied.

It wasn't fine. The daughter didn't sound fine. When I was wondering whether I should ask her or not, she texted me.

"He's left me. Don't be angry with him. It wasn't his fault. There's an older woman at my work, my friend. They're together now. I don't hate her. She's not a bad person. He had to leave me after she fell pregnant. I was sad, but not too sad. People thought we were husband and wife, but you know we never registered so it was fine for him to leave. We didn't need to get divorced. I'm staying in the same apartment. He's still sharing the rent. I'm looking to move into another shared apartment with some single female masseuses. I'm fine. I don't think I loved him that much, and he didn't love me much either. We were together because we liked each other and it was cheaper to live together. I'm sorry. I know you and Dad wanted a grand-child. I'm so sorry, Mum."

I read the messages again. No, she didn't have to apologize.

I had liked the "son-in-law," but I wouldn't forgive him. These days, young people used "love" as an excuse. Where did they put "morality"? Did he pay compensation to the daughter? What could the daughter do? Where could she find another young man? When I once reminded her to register marriage, she joked it would be easier for her to leave him in the future without a marriage certificate. I forgot to remind her it would be more difficult for him to abandon her if there was a certifi-cate. Then I totally forgot about the business as I was trapped in trouble myself.

People in the countryside usually got married at a younger age than those in the city. While the city young people were studying for degrees, the countryside young people were look-ing for people to get married. We weren't that picky, so it wasn't hard to decide who you were going to marry or stay together with. It seemed it took city people many years to decide who they would like to marry after they'd had several boyfriends and girlfriends. The strange thing was, even if they had been careful, city people got divorced more often than us country-side people.

On the other hand, in my opinion, while it was fine not to have a husband, it was important to have a child. What if the daughter couldn't find another man soon? I wouldn't tell Mum, as she was looking forward to having a great-grandchild. She once said her last ambition was to become a great-grandma. In fact, she had never had any other ambitions, so it was her first and only ambition. A family of four generations was most peo-ple's dream.

Maybe I should go to Shanghai to visit the daughter, but who would benefit from it? Nobody. And the train fares would be spent in vain.

When were they going to build those villas and apartments? We could move to town, as the husband wished. Now I also quite liked the idea of investing in an apartment in town, when we had plenty of money. Maybe we could open a hotpot restaurant with the daughter.

Now that the daughter didn't have a man to be with her, I felt a little closer to her and wanted to help her more. But had she been looked after before? I had had a man for over twenty years, and I had never been taken good care of.

What was a marriage for? Was it for company or care?

Who invented the word *love*? What did it mean?

26

Mum said I had wasted money on the hairdo. I agreed with her, but it wasn't anyone's fault. If I'd borrowed an umbrella from the barber, my hair would have been fine. If I hadn't left my scarf there, my hair wouldn't have been messy. Meanwhile, I didn't need a hairdo, as there was no funeral. It would be a waste anyway, even if it had been protected by an umbrella or a scarf.

I wasn't sure whether I should go back to the barbershop to ask about my scarf. I hadn't seen it at home since I had my hair done, but it could be sitting there somewhere.

If the barber saw the scarf, he probably wouldn't think it was mine. I wasn't his only customer, so the scarf could well be someone else's. If he was a careless man, he might even think it was his girlfriend's scarf.

I wouldn't ask the barber about my scarf. It would be embarrassing for me if it were there, as it was an ancient knitted scarf, thin and bare.

I didn't tell Mum about the scarf. She would insist that I go back to the barbershop to fetch it.

I wasn't sure whether the barber had touched my breasts accidentally or intentionally. He had to touch me when he was massaging me, but not my breasts. I felt ashamed of myself. My breasts were not large, and they were not firm either. I wasn't even wearing a bra when I went to the barbershop last time. My breasts must have been sagging. They weren't exciting for men at all.

But maybe, maybe it had been a dream.

Dreams were good. You could do anything in your dreams. Dreams were also secrets. It was exciting to be able to do anything you liked and it was exciting to have secrets. I had started liking to see the barber, but I didn't tell anyone about it, so now I had a secret.

Did I wish the barber had touched my breasts on purpose? Was I cross with him because I wasn't wearing a bra? Or because I thought my breasts were not good enough?

The husband didn't always come home for dinner these days. I didn't ask him who he ate with and where. There was no point in asking him, as he could lie and I wouldn't know if he was lying. It was embarrassing when Mum was here. She must think I was useless as I didn't always know the husband's whereabouts.

Cooking could be boring if you had to cook every day or for one person, especially in winter when the kitchen was cold and dishes would cool down quickly. Mum was here at the moment, so I enjoyed cooking more.

Mum was watching a shopping channel on TV. They were selling kitchen things like woks and soup pots.

"What would you like to eat, Mum?" I asked.

"Something to keep us warm?"

"What about some chicken soup? It'll warm your stomach."

"Good idea."

"Snow is on its way, Mum."

"We can put some dried mushroom in the soup. I brought a pack when I came."

"Thank you. Shall we go out to check the bamboo shoots?" I suggested.

"Yes. They'll boost the freshness of the soup."

Bamboo shoots were nutritious and delicious. The winter shoots were robust and not as common and delicate as the spring shoots.

We did need to go out. It was time to store up some cabbage in the backyard, which was a natural fridge in winter. Sweet potato noodles were also essential in winter. Cabbage, pork and noodles made a house special dish for every household in winter in Northeast China.

Since there was nothing else to look forward to, I looked forward to eating some nice food with Mum, and the husband if he was home.

Mum and I wrapped ourselves up.

I opened the door, but saw the husband.

"It's started raining." He wiped his forehead.

"We were going to the bamboo grove," I said.

"It should be dry tomorrow. The rain here never lasts."

So we stayed in. I chopped the chicken. Mum insisted that she cook the chicken soup.

She opened the cupboard. "Dried chili, Sichuan pepper, bay leaves, chili powder, five-spice powder…"

"We're never short of spices and herbs, Mum."

"You didn't throw any of my spice jars away."

"Why would I?"

"But where's my trowel?"

"Let's cook the chicken soup, Mum."

"Remember: the wok should be hot but the oil cold before you add the chicken pieces."

"I know."

"You don't always remember."

Mum didn't like cooking that much, but she was good at it.

The husband was a bit taken by Mum's chicken soup.

"Delicious. Rich and thick. The chicken's soft." The husband stuffed a piece of chicken into his mouth.

"It's the same chicken soup I used to cook." Mum took a sip.

"It's even better now." The husband nodded.

"The potato makes the dish thick." Mum tasted some soup with her spoon.

"You're a better cook than me, Mum," I said.

"Of course." Mum was pleased.

After dinner, the husband was playing a poker game on his phone while I was knitting a scarf for myself using wool from an old sweater. The wool looked a little better than the scarf I had lost. The TV was on, but the volume was low. It was a replay of one of the wartime spy TV series.

Although whether I looked good or not wasn't important, looking good made me feel good. Perhaps I should buy a brightly colored scarf, but I thought people would raise their eyebrows when they saw it. As a married woman, people would gossip about you if you made an effort to look good: *Are you trying to seduce men?* Bad women, Damaged Shoes like Bubble Tea, usually looked nice.

It seemed my life was no more than existing. Maybe most people lived like this. All I did was earn money, buy food, eat and sleep. Recently, I had been wondering what might happen when the husband or I died. The last outfit, the graveyard. I had neither of these.

The husband threw his jacket on the bed. I picked it up and placed it on the chest of drawers.

"Your mum is strange," the husband said.

"Why?" I stopped knitting.

"I heard her asking you about the trowel again."

"What's wrong with that?"

"It's only a trowel."

"Did you throw it away?" I asked.

"Why would I?" He sounded annoyed.

"She's my mother. She can say whatever she likes to her daughter."

"But why the trowel?"

"It doesn't matter whether it's a trowel or a china bowl."

"Sorry?"

"Mum and I don't really have much to talk about. It seems as though she's trying to tell me off, but she isn't."

"I don't understand."

"No, you don't. You're an orphan."

"Thank you for reminding me." He put the phone down.

After a while of silence, the husband asked, "Have you seen Hotpot recently?"

"No. Maybe we should help her store up some cabbage."

"She's thinking about putting her son up for adoption."

"Why?" I was surprised. "Is it because the baby is premature?"

"No. I think the baby is growing well."

"There is no reason to give the baby up, then."

"She can't afford to bring him up."

"But you mentioned she was getting some financial support from her relatives."

"They can't help her forever."

"The mah-jongg venue renting…"

"That's not much."

"She still gets money from men?" A vague image of a young Bubble Tea appeared before me.

"I don't know."

"She's on the verge of becoming a Damaged Shoe," I murmured.

"What?"

"Nothing."

"Do you want to adopt her son?"

"I want to have a son, but we're too old for such a young son."

"The daughter would look after him when we're old."

I would have said *no* straightaway, but now that the daughter was single, it didn't sound like a bad idea.

"Hotpot might want to get married again," the husband said.

"That sounds more plausible. The baby's in the way." I slowed down my knitting.

"Could the baby boy take my family name if we adopted him?" The husband pressed a hand on mine.

When the husband tugged at my panties, I didn't move away. The night was cold and the heat of the stove was low, so it wasn't too bad when someone touched your skin.

I still felt dry. I had always been dry. Everything about me was dry now, including my skin.

What about Hotpot? She was much younger than me with wrinkleless skin. She looked fresh.

Did she actually know who had fathered her son? Did she have a favorite man she wished to be the father? There might be more than three of those men. How many men in the village suspected they were the father? Maybe they were all helping her as they thought they might be the father. Was the husband one of them? Or was the barber?

The barber was the mostly unlikely one, and the most likely one at the same time. Hotpot had been to the barbershop. I had never seen her there, but the barber wouldn't have made it up. A woman wouldn't visit her secret lover's house openly, but it was fine to visit a barber—a free hairdo exchanged for sex.

And, of course, the most suspicious evidence was the shampoo. It made perfect sense for a barber to give away some shampoo. I felt pain when I was imagining them together. He had a nice upstairs room. Most importantly, he had offered Butcher a job. The barber could be the man Butcher caught in bed with Hotpot. He arranged Butcher's shifts in the shop, so he knew when Butcher wasn't home.

The barber's girlfriend wasn't home right now. I didn't know her well, as she had hardly lived in the village before she moved back with the barber. The husband had an impression that she had left the barber, and the barber told me she wasn't home. Had the barber implied something when he said she wasn't home? Did he touch me to test my reaction? Was he a womanizer?

It might be a good idea to pay a visit to Hotpot.

I would take my wheelbarrow with me when I went to the shop with Mum, and I would take some cabbage to Hotpot. If Mum liked the baby too, I might consider adopting him. It could well be the husband's son. It seemed a crazy idea, but it could be wrong or right, so a fifty-fifty chance.

Without the baby, Hotpot could move anywhere to find work or a man to give her some financial security. There was no hope for her while she was stuck in a remote village.

When there was some youth left, there would be some future. This village, like an elderly person, was dying slowly, unless the property developers turned up one day. Then we would have either money or villas or apartments, and new people would come to bring some dynamism to the village. It wasn't the right place for Hotpot and her son.

I looked forward to meeting the baby soon. I would play with him.

Now I wished the husband was the father.

27

Mum and I were going to the shop. I wrapped my scarf around my neck after putting my coat on.

"Are you going to wear this?" Mum pointed to my newly knitted scarf.

"Yes." I nodded.

"But can you wear something more colorful? What color is your scarf?"

I looked down around my neck. Yes, what color was it? Brown? Gray? Beige? Yellowish?

"Mum, nobody will see it," I said.

"I will. So will you."

"I'll buy some colorful wool."

"I'll buy a scarf for you."

"You don't have to, Mum."

"At least your hair is a nice color. I don't like to see grays in my daughter's hair."

"I've got a good barber."

"But I don't like your wrinkles."

"Mums never like their daughters' wrinkles."

"Talking about daughters, how is yours?" Mum asked.

"She's fine."

"Tell her I want to be a great-grandma." Mum squeezed my arm.

"What about being a grandma again?"

"Are you pregnant? You still sleep with your lazy husband?"

"No. A young woman in the village has put a baby boy up for adoption."

"So you don't sleep with your husband?" She looked into my eyes.

"Mum, I want to adopt the baby." I ignored her question. She probably wasn't asking.

"You're too old to have a baby, but having a son is always good."

The shop was full of people. They all needed to store some food for the winter. We filled the wheelbarrow with twenty heads of cabbage and twelve packs of sweet potato noodles. Mum insisted on paying the bill.

On our way to Hotpot's house, Mum offered to push the wheelbarrow.

"I know I'm old, but I can still do most things myself."

"Don't carry heavy things when you're on your own, Mum."

"No, I won't. I'll look after myself. I want to be a great-grandma. I need to be alive."

"I'm glad you like the idea of adopting the baby, Mum."

"Why not? A good child is a great treasure. I'll help you look after your adopted son."

"But you'll move back to the brother's."

"If I'm busy here, I won't. They don't care," Mum said.

I didn't respond to Mum. I saw someone walking out of Hotpot's house—a tall, slim man. My eyes weren't that sharp, but I could see the man was lame.

"What's wrong with you? Why did you stop walking?" Mum turned around and called out to me.

Hotpot was surprised when we brought in the food from the wheelbarrow. She was tidying her dining table. Half of the table was covered with baby bottles, baby clothes and all kinds of leaflets.

"Big Sister, Big Auntie, thank you."

"It's easy for us." I started placing the cabbage and noodles on her dining table.

"You're a nice family." Hotpot picked up the baby clothes.

"There's no mah-jongg today?" I asked when I sat down.

"They don't come every day."

The baby was asleep.

"Are you sure you want to give up your son?" I asked.

"I can't afford anything nice." Hotpot looked around her living room.

"What about Butcher's relatives? Have you told them what you're going to do with your son?"

"Nobody cares. They don't think he's Butcher's son."

"Did they say that? I'm so sorry. That must have hurt you."

"I don't mind." Hotpot shrugged.

"It wasn't nice to say that." Mum joined the conversation.

"Maybe they were right. I've slept with other men."

"Do you still not want to find out who the father is?" I asked with a quickening heartbeat.

"He could be Butcher's son anyway." Hotpot fiddled with a baby bottle.

"That's possible." Mum nodded.

"How much money are you prepared to pay?" Hotpot turned toward me.

"Are you selling your son?"

"No, but I've spent money on him. I can't give him away and lose money."

"How much are you thinking about?" I asked.

"I don't know. I've never done this before."

"We'll think about it. We'll come back another time," Mum said.

"Okay. But some other people have shown interest in him too."

"Is any one of those men interested?" I asked.

"Not really." Hotpot shook her head.

Then she added, "They still want to sleep with me, but I'm recovering from my cuts."

"You shouldn't let them touch you," I said.

"They come to see me with presents."

"Don't let them touch you."

There was no answer.

Mum was doing some sewing while I was chopping the cabbage. We were going to eat pork noodles with cabbage and steamed buns for dinner. Imagining the fresh taste of the warm soup, I felt contented.

The husband didn't come home until after dark.

"I've had dinner," he said. "Are you having pork noodles? I'll have some."

I wondered who he had had dinner with, but I didn't ask.

"The soup's delicious," he said while he was slurping.

"We've given some cabbage and noodles to Hotpot."

"You're kind. Did you like her son?"

"Yes. She asked me how much money I'd be willing to pay."

"It's not unreasonable," the husband said.

"Maybe."

He stirred his noodles slowly and didn't say anything.

Mum went to her room after dinner. She wanted me to talk with the husband about the baby. She would like to have a baby at home, but as we might have to pay Hotpot a lot of money, she wasn't sure whether it was worthwhile.

The husband offered to dry the dishes.

"If we adopt the baby, our life will be very different," I said.

"I know. I'll look after him when you're doing your funeral crying."

"It'll be many years before he grows up. I'll be too old."

"We don't have to adopt him if you don't want to."

"We've got the daughter. She'll look after him after we've gone, I suppose."

"Yes. If she hasn't got children, it'll be like her own son."

"But I do wonder who the father is."

"Nobody knows. Even Hotpot doesn't know."

"In a few years' time, it might not be difficult to see which man in the village her son looks like."

"You're right."

"What if the man wanted to claim the child?"

"You're worrying too much about nothing."

Having a baby at home wouldn't be a big problem at first, but then he would have to go to school. The baby seemed to be healthy, but we had no idea whether he was bright or not. If he took after his mother, Hotpot, school would be a burden for him as well as us. If he couldn't go to university and get a good job, he might not be able to find a wife. The money we'd been saving was for our old age, not for feeding a young man.

Maybe I shouldn't worry too much about the future. I might not be around for long enough to see all that happen.

It might be fair to ask the daughter for an opinion.

It was another cold night.

The house was cold, and I felt cold. I might have forgotten to keep the stove open. I wished I could be hugged, just for warmth.

I huddled up in the duvet. I could see the barber in the dark when I closed my eyes. He was walking out of Hotpot's house. Was it someone else? Was I imagining?

I remembered seeing a new sack of rice and a pile of corncobs behind Hotpot's front door when Mum and I left her house. Did the barber give her all that as presents? She said *they come to see me with presents.*

I curled up and folded a corner of the duvet under my shoulder.

The husband was already snoring.

28

Late one morning, when I arrived back home with some chicken poo from Little Sister's, I saw a carrier bag under our porch.

I opened the bag. There were about ten cobs of corn. They were big and fresh. They must have just been picked. Who had left them for us? Or for me?

I was one of the very few people around my age in the village who took university entrance exams, and the only girl. Two or three of them went to university and I had hardly seen them since. The girls who went to school with me had mostly married men in other villages, and some in town. Girls were not encouraged to marry in the same village, since most families were related. Still, some women who had been in the village all their lives, like me, had either married men here or had been live-in daughters. Among them, there must be some people who still liked me, so they were giving me free food.

It wasn't the first time I'd found food under our porch. I'd found sweet potatoes and onions as well over the past years. Not a lot, but enough to show that I wasn't altogether worthless.

Mum was busy with her sewing every day.

"You haven't done any work since I came. It's been nearly a month."

"I want to keep you company. I turned down a couple of jobs recently," I said while I was chopping some pork for dumplings.

"Money won't walk to you if you stay at home."

Mum showed me the outfit she was making. "Look at the stitches." She was pleased.

"They're neat and fine, Mum."

"The outfit will be burned with me. Who cares whether the stitches are good or bad?"

"Mum." I didn't know what to say.

"Don't be upset. We all have to walk the same journey."

"You'll have a very long journey, Mum."

"Nobody knows. At least I don't need to worry about my last outfit."

"It's been beautifully done."

"I still feel guilty about your dad's last outfit. I didn't pre-pare it for him."

"We had a good-quality one made for him." I tried to comfort her.

"Do you remember? When you were still at school, he be-came so ill that we all thought he was going to die."

"Yes, I do." I nodded.

"I had begun sewing his last outfit, but then he recovered."

"It was odd, wasn't it?"

"Yes. I found his unfinished outfit in my wardrobe. You didn't throw it away."

"I didn't know it was there."

"The fabric still looks new."

"It has to be wasted. You can't use last-outfit material for anything else."

"I don't care. I'm not superstitious." She shook her head.

"What are you going to do with it?" I was curious.

"Make your husband's last outfit with it."

"I can't."

"What's wrong with that? It'd be a shame to waste the fabric."

"He'll be angry, Mum."

"Why?"

"He's not old. There are many years ahead of him."

"It's better to be prepared. Just tell him he'll be better off with a last outfit if you die before him."

Mum had always been the decision-maker at home. I believed most households in the village were run by the wives or the old mothers. It didn't seem to make sense, as men would like their wives to obey them. When young men looked for girlfriends, the first criterion they and their family had for girls was "obedience." The reality was that the wives were the ones who did all or most of the housework, so they were responsible for family matters. The wives did ask for the husbands' opinions, and they tended to agree, so they thought they were making decisions. For most men, doing nothing was a good choice.

Mum wasn't wrong, as the husband's last outfit had to be made sooner or later. So did mine. Everybody needed one. Making the last outfit for your husband when he wasn't too old was like saying *I'm preparing for your funeral.* In theory, it was a considerate gesture, but it would probably make the husband furious. He wouldn't even let me explain. On the other hand, I was reluctant to say it was Mum's idea. He didn't know anything about Dad's unfinished last outfit.

I wasn't convinced by Mum's idea about the husband's last outfit. I would only consider making it when we were old—about Mum's age—or when we were ill. The husband was the husband, so whether we got on well or not didn't matter. I would wish him longevity in any case. I would wish everyone longevity, ironically, as a funeral cryer.

Mum might forget about the idea of the husband's last outfit soon. I wouldn't mention it to her or remind her of it.

"Do you believe your mother had your brother with another man?" The husband was still in a bit of shock.

"That's what she said."

"I don't care as long as she gives us money."

"At least I'm Dad's daughter."

"Who knows?"

"I don't know."

"When is she going to give you the money she's promised?" the husband asked.

"Soon."

"How soon is *soon*?"

"Soon."

"What if she dies suddenly?"

"She won't die suddenly." I was cross.

"You know it happens. Your dad, Butcher and Bubble Tea."

"You're not wrong. We all have a fair chance."

The husband didn't say I was a strange and stupid woman. I had thought he would be more annoyed with me for not pushing Mum about the money, but he didn't seem to be. Maybe he wasn't that bad a husband. Maybe he still liked me but didn't want to admit it.

I turned toward my corner. I wanted to sleep. Thinking about money and death gave me a headache.

"We're different from your mum. She can see the end of her life, but we still have a future. We're going to adopt a baby boy, and the daughter is going to have a baby." The husband pulled my shoulder.

"Neither of these babies exists here. We don't know whether we're adopting Hotpot's son yet."

"At least your mum doesn't need a lot of money. We need money for our old age as well as our grandchildren."

"I'll ask her."

The husband tugged at my panties. I pushed his hands away.

"How many women have you slept with in your life?"

"Why do you ask me a question like that?"

"I'm the wife."

"Would you believe what I say?"

"I don't know."

"Two or three."

"Two or three?"

"Does it matter?" The husband tugged at my panties again.

I tucked the duvet under my body. "I'm cold."

"How many men have you slept with?"

"You know you're the only one." I remembered our first night.

"I don't know, but no man wants to sleep with you anymore."

"I'm old and ugly."

"You don't look that bad."

"Do you think Hotpot is a bad woman?" I asked when the husband put his hands under my top.

He paused. "Why do you ask?"

"She's slept with men for money and presents."

"She needs money."

"She's not supposed to do that. Selling sex is illegal."

"But she doesn't harm anyone," he said.

"She did when Butcher was alive."

"Maybe it was Butcher's idea."

"Did she tell you that?"

"No. I guessed."

"But do you think she's bad?" I asked again.

"I don't know."

"Is a woman bad if she's slept with more than one man?"

"If you think she's bad, she's bad. You don't have to ask me."

"You don't think she's bad because she's pretty." I didn't want to continue the conversation.

"You used to be pretty too." He pulled my shoulder again.

His breathing was heavy, and so was his weight on me.

My ribs hurt, but I decided not to complain.

I was tired. Soon I would fall asleep.

29

Since the daughter moved away from home, I hadn't worried about her until recently.

After she left school, she went to a training college to learn beauty and massage with a couple of her good friends. They found jobs in a massage parlor in Shanghai. The daughter was excited, and even I thought it was an opportunity to make a good living. Although there was hardly any paid leave and the girls had to work long hours, there was free food and accommodation, so things seemed to be fine. Her circumstances were much better than mine when I went to Nanjing for work.

Once, on the phone, the daughter said some of the masseuses were making a fortune. They went out with customers as escorts. She said she had only gone out to restaurants with some customers. They would pay her money, the price of a full-body massage or two foot massages. She promised me she wouldn't do it again.

When she next spoke to me, she was considering leaving her

job. She met a man at the massage parlor. He was a customer. He said she shouldn't work there, since some people believed masseuses were also prostitutes, which made her angry. He said he wouldn't have said it if he thought she was a prostitute.

They had a couple of paid dates before the man asked the daughter to be his girlfriend. To please him, she started looking for a more *respectable* job. However, she stayed on in the massage parlor, as the pay there was much better than any other job she could possibly find. What could she do? The boyfriend wasn't too happy about her decision, but he couldn't do anything about it. As a taxi driver, he didn't earn a lot himself. She moved in with him soon after that, so that was like a compromise.

I didn't show my disappointment when I heard about the daughter's boyfriend. I had hoped she might find a Shanghainese boyfriend. The man didn't have to be young or rich. With a Shanghai residence, my grandchildren would have a higher starting point in their life than us.

Did the daughter's boyfriend compensate her for being unfaithful and leaving her? She'd had a miscarriage, so another one in the future was possible. What if she couldn't have children any longer? She would be dumped again by someone else, or she might not even be able to find a boyfriend or husband. Nobody would take care of her when she was old and childless after I was gone.

A child. Yes, she needed a child, in case she couldn't have her own. There was a child available for adoption now.

Thinking about the daughter, I decided to pay another visit to Hotpot as soon as possible, before she accepted money from anyone. I might not need to worry too much. I doubted anyone else in the village would want to adopt her baby, but you never knew; word like this would normally be spread quickly, and a healthy boy available for adoption would be highly sought-after. People in other villages, towns and even cities would travel to view the baby boy if they knew about it.

★ ★ ★

Mum wasn't sure about my idea of getting the baby for the daughter. She thought at least I should ask the daughter first. It was always awkward for a single young woman to adopt a child, and gossip would be unavoidable. Not many women could stand having a reputation for infertility.

"*I* am going to adopt the baby, not the daughter," I explained.

"Remember: if you adopt him, I'll pay and I'll help look after the baby."

"If the daughter wants him in the future, I'll let her have him," I said to Mum.

"He would always be her brother. I'm sure she'll look after her younger brother. She doesn't have to be the mother."

"He can take care of her when she's old."

The husband only had ten dumplings for dinner, which was less than half his normal portion. I suspected he had already eaten somewhere else, but didn't want to miss the dumplings.

"I've seen Hotpot's son again," I told the husband.

"He's cute, isn't he?"

"Yes. But I think there's something wrong with him."

"I haven't noticed that."

"I can't tell what it is."

"It's probably your imagination."

Was it my imagination? Was it because I didn't want to adopt the baby? Did I want to?

"What are you thinking about?" the husband asked.

"When I have to pay, I'd better be careful," I said.

"Maybe because he was premature?"

"I don't know."

"But something has just occurred to me," the husband said. "You'd better check with the government. We might be too old to adopt a child."

"Is there an age limit for adopting children?"

"I have no idea. I assume so."

★ ★ ★

The cold hadn't been quite so extreme for a couple of days. There had been some rain. Mum said the bamboo shoots should be growing well. I asked her whether we should take a look, but she wasn't so keen. She'd nearly finished making her last outfit, so she didn't want to leave the house at that moment.

I used to check on the bamboo shoots with other women in the village. It was good fun, as it was also a good chance to gossip. We dug together and shared the shoots as well.

I found a wicker basket in the shed and put the new knife in it. Mum said it would be better if I hadn't thrown away her trowel. I could use the trowel to dig the bamboo shoots with and cut the ends of the shoots with the knife. I felt frustrated and wronged, but I didn't protest.

It took me a while to clean the basket, as it hadn't been used for a long time. Dad had woven the basket. He made it to show the brother and me that he could do manual work as well as calculations. It wasn't bad at all. Mum said it was hard to make a bad wicker basket, unless you were exceptionally clumsy, since the wicker was springy, so it would adjust itself even if you made a mistake. However, I had tried to make a wicker basket before; I wasn't successful.

I left the basket and the knife by the kitchen door. Mum and I would go to the bamboo grove after she finished making her last outfit. She wanted to give some bamboo shoots to the brother if we managed to dig a lot.

As I'd wished, or, rather, expected, deaths were coming in the cold weather. I had a couple of crying invitations in town in the next week. I needed a hairdo more than bamboo shoots.

I quickly got changed and put a bra on. I was wearing the daughter's old blue sweater, so I didn't look too bad. My cheeks felt hot when I remembered what happened the last time I was in the barbershop.

★ ★ ★

The barber looked awkward, or perhaps surprised, when I entered the barbershop. He was shouting at someone on the phone. I was embarrassed as I hadn't knocked, but the door had been ajar.

"I'll call you back later." He sounded impatient when he put his phone into his pocket.

He waved to me. "Hello."

"Hello."

"It was my girlfriend. Sorry. We sometimes argue."

"It's okay. Everyone does."

The room was warm, unlike my house. I took my coat off and put it on one of the dressing tables. Then I saw my missing scarf. It had been folded neatly and was lying in front of the mirror.

"Somebody left this scarf here. Is it yours?"

"No. It's not mine."

"I don't have many customers. I'll find the owner easily enough," he said.

"It's an old scarf."

"It is old, but well-knitted."

"It's not bad."

"What do you want me to do with your hair today?" the barber asked.

"A hair wash and a bun."

"Do you want color?"

"Maybe not."

"Yes, you don't need a new color yet." He picked a couple of strands of my hair.

"Do a tight bun for me. I've got a crying job the day after tomorrow."

"You can come tomorrow instead."

"No. There's always stuff to do the day before the crying job. I get nervous too."

"You're such a good funeral cryer. I never knew you got nervous."

"Maybe *nervous* isn't the right word." I corrected myself.

"What is?"

"*Stressed*. I want to do a good job"

"Your clients are lucky to have you cry for them."

"I don't know."

"Will you cry for me one day?"

"Don't joke. It isn't funny."

"I'm not joking."

When the barber was drying my hair, my earlobes felt ticklish. When the daughter was taking her massage course, she told me the ears were crucial in making people feel comfortable. Although in theory massage was clinical and breaking through your body with pain, people wouldn't come if there was no comfort. I didn't know or remember whether the barber massaged my earlobes the last time. At the moment, his fingers were touching my earlobes subtly and accidentally with the movement and the noise of the hair dryer.

The noise of the hair dryer stopped. The barber started combing my hair with slow, deliberate strokes.

"Is your girlfriend home?" I asked.

"No."

"Is she still away?"

"Yes."

"When will she come back?"

"I don't know. I don't care."

I didn't expect that answer. I didn't ask any more questions.

"If your bun gets messy or loose, come back tomorrow. I'll redo it for you," he said when I got to my feet.

"Thank you."

"Have you ever thought about having short hair?"

"No."

"I think you'd look nice with short hair. You'd look younger."

"But I need long hair for my job." I felt my bun.

"Do you?"

"Maybe I don't. I just assumed so."

"Here's a magazine. You can have a look at the short hair-styles."

I took the magazine. "I'll take a look, but I only need to look nice for the funerals I cry for."

"It's also good to look nice when you're not working."

"Nobody would care what hairstyle I have. I don't care either." I shook my head.

"I care," he said.

"Oh." I didn't know what to say.

"I'm a barber. I care about people's hairstyles."

"Of course."

"It's also nice to look nice when you go out."

"I never go out."

"Neither do I. Maybe we can go to town together sometime."

"I haven't got anything to do in town."

"We can have lunch together. There are nice restaurants in gū shān zhèn."

"Maybe. But people will see us."

"They won't."

"They will." I remembered what people said about him and me.

"We'll see. By the way, you've never asked me to order anything for you. You've got my number."

"I don't need anything."

"I'll phone you when we've got something nice in the shop."

"Thank you."

The barber's mobile phone rang when I was leaving. I half closed the door behind me. I wondered whether it was his girl-friend again. Were they arguing or making up?

He asked me today whether I would cry for him one day. Did he mean whether I would *cry* with tears and sadness or *cry* as a funeral cryer?

I was walking into a headwind. My eyes and ears were hurt. I lowered my head and sped up toward home.

Then I felt my eyes wet. Was it because of the wind?

My fingers were cold and stiff, and it took me a while to turn the key in the door.

I walked straight to the kitchen and put my hands over the kettle on the stove. The husband was sitting near the stove, eating some pot noodles.

"Have you got a crying job?" The husband stared at me.

My newly done bun said it.

"Yes. Not a lot of money, though," I said.

"Better than staying at home doing nothing," he said.

The funeral would be in a nearby village. It wasn't a big job, as the family wasn't rich. For me, it was about the atmosphere of the funeral and the sincerity of the funeral goers. For funeral goers, it was true that you had to pay to go to a funeral, like you would pay to go to a wedding. You invested time, money and your emotions—one was sorrow, and the other was joy. They were both important expressions of emotion to mark the start or the end of a journey.

I couldn't help recalling Dad's funeral. It had been a short-notice death. If I remembered rightly, Mum was more angry than devastated. Her anger was a projection of her helplessness. For Mum, she hadn't been able to take care of Dad during his final years. If Dad could have lived for a long time in the care home, she would have felt less guilty.

I didn't know how close Mum and Dad had been, but they were not estranged like some older couples I knew of. If I was honest, their relationship had been better than that of the husband and me. Dad's funeral could have been better organized if we'd had more time to prepare. The funeral was also faulty because of my crying. I had never discussed it with anyone, but I thought that my job as a professional funeral cryer made it hard to tell whether my crying for Dad was heartfelt or not. Of course, as a daughter, people wouldn't and shouldn't doubt my genuineness.

By the time Mum died, I would hopefully have retired as a funeral cryer. Then I would cry as a daughter, and there would be no trace of any professionalism in my crying.

Perhaps I should stop being a funeral cryer before anyone else in the family died. Since no one would be able to predict any death, the sooner I stopped my job, the less damage there would be. I would like to cry for my family as a family member. If I were the first to die from now on, I wouldn't have to worry about anything or anyone.

But what source of income would I have if I didn't work as a funeral cryer?

None. That was the answer.

I had no choice but to be a funeral cryer.

30

Mum wanted to show me what she had made. I entered her room with her.

To my surprise, there were two identical tops and two pairs of trousers on her bed.

They were bright red.

"Feel the fabric. It's fine and soft." Mum picked up a top.

"Yes. It smells nice too." I touched the fabric.

"My fingers are sore, but I'm glad the outfits look pretty."

"They look comfortable too."

"I don't think I need to feel comfortable then."

We sat on her bed. Mum took my hands.

"I'm not worried now," Mum said.

"Mum, I'm sorry."

"Why? You've got nothing to apologize for."

I didn't know. Was I sorry that I didn't make the last outfit for Mum? Or was I sorry that Mum would die long before me?

"You've made two layers, Mum?"

"No. Never two layers, never an even number." Mum shook her head.

"But…"

"I've made two outfits, not two layers."

"Why?" I was confused.

"One for me, and one for you."

"One for me?"

"Everyone needs their last outfit. You have probably many years ahead of you, but it doesn't mean you don't need to plan ahead."

"You're right, Mum."

"Now you've got your last outfit ready, I won't worry about you."

"Thank you, Mum."

"I'm not scared of death any longer. I'm ready to die now, whenever and wherever."

"Shall I try my outfit on, Mum?" I asked quietly.

"No. You never try on your last outfit. Other people put it on you—after you die."

"Okay."

Mum started folding one of the tops. "I've never worn something so beautiful in my life."

"Good color."

"By the way, I've sowed some spinach and pak choi seeds in the backyard." Mum changed the subject.

"Thank you, Mum. It must have been cold outside."

"It was cold, but I didn't mind."

"I think it might snow soon."

"Your backyard isn't very beautiful. I think you should grow some flowers there."

"I'll buy some seeds in spring."

"Your husband is a man of leisure. Maybe he can make a flower bed."

"He doesn't know how to do it."

"He can learn."

★ ★ ★

The husband had no interest in flowers, but was into the idea of building a flower bed.

"It sounds interesting. I've never built anything in my life."

"I hope it's not too hard."

"I can work it out. I'm not stupid."

"I'm going to grow roses in the flower bed."

"Are they expensive?"

"More expensive than vegetables I think."

"By the way, how much money are you willing to pay to adopt Hotpot's son?" the husband asked.

"I'm not sure."

I didn't tell the husband about my last outfit. I'd been around death for long enough not to be shocked at the sight of Mum's last outfit, but mine made a difference. There was a natural queue for people to be born and to die, and the majority would take turns. There were queue jumpers, mostly unintentional, and you never knew if you would be one of them.

When people said I brought bad luck, I couldn't really care too much. I had to make a living. Sometimes I thought perhaps I already had the immune system to deal with the bad things including death. There was an old saying: you defeat poison with poison.

It wasn't that I wanted Mum to die before me, but it wasn't fair if I died before her, and she wouldn't want it either. With my last outfit lying in the house, I had to contemplate my own death all the time. To make it worse, according to Mum, I was going to make a last outfit for the husband. I didn't know what would be better—or rather, less awful—telling him now or just informing him when it was done?

I'd been a responsible grown-up, a good enough daughter, wife and mother. If everything happened in order, chronologically, I would die after Mum and the husband, and I'd organize their funerals professionally. They would no doubt have better-than-average send-offs. If I died before both of them, who would make arrangements for them? My many years of being a good woman would be in vain. I couldn't bear the thought of not crying for Mum. Therefore, I must try to live as long as possible. I wasn't allowed to die too soon. Moreover, I wanted to live a better life to make myself more worthy.

But what was a better life?

It might be too late to have a better life, but I would try.

First of all, I would work as much as possible and save money. At the end of the day, money would talk, as you would need money for everything when you were old and ill. Secondly, I would smile more. Mum used to say I didn't smile enough, so I sometimes looked unhappy when I was fine. She said women should always smile, more often than men. Thirdly, but not lastly, I would adopt Hotpot's son, even though there might be something wrong with him. I would try my best to smile for the husband. It wouldn't be easy since we didn't look at each other when we were talking.

I should also make the house look nicer. When I was thinking what needed to be done to Hotpot's house, I realized my house didn't look better than hers. Maybe I should wash the curtains. I didn't remember the last time they were washed. They didn't look dirty, but they couldn't be very clean. Perhaps it would be a good idea to buy some new ones. We only had curtains in the bedrooms, and they were put up when we got married. Mum and Dad had never had curtains before that. I had seen curtains in living rooms in films and TV series, not in real life. Who would bother looking into your living room, especially in a village like ours? It was a waste of money.

I would declutter the house. Maybe Mum's trowel and bowl would turn up after the house was turned upside down.

Then, there was the daughter…

★ ★ ★

On the bus to my funeral job, I received a text from the daughter. I was surprised but relieved. Her boyfriend had come back to her. She said she would call me to tell me the details. To be honest, I wasn't interested in the details as long as they were together again.

For now, I would concentrate on the new funeral-crying job. I wanted to be paid and buy some new curtains with the cash.

I didn't ask or tell Mum about the curtains, since she might be opposed to my idea. I had been used to listening to Mum, although she had never said I had to obey her all the time. It seemed natural for me to follow her advice, unlike the younger generation. The daughter had always had her own ideas. To be fair, I had been a little more adventurous than most people around my age. When I went to Nanjing, it was a brave move, but I asked Mum and Dad for permission first. The curtains weren't for Mum. Why should I ask her for an opinion?

What color curtains should I buy?

Our old curtains used to be bright red, the standard color for newlyweds. The brightness had aged and evolved into a shade that I was unable to put a name to. Before I decided to buy new curtains, I had hardly noticed them. In fact, over the years, the curtains were always drawn and almost untouched as if they didn't exist.

I wanted to have some new curtains to make my bedroom look nice.

This time, I wouldn't leave them untouched.

31

The curtains were so heavy, but I managed to carry them home, as I wanted them badly.

Mum and the husband were surprised to see my purchase.

"Why did you waste money on curtains? Our curtains are fine." The husband didn't sound pleased.

"The old curtains aren't fine, but the new curtains aren't necessary," Mum said.

"So it's a waste. Can you take them back to the shop?" the husband asked.

"No, I don't want to." I flattened the curtains out on the dining table.

"The color's nice. Similar to the old curtains." Mum felt the curtains.

"I was going to choose a different color, but couldn't find anything," I said.

"But this red is too dark," the husband commented.

"It's not dark. It's rich." I corrected him.

"The color doesn't matter as long as it's not black or white," Mum concluded.

"What are you going to do with the old curtains? Are you going to throw them away?" the husband asked.

"We can give them away. In our village, many people don't have curtains," I replied.

"That's because nobody needs them, including us. I hardly remembered we had curtains."

I wiped the old curtains carefully with a damp cloth. They didn't look too bad. For a moment, I nearly regretted the decision to replace them. But then I thought they *were* old, although they didn't look that old. It seemed poignant to me when I realized they had been neglected for over twenty years. They had been the silent witnesses to my married life.

"I bought the curtains with the money I was paid today. There's still some left." I emptied my bag and left the paper notes and coins on the bed.

"So you weren't paid much today?" The husband counted the money.

"They weren't a rich family. The curtains weren't cheap."

"The new curtains aren't that good. The old ones look okay to me."

"The old curtains are older than the daughter."

"I don't care. Why did you want to change the curtains in the first place?" The husband sounded annoyed.

"The old curtains were just too old."

"You're a strange woman, and stupid." The husband raised his voice.

I hoped Mum didn't hear him.

Maybe the husband was right. We didn't need new curtains, and we didn't even need curtains. To make myself feel less bad,

I had to find someone to give the old curtains away to. I would feel guilty if we had to throw the old curtains away, since there was nothing wrong with them apart from being old. The trouble was that I hardly met people in the village, so it would be odd to ask people whether they would like to have my old curtains. If I asked the right person who wanted or needed some curtains, I would be lucky. However, it would be offensive and embarrassing if I asked the wrong person. Not many people would accept other people's unwanted stuff.

According to the husband, I was a strange and stupid woman. I would show him what strange and stupid meant. I would start making his last outfit. I didn't care whether he was angry or not, as I was strange and stupid. I might even tell him that he had to die before me.

I asked Mum for Dad's unfinished last outfit. I was going to make the last outfit for the husband.

"I thought you didn't want to make it yet."

"It is better sooner than later," I said.

"You're right."

"It's one thing out of the way," I said.

"Don't argue with him if he gets cross about the outfit."

"I won't."

"By the way, if you don't adopt that boy, I'll go back to your brother's soon."

I wouldn't be able to adopt Hotpot's son. I had asked the daughter to find out about the adoption rules. I told her I was asking for a friend. The rules disappointed me. In most cases, you should be childless if you wanted to adopt a child, and I was also far too old in any case. And the daughter was too young to adopt a child.

I should have expected all this. I didn't care what the husband thought, but I didn't know how to explain to Mum. Would she be disappointed?

★ ★ ★

The barber combed my wet hair slowly. "You've got another crying job again? You're doing well."

"Yes, but not too soon. I want to treat myself," I said, feeling slightly awkward.

"It's nice to treat yourself. I hope more people will treat themselves. I want more people to visit my shop." He smiled.

"Why have you got three hairdressing chairs? You're the only barber here. You can't use three chairs at the same time."

"When people have their hair dyed or permed, they can sit there, waiting," he explained.

"But have you had three customers at one time?"

"Unfortunately not. I've only needed one chair most of the time, occasionally two."

"Aren't they a waste of money?"

"You can say that, but we all have things we don't need."

"Yes." I remembered my old curtains.

I was sitting right in front of one of the two windows and noticed there were no curtains.

"You have no curtains," I said.

"No. My girlfriend used to have curtains."

"Where are the old curtains?"

"She threw them away. Her late husband died in this room, so she thought the curtains would bring us bad luck."

"I didn't know he died here."

"When he became ill, he wasn't living here. He wanted to die in his home village."

"So he wanted to die at home and in the end died at home."

"Yes."

"But are you going to put some new curtains up?"

"Yes and no. Curtains look nice, but they're not cheap, and we don't really need them."

"I have some nice old curtains. I can give them to you."

"Why don't you want to keep them?"

"I've bought some new curtains."

"If you don't need them anymore, I'll have them."

"Is she back yet?" I didn't know why I changed the subject.

"No."

"When's she coming back?"

"I don't know."

"So you have to cook all the meals yourself?"

"I do. Sometimes I eat pot noodles. Nice and simple."

"You can sometimes come to my house for dinner. My mum's staying, so we always have nice dinners."

"That sounds good. Thank you."

I looked in the mirror. "My hair doesn't look bad."

"It looks good."

"Do you want to use this scarf?" The barber handed *my* scarf to me when I was about to leave.

"No. The owner might come back to look for it."

"They might not. It's a warm scarf and it's lying here doing nothing."

"It's not mine. I don't want to steal it."

"It's hand-knitted, good stuff," he insisted.

"No."

"It's cold and windy today. You haven't got a scarf or hat with you."

"Okay, I'll borrow it."

"You can keep it until someone wants it back."

On my way back home, wrapped in my tatty scarf, I couldn't hold my tears back.

As a middle-aged woman, no, an older woman, I didn't have a good-quality scarf. I had been to Shanghai and Nanjing and had seen many beautiful things for women. I had liked many nice things, but had thought it a waste of money to buy any of them for myself. As for scarves, I grew up wearing hand-knitted sweaters and scarves, and I never thought there was anything wrong with them as long as they were warm. But why wouldn't I admit the scarf was mine? Maybe the barber knew it was mine. If he had noticed me, or liked me, he would know it was my scarf, so he returned it to me. However, I would return it to him. I had to keep pretending it wasn't mine even if I thought he thought it was mine.

If I didn't buy anything nice for myself now, I would never have any chance.

Not just a scarf. There were many nice things I should have and should buy.

32

I was sitting on the sofa, sewing. The husband was cracking sunflower seeds while smoking. The noise he was making was annoying, but I didn't say anything. If I complained, he would shout at me or make a louder noise.

"What are you making?" the husband asked.

"A jacket."

"What kind of jacket? It looks like a men's jacket."

"It *is* a men's jacket."

"Are you making it for me?"

"Yes."

"I don't want it. Who wants to wear handmade clothes these days? Machine-made ones are better."

"It's not for you to wear now," I said slowly.

"What?"

"You won't know when you're going to wear it."

"Why?"

"You don't need to know."

"I'm not interested." He blew a smoke ring.

I put my sewing stuff into a basket and stood up. I would go to talk to Hotpot. I had to tell her that I wouldn't be able to adopt her son. I hoped she had already accepted an offer from someone.

Hotpot had decided to keep her son.

"I'm moving back in with my parents. They've forgiven me," Hotpot said.

"Forgiven you for what?"

She said quietly, "I've been a Damaged Shoe since I was sixteen."

"You're not."

"I *was* a Damaged Shoe. That was why I had to marry an older man. Nobody wanted me."

"You're a mother now. Forget about the past."

"My parents have forgiven me because I've given them a grandson. I'll try to be a good woman for my son."

"Do they live far from here?"

"They live in qīng shuǐ zhèn"—Clear Water Town—"about an hour on the bus."

"I know where it is. I went to secondary school there."

"My parents have a dumpling bar. I can help them."

"Do you need any help before you move?"

"I'm okay. I can find plenty of people in the village to help me pack."

Now that Hotpot's son wasn't available for adoption, I felt a little lost. Soon she and her son would disappear from my life. When you didn't see someone and didn't know how they were doing, it seemed they didn't exist.

Perhaps my own existence was more important for myself.

There didn't seem to be anything I could do to make my existence better. Just as I had resolved to smile in my life, I noticed that most people didn't smile. Mum didn't smile—it was how she was; Hotpot didn't smile, because there was nothing for her to smile about.

The husband didn't smile at me, and I didn't smile at him. I didn't feel like making any effort, so unless he made me genuinely happy, I wouldn't smile for him. It was all very fair. But when was the last time he made me happy?

If I couldn't smile naturally at the husband and he couldn't at me, how could we live together? How had we managed to live together and sleep together for so many years without smiling at each other?

Then I realized the only person who smiled at me was the barber. He seemed to be happy to see me. Did I smile at him? I wasn't sure. I hoped I didn't look too miserable to him.

Since we weren't adopting Hotpot's son, Mum would return to the brother's. For me, it was something of a relief. I didn't want Mum to find out too much about my life, especially my feelings for the barber, which made it hard for me to face her. She had eagle eyes, like any old mother, and her directness would shame me. The brother's place was better for her.

The brother had always been a reasonable man, more intelligent than average men. An average man in our village or any nearby town was nothing near smart, but he was still Mum's pride.

The brother disapproved of the husband's idle style, but he never said a word. Occasionally, he would send some cigarettes to his brother-in-law. The brother was making a good living, so he probably didn't mind how much money he would receive from Mum and Dad. Traditionally, Mum should give all or most of the money to the brother, and he might give some of it to me if he was generous. However, if the brother wanted to divorce the sister-in-law, as Mum wished, it would be better if he didn't receive any money now.

Whoever the brother's real father was, he was Mum's son. He must be happy to have Mum back.

Before I worked as a funeral cryer, I hardly thought about death. People didn't discuss death—it was taboo, so nobody would. I always maintained a high degree of awe and fear of death. Since I started crying at funerals for a living, I had been used to witnessing death and saw it as normal. It was normal, but not many people were willing to admit it.

It was hard not to think about my own death after helping prepare many funerals, especially now I had a last outfit. One of the things that struck me most was it seemed that people wouldn't care what kind of person the deceased had been. Good or bad, all gone.

Another was that what many funeral goers really minded about was the food they would eat after the funeral. It had to be a feast, otherwise they would think the bereaved family were stingy or they didn't love and respect their so-called beloved deceased.

Then there was the scale of the funeral. The more money spent, the more respect would be earned from the funeral goers. The funeral would be the subject of gossip for a long time if it was either luxurious or spartan.

On the other hand, nobody cared whether tears were genuine as long as they looked genuine. Even if your heart was broken, there was nothing you could do to bring anyone back to life. Sometimes, it could even be a relief for the family when someone died. You never knew for sure, but I could sense it and I had experienced that on several occasions.

If I told Mum how I felt about death, it would upset her, as it was like I wouldn't care if she died. Mum said she wasn't afraid of death, but I didn't know whether she meant it.

We always cared what other people would make of us when we were alive. If we were busy creating an image for other people to see, it meant our real selves weren't important. Why couldn't we live however we wanted and ignore other people's opinions? Everyone was *someone else*.

Each night before bed, I did some sewing. I preferred the daytime, so I didn't want to waste it making the husband's last outfit. He hadn't asked me about it since the first time he saw me making it. Had he guessed what it was for?

Mum had packed her suitcase, but hadn't decided on a date to leave. The brother had said he would send a driver to collect Mum, but I wanted to take Mum in a taxi. We would go to gū shān zhèn, Solitude Mountain Town, first to cash her check. The money would go into the husband's account, and we would transfer some of it to the brother in the future when he asked for it, or after he was divorced.

"I've put our last outfits in the bottom of the chest of drawers," Mum said when we were having dumplings.

"Okay."

"You need to tell your husband about our last outfits. It's a good idea to let him know that we both have our last outfits ready."

"Are you going to tell the brother?"

"Yes. Everybody. Your daughter, your sister-in-law and their son, your nephew. Your sister-in-law will be glad, for it saves her the trouble making a last outfit for me."

I thought we probably didn't need to tell everyone where the last outfits were. If one of us died, the other one could tell other people about the outfits. Of course, there was the possibility that we might die together, in a car accident or something. Who would know?

Mum had tidied up her bedroom, but I hadn't tidied the house as I'd planned. I hoped she wouldn't ask about her missing items before she left. She wouldn't need any of them in the brother's house.

"Remember to finish making your husband's last outfit." Mum reminded me.

"Yes. I'll tell everybody in the family once his last outfit has been made."

"Keep it in the drawer with our last outfits."

"I will, Mum."

"I don't know which one will be used first," Mum said quietly. I pretended I didn't hear her.

The husband was playing on his phone while I was sewing his last outfit.

"Are you still making the jacket for me?" the husband asked.

"Yes."

"I won't wear it."

"It's not for you to wear now. I've told you."

"What? What do you mean?"

"It's part of your last outfit." I stopped sewing and placed the unfinished jacket on the bed. I waited to see him explode.

He stared at me in disbelief. He moved his lips slightly, but didn't make any sound.

I felt some guilt, but didn't want to say anything.

He heaved a sigh and said, "Thank you."

I tried to sense some sarcasm in his tone, but there seemed to be none.

"If you're angry with me, tell me. I'm sorry I'm making your last outfit."

"I'm not angry." He shook his head. "Are you making one for yourself too?"

"No. Mum's made one for me."

"I wouldn't mind if I didn't have a last outfit prepared, like your father. It's easy to buy one."

"Dad had an unfinished outfit."

"Unfinished outfit?"

"Dad was very ill one year. Do you remember I took a lot of time off school looking after him?"

"I didn't know."

"We thought he was dying, so Mum started to make a last outfit for him."

"Why didn't she finish it?"

"He recovered."

"Where's his unfinished outfit?"

"Here." I pointed to the pile on the bed.

"What? You're making my last outfit because you and your mother don't want to waste the fabric? Do you think I'm going to die soon? You're hoping for me to die soon. You and your mother."

His voice was angry and loud. I was worried that Mum might hear it. She must have heard him, but probably couldn't make out all the content. As long as she didn't come to our room to get involved, it was okay.

I didn't respond to the husband. I sat still, listening carefully, trying to hear any movement from the direction of Mum's room.

Nothing.

The husband picked up his—or rather, Dad's—unfinished last outfit and hurled it into the far corner of the room.

He shouted, "You're not just stupid and strange, you're also evil. You and your mother. You're a pair of bitches."

I didn't move.

I felt as angry as him, but I thought I deserved his anger and swearing.

33

The husband had gone out. He might have gone to play mah-jongg, but he might have gone to do other business. Hotpot was moving soon, so he might be visiting her and helping.

The husband and Hotpot had most probably slept together. She was a young woman who would sleep with any man who was willing to give her money or presents, and he was a man whose wife was old and ugly.

He would want to spend some time with her, as he might not see her again soon. I wouldn't stop him. If we all might die at any time, why couldn't we do whatever we wanted to? And if he could do whatever he wanted, I could also do whatever I wanted.

The barber had put the curtains up. They looked better in his shop than they did in my bedroom. They didn't look too old or tatty when they weren't dusty, as the faded bright red had transformed into a stylish shade. If I had wiped the curtains when I thought about getting rid of them, I wouldn't have bought the new curtains.

"The curtains look good," I said.

"Yes. Thank you." The barber sounded pleased.

"Thank *you*. Thank you for having them. I don't like wasting things."

"They'll look better when they're drawn."

The curtains were drawn, so the room suddenly became dark.

I felt embarrassed. There was a strange silence in the air.

The barber quickly opened the curtains halfway.

"You can have a free hairdo today." The barber snipped his scissors in the air.

"No."

"You've given me some nice curtains."

"They're old and unwanted."

"They're still nice."

"No. I gave the curtains to you for free."

"A free hairdo is a thank-you token."

The barber was going to give me a head massage. The chair had been lowered as far as possible. Although I couldn't lie flat, it was comfortable enough as a chair. Because the curtains were half-drawn, the light was a little dim, even with one ceiling lamp on.

"Your girlfriend hardly stays in the village," I said.

"There's nothing for her to do in the village," the barber said.

"Does she grow vegetables?"

"No."

"She doesn't like to live in the village, does she?"

"No, she doesn't."

"Do you think you might move back to the city?"

"I don't want to."

"Sometimes it's not too bad living in the countryside."

"The air is fresh here."

"The village is smelly, though."

"Smelly? I don't think so."

"That's why I go to the bamboo grove for a walk. The air there is fresh."

"We can take a walk there together," he suggested.

His fingers lingered behind my ears.

"Nobody will see us. Nobody goes there," he said to me.

"But people will see us walking to the bamboo grove."

"We don't need to walk there together. We can meet there."

"Let me think about it."

"You look really nice," the barber said when he shook the apron.

"Thank you." I felt my hair.

"Do you want some tea before you go?"

"Thank you, but I need to go."

"You don't need to hurry."

"Mum's home."

"It won't take you long to drink some tea. You know I've got a nice room upstairs."

"It's your girlfriend's room too."

"She's got her own room."

"When will she be back?"

"I don't know."

"Do you miss her?"

"I'm okay."

"But you're always alone."

"We're not young. It's fine."

"You must be bored. Do you play mah-jongg?"

"No, I don't."

"I don't, either. I'm going now."

"You're welcome to have tea anytime. You've got my number."

Maybe I shouldn't have asked the barber about his girlfriend. I was also tempted to ask him whether he was lonely. Was it possible that they had separated? I had no idea whether they had a good enough relationship. Most people of my age weren't fussy about relationships. They ate and slept together, and they pooled their money together. There wasn't much joy to think about. I wanted to be happy, but I didn't know how to achieve that.

I sometimes wished I was on my own. If I was alone, I could see any man without needing to feel guilty. There were scenarios in which I could be alone: if the husband and I got divorced, or if he died. If he died suddenly like Butcher, I would be a widow. If he were murdered... But who would murder him? Nobody hated him enough to kill him and he wasn't rich enough to make killing him worthwhile.

Suddenly, I felt a sharp pain in my left palm. The needle had slipped and the point pricked into my skin. I had been fantasizing about death while I was sewing the last outfit for the husband, for him to wear after he died.

I realized I was jealous of the barber's girlfriend and the feeling hurt my chest. I wished she didn't exist, then she wouldn't be in my way. Did I wish her dead? When I watched films as a child, I was scared to see blood, never mind death. I thought everything in films was real—that was how I first witnessed death. After two sets of my grandparents died one by one when I was little, my grief and fright diminished over time. Then I started crying at funerals for a living, and the fear of death eventually turned into numbness.

It was sad that death had become normal to me. It wasn't a feeling one should experience, yet it wasn't bad for me professionally. For the last few years, I had managed to cry at funerals without much real emotion for a variety of deaths and a wide range of ages, though still feeling overwhelmed at times.

I shifted my mind back. I sensed that the barber was lying about his girlfriend. If he had complained about her having been away for too long, I would think he was telling the truth. There should be some details, like, where she was or what she was doing if he wasn't lying. But, no—there were no details.

There was something strange too. According to the husband, the barber sometimes played mah-jongg, but the barber said he didn't. One of them was lying? Who?

I also remembered hearing the quarrel between the barber and a woman. I had assumed he and the woman were arguing over me. However, it could be any woman. There must be other women who were wearing *tight* jeans.

What would he want to do to me if I went to his "nice" room for a cup of tea? Would he want to touch me and kiss me? Would he want to have sex with me?

If the barber and his girlfriend hadn't split up, she should return to the village soon enough. There was no way that someone would leave their partner on their own at Spring Festival.

I wondered what the barber would have to say if his girlfriend didn't turn up for Spring Festival.

34

The husband had been irritated with me since he learned that I had given the curtains to the barber. In fact, perhaps he had been irritated with me since I started making his last outfit.

"Why did you give the curtains to the barber?" the husband asked. It was more like telling off.

"Sorry, I should have told you first."

"It's not about that. I want to know why you gave the curtains to the barber."

"Why not?"

"He's a man. You're a woman."

"So…"

"When you gave him the curtains, there was no one else in the barbershop. You shouldn't be with a man in a room on your own."

"When I have my hair done, no one else is there either."

"But it's different when there are curtains, especially when the curtains are drawn."

"He keeps the curtains open during the day."

"It's easy to draw the curtains."

"What will happen if the curtains are drawn? Do you think he's going to do something to me? I'm an old and ugly woman."

"You're still a woman." He sounded impatient.

"You've told me no man wants to sleep with me."

Mum and I went shopping in gū shān zhèn, Solitude Mountain Town. She bought a blue wool-blend coat for herself and a green woolly scarf for me.

"Green is too beautiful for me. I'm too old for the color," I said.

"That's why you need green to make you younger."

"It won't make me younger."

"It might make you look a little younger."

"But nobody cares."

"You can care for yourself."

"You should care for yourself too, Mum. Dad cared for you, didn't he?" I asked.

"He cared *about* me, but he didn't care *for* me."

"Dad listened to you."

"Yes."

"At least he always needed you. He relied on you."

"So he cared for himself."

"But he wasn't mean to you."

"No. I sometimes miss him."

Mum looked into the distance. Her eyes looked moist. Were there tears? Maybe it was only the reflection of the sunshine.

Since Mum was going to transfer the money to the husband's bank account, I took his ID card with me. Unfortunately, we couldn't do the transfer. The check had to be cashed into Mum's account first before any transfer. The clerk also said that the sum of the check was too large, so we would have to transfer

the money in the bank's headquarters in Dalian. As for applying for a bank account, it was easy. I only needed my ID card
and proof of address.

"I'll ask your brother to apply for a bank account for me as
soon as possible. You must have a bank account too. I'll transfer
the money into your account, not your husband's."

"Once we've done our bank accounts, we can take a day trip
to Dalian."

"Buy some nice clothes for yourself. Don't wear your daughter's clothes."

Dalian was almost as modern and rich as Shanghai, but I had
never visited it properly as it was almost on our doorstep. I tried
to remember where I had been in Dalian on my only trip there.
I had only caught a glimpse of the city in a hurry. I didn't even
go to its beautiful seaside. All I remembered was I felt so awkward as neither of us had any money to spend in shops.

Before I called a taxi for Mum, we went to a Korean noodle
bar for a light dinner. She ordered some Korean fried dumplings.

"Your dad and I sometimes came to town for lunch. He always ordered these dumplings."

"When was that? Before you were married?"

"No. When you were at secondary school. Your brother had
a job, so we had some money to spare."

"Do they still taste the same?" I picked up a dumpling with
my chopsticks.

"I don't remember. We didn't come here that often. Then
he became ill."

"You didn't come here again after that?"

Mum dipped her dumpling in the chili sauce. "No. I thought
it might be better to save money for future hospital treatment."

"Do you want to buy health insurance, Mum?"

"I've lived enough years. Even if I'm terminally ill, it doesn't
affect my life span."

"You're not that old, Mum."

"I *am* old. I'm nearly in my mid-seventies."

"People live much longer these days."

She nodded. "That's why you need health insurance."

"It's not cheap."

"You've got money from me. You can afford it now."

"I'll consider it."

"By the way, don't mention to your husband about your bank account."

Mum and Dad's generation didn't talk about love. Even our generation hardly did. We all grew up learning to love our leaders and our Party as well as our motherland. The daughter's generation started to go on about love, and there seemed to be too much so-called love around the world these days.

Love was a strange thing, since you could never touch it or see it. From the few popular novels I had read, I appreciated that one could always feel love. But how? How could you know it was love? What happened when love happened? Love wouldn't make you rich, and it wouldn't help you to live longer, either.

I'd heard that love was more important than many things, but I didn't think it was more important than money. If you didn't have enough money, you couldn't even get married or have children, for everything cost money. However, being alive was the most important thing. Even if you were a millionaire, you wouldn't be able to spend your money if you were dead. Being alive was something puzzling too. Nobody chose to be born, but you needed to be thankful to your parents.

As I was growing older, I felt death wasn't far from me, but had no idea where it was. We didn't do much to prepare for death in most cases, but I was preparing for the husband's death by making his last outfit. Having the outfit ready was an essential part of a funeral. You made it for the dead body and it disappeared with the body in the fire. Sometimes I was confused.

When we were born, we were naked, so it would make sense that we are naked when we leave this world. But that doesn't make sense, as we wear clothes when we are alive.

I felt exhausted and helpless when my head was filled with wandering thoughts about death.

The husband came back home late. I was already in bed.

He didn't have his keys on him, so I had to climb out of the duvet to open the door for him. I shivered when the wind blew into the house. I had asked him many times to take his own keys, but he just ignored me. It seemed it was women's duty to be home and open the door for men.

He shuffled through the bedroom door and slid under the duvet with his clothes on.

I was about to complain, then I thought that, since he was in his place, it didn't matter as long as he didn't make my side of the bed cold or dirty.

"Once I don't feel cold, I'll take my clothes off," the husband mumbled.

"You should."

"The room's so cold. You don't keep the stove open at night now that your mother's not here."

"We don't need it now. We're not old. Mum's body isn't as warm as ours."

"My body's never warm."

"It's too expensive to keep the stove open all the time."

"Hotpot's house is even colder," he said when he was taking his jacket off.

"Did you go to her house today?"

"Yes, I went after mah-jongg, only for a little while."

"What did you do there?"

"I helped her pack."

"She did say she had plenty of people helping her. Plenty of men, I guess."

"Did she say that?"

"You're one of her 'plenty of men.'"

"I'm sure you will help her as well."

Mum had returned to the brother's home and there was no baby. It seemed life had gone back to its old form. Maybe it wasn't back to normal, as I would have my own bank account. And most importantly, I would keep a lot of money to myself and I would be in charge of it.

The husband hadn't nagged about moving recently. Once Mum's money was in my account, I would decide whether we were going to buy an apartment in town.

Although I was thinking about the daughter when I was considering adopting Hotpot's son, I had never mentioned it to her. I would like her to have her own children. Your husband or wife might care about you when you first lived together, but your children were the only people who would be close to you. Even if your children might not take good care of you, they were your own blood and they were the people who would send you off. I wondered whether that was the real purpose of having children.

Sometimes, I felt unsettled and vulnerable when I thought about myself and the daughter. I didn't choose to be born and my life hadn't been the best, but I had repeated my parents' actions. Although it wasn't my fault that *I* was alive, it *was* my fault that the daughter was alive. If she wasn't living a good life, it was my fault.

When I saw people's gloomy faces, and they often were gloomy, it was like seeing my own face. I had been to more funerals than weddings, but there had been enough weddings for me to observe. Whenever there was a wedding, people would make a great effort to ensure a happy atmosphere.

The newlyweds would smile and most likely laugh inwardly. It was probably the first and last time they would receive so much money and so many good wishes in one day, especially the money. It would cover the cost of the wedding with plenty left over. Everyone knew what the bride and groom would do after all the guests had left—counting money and having sex, most people's joint-favorite things in the world. In many cases, the sex was lacking, since the groom would already be drunk. Even if they weren't drunk, preparing for the wedding would tire the bride and groom out, so he might not have enough energy left for proper sex. I knew all too well about it from my own experience. Naturally, life after the wedding could only go downhill if they'd just had the best day of their lives.

I hadn't been invited to any weddings since I became a funeral cryer, but I wasn't unhappy with anyone. I wouldn't invite a funeral cryer to my wedding myself. To be honest, not many people liked to be invited to weddings. You never knew how much gift money would be sufficient, so you had to give more than you were comfortable with. People would pay you back when you invited them. In my case, it would be when the daughter got married. These days, a lot of young people didn't marry young like in the past. Some of them didn't want to get married at all.

It would be worse for childless couples, as no money would be returned. It was also bad for people with very young children, as it would be many years before their children got married and the people who were supposed to give you money back might not be around anymore. Most people would keep a book detailing how much money they had received at their wedding, and they would give a little more than they had been given. A rise due to inflation was reasonable, and it was also a courtesy to pay back more. That little extra showed that you cared about them, and about the community.

It was sad the community in the village was in the process of disintegrating. When I was little, our village was called a commune, which meant a public society, or a public community. We didn't use to have locks on our doors and you could go in and out of people's houses freely. People would even take shortcuts through other people's front and back doors. Nobody would worry about thieves either. There was nothing to steal in any case. The village was an extended family for everyone.

I always thought if I could turn the clock back twenty or thirty years, I would still have friends and nobody would think I carried a lethal atmosphere. Everybody was everybody's sister or brother, so everyone was part of your family. How could your family turn you away because you were a funeral cryer?

The husband had fallen asleep. He had tugged at my panties when we went to bed, but I didn't let him take them off.

At some point, I was curious about other people's sex lives. Nobody had told me in detail, but I had guessed from snippets of conversations over the years. People would laugh at you if you still had sex in your middle age. I found sex awkward, as it made me feel ashamed about my body.

For example, my breasts were like sacks, but worse than sacks. A sack could be filled up with rice or wheat and be plump. What could I be filled up with? At the same time, my nipples were dark and ugly, not that other people would see them, but I didn't like them. I believed the husband didn't like my breasts and nipples.

These days, some people called having sex *making love*. I imagined it could also be called *making hate*.

During the early days when the husband and I were together, I didn't think too much about my feelings. Sex was a natural part of marriage, so it wasn't anything you chose to do or not to do. It took me several years to get familiar with sex and used to it. There was a saying, practice makes perfect, but it didn't seem to apply to sex. After enough practice, there was no excitement or curiosity left. It became a frustrating routine when we knew how to do it, but didn't know how to do it well. If you weren't attracted to each other, it would be pain and torture. How could people who didn't like each other sleep together?

It was difficult to know what the purpose of life was. I had never learned about it anywhere. Mum and the daughter were the only people I cared about now. I had to live for them. They were my blood relatives, so I had to care. I had no choice and there was no way to escape my responsibilities. Although I also thought about the brother sometimes, he was his wife's responsibility. I wouldn't say I didn't care about the husband at all, but it was conditional: how much I cared about him depended on how much he cared about me.

Mum didn't want me to do anything for her. As long as she didn't have to worry about the brother or me, her life was fulfilled. I would make sure she believed I was fine. I didn't expect the daughter to do anything for me.

Now I would also like to be kind to myself. Maybe I should buy a new bra to lift my breasts. Although nobody would see my panties, I would get rid of the tatty ones. All my panties were tatty, though, so I would get rid of the tattiest ones.

For the first time in my life, I wanted to treat myself to some lovely underwear. The husband was the only man who had seen my naked body, but he'd never told me whether it was beautiful or not. He stripped me for his own convenience. Were all men like him?

I couldn't understand why I wanted to like my body when I was old and ugly now. I wanted someone else to like it too. Pretty underwear would make my body more beautiful, or at least less ugly. Maybe someone wanted to see my body in some beautiful fabric? The barber? Maybe I wouldn't feel embarrassed about my body if I wore some nice underwear? Would the husband look at me and be nice to me if he thought I looked nicer?

Perhaps I wasn't beautiful. But could a man just tell me I was beautiful?

Mum said there was some fabric left in her wardrobe. I would have a thorough look to choose something and sew a skirt or a dress for myself. It would take me a long time to make clothes, but it didn't matter if they would make me look pretty.

Then I thought I should finish making the husband's last outfit first. Nobody knew what might happen to him, or to me, tomorrow.

If I managed to finish making the husband's last outfit, it would be easier to sew clothing for myself: *practice makes perfect*.

35

The husband was annoyed that Mum hadn't managed to transfer the money.

"Couldn't the bank be a bit more flexible?" He frowned.

"No. Mum's never had a bank account in her life, like me," I said.

"Not everyone needs a bank account."

"She needs one now."

"It's easy to get a bank card done."

"She didn't have her ID card and home-address proof with her."

"Once she's got her card, I will go to the bank with her," the husband offered.

"I can go."

"She'll transfer the money into my account, so it would make sense that I go."

"I'll let you know."

"I hope she doesn't change her mind." The husband sounded worried.

"It's her money. She can decide what to do with it."

I trusted Mum, but she had the right to change her mind. If Mum gave me the money, the husband wouldn't know, since he wouldn't know that I had my own bank account. He had to behave himself if he wanted to spend my money.

I shouldn't wait for Mum's money. The most reliable money was my own earning.

In the past, winter had been a good time for my job. I had always earned more money in winter than any other season. This year had been different, though. I hadn't had many jobs yet, and it would soon be Spring Festival, and then it would be spring. When it was warmer, there would be fewer deaths.

On the one hand, I was glad that not many elderly people had died. I tried to think how many elderly people there were in my village—there were enough. They would hate me so much if they knew I was counting them. I must be the last person they would like to see, since seeing me would remind them of their coming death and funeral.

Even if some elderly people didn't die soon, their longevity had a limit. I still had at least ten years left in my job, so my income would be guaranteed. For the first time, I didn't worry about my job. As long as there were people dying, I wouldn't be out of work. I realized that I actually had a good permanent job, as I wouldn't lose it.

Since I had an unemployed husband, being financially capable was the most important thing for me. Money had been an issue all the time, even when the husband was also working. Although we earned good enough money as a comedy duo, household expenses as well as money we spent buying flour and rice from our fellow villagers didn't leave us much to save. Now, as a middle-aged man, it would be impossible for him to find anything well paid, and he was too lazy to do odd jobs. I felt like I was in a raft on my own on the sea, risking drowning.

There were still fields around the village the husband could rent. The village committee still existed, but I didn't know what they were doing at the moment. I learned from the husband that the committee had been thinking about setting up a business, like some other villages had done, but nothing concrete had happened here. A clothes-making company or a toy factory, which was what had been discussed with some business people from cities. I wouldn't mind being a seamstress or a toy assembler on the production lines.

The reason business plans didn't manage to go ahead was due to transport difficulties. There were no direct trains to big cities from our area, and there were mountains around here, which made building major roads difficult and costly. For the same reason, the rumored development plan hadn't taken place and the apartments and villas still only existed in the villagers' dreams.

There was less than a month before Spring Festival. It was the traditional Chinese New Year period.

Hopefully the daughter would come home soon. She was only home for a week last year. Traveling was a pain around Spring Festival. The prices of train tickets rocketed up, and it was almost impossible to get ahold of seat tickets.

I had experienced the train chaos myself, but things were worse these days. I had seen tens of thousands of people sitting on the train-station floor on TV, and you could hardly move in the crammed carriages.

The daughter had never described her train journeys in detail, as she found them too frustrating to talk about. She had to change trains three times before taking a bus to gū shān zhèn, Solitude Mountain Town, and then to our village. She had never brought her boyfriend home for Spring Festival either, since he had to go to his hometown to visit his own parents.

I had a couple of crying jobs before Spring Festival. It was always an extremely difficult situation if a family member died nearer the holiday, when preparations for the festival would have to continue and a funeral had to take place as soon as possible. Death didn't wait for you, and funerals couldn't be long delayed or postponed. Then you wouldn't be able to enjoy Spring Festival, since even the slightest sign of happiness would be seen as a betrayal of your deceased loved one.

"Are you sure you want to have your hair cut?" The barber snipped his scissors in front of me.

"You said I would look younger with short hair."

"But I won't take responsibility if you don't like the haircut."

"I'll take responsibility myself."

"I'll try my best to make you look more beautiful. And trendy."

The atmosphere between us was ambiguous and awkward.

Nobody else had used "beautiful" to compliment me.

When I saw the pile of my hair on the floor, a feeling of loss hit me. I had seen my long hair as a symbol of my youth. I knew those days had long gone, but while my hair was long, I told myself that I hadn't finally bid farewell to my youth.

"Are you all right?" The barber stopped sweeping the hair.

"Yes."

"Your new hairstyle looks nice."

"Thank you."

I felt so embarrassed that I kept my face lowered while I was shedding tears. Then I felt hands on my shoulders. I thought I should remove those hands, but I didn't.

The barber wiped my tears away with his fingers.

"Why are you crying? Don't you like your new hair? I'm sorry."

"I do. No. I don't know." I shook my head.

"You look beautiful."

The barber's hands slid down to my waist and his body touched mine, and soon his chest was pressed against my breasts. A sensation was aroused from my breasts and my body became soft. I tried, but not hard, to move, while his arms were wrapped tightly around me. His body was rubbing slowly against me, hard and hot.

"You're fragrant," he whispered into my ear.

My earlobes felt ticklish.

After a while, the barber's hands started searching between the layers of my clothes. I held his wrists and stopped him, as I realized I hadn't bought a new bra and my panties were old, with loose elastic.

He released his hands from me. The room wasn't bright. The curtains were drawn. I recalled the conversation between the husband and me. If he was here, he would be furious to see the drawn curtains, even if he had no idea what had happened.

Yes, the curtains. The barber wouldn't have dared to do anything to me if there had been no curtains. I wasn't angry with the barber, but I felt humiliated by my reaction. I only stopped him because I wasn't wearing nice underwear. At some point, I had trapped myself in the situation with the curtains. I didn't even know when he drew them.

The barber switched on one of the lamps on the dressing tables.

The light dazzled me, and I blinked.

"Your hair looks lovely," he said to me.

"Thank you."

"You're a good customer."

"You're a good barber."

"Thank you."

"Do you remember that young widow?"

"Hotpot. She was also my customer."

"She's moved back to her parents' house."

"I didn't know that."

"I used to have hair like hers. Rich, shiny and smooth."

"You shouldn't compare yourself with her."

"I'm not comparing. I can feel my youth's going when my hair is thinning."

"We all have our prime time in life. They come at different times."

"I don't know what *prime time* is." I shook my head.

"Your best time could be any age. It's got nothing to do with the appearance or length of your hair." He stroked my fingers.

"You talk like a knowledgeable teacher."

"I worked in a school when I was young, but I wasn't a teacher."

"What did you do?"

"I helped run the maintenance office. My job was to make sure all the sports apparatus and facilities were safe."

"Did you like the job?"

"It wasn't bad. I did a lot of exercise at the same time."

"You must have been fit."

"I'm still fit."

"Are you?"

"I've got muscles everywhere."

"I don't believe you."

"I can show them to you."

"No. Don't."

"Sometimes I helped at the school canteen."

"So you can cook?"

"Not my favorite thing. I got to know some shop people when I was working at the canteen."

"Then you opened a shop yourself."

"Correct."

I searched my bag. "I'll pay before I forget."

"You don't need to pay."

"Why not?"

"I don't want you to pay me."

"I want to pay."

"You don't have to pay."

I kept quiet, but handed him the money. "I'll pay."

He accepted the money.

I took out my old knitted scarf to cover my hair and face, as it was windy and cold outside. I'd kept the scarf in my bag and meant to return it to the barber. I would wear the green scarf Mum had bought for me when I saw him next time. I was keeping it in the chest of drawers. I had planned to wear it at Spring Festival.

The barber brought me into his arms when I was near the door.

"I'll wait for you," he said.

I kept my scarf on after I arrived home. It was almost as cold inside the house as it was outside. We only kept the stove on now for a couple of hours after dinner. Maybe we could eat hotpot to make ourselves warm. No, I would wait until the daughter was home.

I made some green tea before I texted the daughter.

"How are you doing? How's your job? Grandma's left now. She's been well. She misses you. Your dad is the same. He still likes his mah-jongg. This year we haven't had proper snow yet. It's snowed several times, but it's never settled. Have you bought your train tickets? The sausages are dry now, ready for you to take some to Shanghai with you."

Telling the daughter about Mum reminded me of the money she was going to give me. Although she said she wanted to give the money to me because the brother wasn't Dad's son, the main reason was that she didn't trust the sister-in-law. I was still tempted to ask the brother whether he knew he wasn't Dad's son. I might wait until after Mum transferred the money to me.

Mum didn't trust her son-in-law either. I would have my own

bank account soon, so she wouldn't worry. She didn't think the husband and I would get divorced, but she was reluctant to let him have her money.

Mum said she would give some of her cash to the brother. Most of it was from the savings I gave her many years ago. She said I might have forgotten about it, but she didn't touch my money after she spent some of it on my wedding. Mum said I was a good daughter, and she and Dad were grateful.

I unpacked the green scarf and flattened it in front of me on the duvet. The husband was playing mah-jongg somewhere, so I wouldn't cook until he came back, and I wasn't hungry anyway.

While I was feeling the scarf, my mind returned to the barbershop. The curtains, those old curtains, looked nice in the barbershop. The barber had said I was fragrant. What did I smell of? Was I really fragrant?

The husband had never said I was *fragrant* and I had never thought about whether I was fragrant or not. I knew there was something called perfume, bottles of scented water, expensive water. I had seen bottles of perfume in my employers' places while I was in Nanjing, but I didn't pay any attention then. I'd never worn any perfume in my life, let alone owned any.

What were the barber's intentions? If I had let him touch me with his lips, what would he have done? If I had worn a new bra and if my panties were not worn-out, would I have let him take them off?

Did I want him to touch me?

And…where was his girlfriend?

The daughter replied. "I'll come home for Spring Festival. I'll try to get train tickets. Homemade sausages are delicious. Thank you, Mum."

The tickets would be expensive. I would give her some money.

I would show the daughter my last outfit, so she would know she didn't have to prepare one for me.

I would also show her dad's last outfit to her if I'd finished making it by then.

Most importantly, I would tell the daughter her grandma's last and only remaining ambition in life.

Her grandma wanted to become a great-grandma.

36

I had waited outside the restaurant for over half an hour before I decided to leave. Before the banquet, someone had told me briefly that the payment would be made quickly on-site, so I sat waiting near the reception.

I was asked to join the tofu banquet, but I declined the invitation. I wanted to buy a new bra and some new panties, so I needed to leave soon enough. I had also planned to apply for a bank account, but I had forgotten to bring my proof of address.

I could hear the usual noise you would hear at a restaurant. Then people started arguing, followed by some crying, not the grieving crying, though. It was angry crying mixed with screaming. It was the last noise you would like to hear after a funeral.

The argument must be between the two families. The man had died by suicide, and from the chitchat I had overheard, the wife had been unfaithful to him. I didn't know how long the argument and crying would last for, so I left the restaurant without being paid. If I didn't leave, the shops would be closed by the time I arrived in the town center.

I wasn't worried about the payment. They would pay me, otherwise they might be worried they would be living on borrowed time. It was the custom. You could owe people money on any other occasion, but not the funeral service fees.

I didn't know whether the chitchat was true. How could a man kill himself because of the wife's infidelity? I wouldn't do it. If the husband had slept with other women, including Hotpot, I wouldn't hurt myself. Instead, I would try to live a better life.

I entered a nice-looking shop. Most shops in town looked similar, but the prices varied. To my surprise, some bras and panties weren't too expensive. I was glad to find out that I could afford a pretty lacy bra with my cash. When I was paying the shop assistant, she gave me a sideways glance as if I were doing something wrong. Maybe she thought I was too old and I didn't deserve a lacy bra. I also saw some colorful skirts and sweaters. I took a look at the prices. They were too high for me.

On the bus back home, I tried to think how many times in my life I had worn a skirt. I'd had a couple of skirts when I was young, but they must be too tight for me now as I had put on weight. They must be somewhere in the house. I would find them and unstitch them to try to enlarge them. It was only the beginning of January, so it would be a while before it was warm enough for me to wear skirts.

The husband wouldn't notice whether I had a new bra, but he would see me wearing skirts and he would think I was crazy. He would possibly make sarcastic comments about me, but I didn't care. If it was too difficult to alter the skirts, I would try to make one skirt using the fabric Mum kept in the house. For me, having one skirt was probably enough, not that different from having two or more.

I would ask the daughter to bring home some of her old clothes she didn't want to keep, some colorful clothes, something out of fashion for her, but fashionable enough for me. If she had some unused old makeup, I wouldn't mind having it.

Mum said I should stop wearing the daughter's clothes. Why? They looked nice and I liked them.

The husband was annoyed that I came home without the payment. He said I should have waited. I knew he was right, but I didn't tell him the reason why I hadn't waited. Buying pretty underwear would seem a crazy reason to him. He scolded me for being impatient, and I didn't protest. I didn't show him my new bra either.

"You're the stupidest woman I've ever met." The husband was still complaining when we went to bed.

"I'm sure they'll pay me."

"How do you know?"

"It was for the funeral. If they didn't pay, they would be cursed."

"Cursed by what? Who cares?"

"People who owe me money care, the bereaved."

"No. These days nobody cares about promises and morality."

"I'm sure they'll pay."

"I can't understand why you didn't wait."

"I had to hurry to catch the last bus," I lied.

"It's 499 yuan, not a little money. You stupid woman." He raised his voice.

I didn't respond.

I used to be nervous and get worried when the husband told me off. I thought I must have done something wrong to make him angry. He always said I was a stupid woman, but I wasn't sure what level of stupidity he thought I was at, but now I knew I was the stupidest woman. Over the years, I had been used to being a stupid woman in his eyes. But was he stupid enough to have a stupid wife? Our conversations often ended when he said I was a stupid woman. When I heard him saying it, I gave up. I gave up continuing whatever we were discussing. No, we didn't discuss things. We mostly disagreed with each other when we talked.

When I opened my eyes in the morning, the husband had already left home. Recently, most days he had been going out earlier than before.

I was going to get a cabbage from the backyard, so I opened the door. It was all white. I didn't know it had snowed the night before. I didn't see or hear any snow falling. The curtains were drawn and the husband and I were bickering.

On such a cold morning, the husband would rather go out than stay at home with me. I didn't mind him not being home, but the fact that he was so obsessed with mah-jongg struck me and made me wonder what was the most important thing in one's life. Some fun, maybe. As long as something would give you some fun, you would just do it. It didn't matter what it was, whether it was mah-jongg or something else, it was the fun that attracted people.

I could go out too to have some fun. Where could I go? There was hardly anywhere I could go in and around the village. The bamboo grove? The grocery shop?

Right now, there was no reason for me to visit either of these places. The village was covered in snow, so the best place was home. I also realized there were so few places for me to go to even when the weather was pleasant.

I could always go to the barbershop to have my hair done, and I had a new bra...

The daughter replied to my text: "Mum, you can have my clothes. I will bring some home. You can take a look in the wardrobe. I left a coat there. I haven't got train tickets yet. I might have to wait until the last minute."

"Thank you for the clothes," I quickly replied.

I found a puffer coat in the wardrobe in Mum and Dad's bedroom. That was the only wardrobe we had. I mainly stored bedding in the wardrobe. There was a chest of drawers in our bedroom and there was more than enough space for our clothes.

The daughter's coat was longer than mine, slightly below my knees. I put it on, and it fitted well. It would be too big for the daughter. The coat was as new. The daughter was wasteful, like many other young people.

I wrapped the new scarf around my neck. I looked at myself in the makeup mirror. The green scarf and the gray coat looked good together. I wished I had a full-length mirror. I needed someone to tell me how I looked. The only person I could think of now was the barber. I didn't need a hairdo yet. In fact, I didn't have to go to the barbershop as often as before with my short hair. I could go there for a cup of tea, though.

The snow looked deep. I had put on my Wellington boots, my feet feeling damp and cold. The barbershop wasn't far away, but I would go somewhere else on the way. I didn't want to leave a clear path in the snow with my Wellington boots, as I didn't want anyone to notice where I had been.

It wasn't insane to go for a walk. The air was fresh and I didn't feel too cold, thanks to the daughter's coat and my woolly scarf. After the snow, the village didn't smell of pig poo and chicken poo. My boots were heavy and clumsy while I was heading to the bamboo grove, but my heart was light and bubbly. I stopped in front of the grove. It was covered in white, and I could see clumps of snow falling from the leaves. It was a silent world, my world.

I took a detour along a couple of paths before the barbershop caught my eye. I turned around and saw my footprints in the deep snow. I didn't see anyone else while I was walking, and the only noise I could hear was the crunching from my boots. I didn't normally like to wear Wellingtons, but with the daughter's long coat, the boots looked like those fashionable boots young people wore. I must look nice from a distance.

I didn't have any gloves on, but my hands were warm. I had wrapped my old knitted scarf around my hands, the scarf that the barber had thought was someone else's and lent to me.

The barber looked surprised, if not delighted, when he opened the door for me.

"Hello," he said.

"Hello," I said.

"Do you want to have your hair done?"

"No, I don't need to yet."

"Do you want to have a cup of tea?" he asked.

"I'm returning this scarf."

"Keep it. Nobody's asked about it."

"But it's not mine. Someone will ask for it."

"Just keep it until someone asks for it."

"I've got a new scarf. My mum bought it for me." I pointed to the scarf I was wearing.

"It's beautiful."

"Thank you."

"Do you want to come in? It's cold outside."

"The snow is deep. I didn't see anyone."

"Most people wouldn't go out today."

He let me in and unwrapped the old scarf from my wrists, his fingers brushing the backs of my hands.

He folded the scarf neatly and placed it on one of the dressing tables.

"You look...lovely today." The barber pulled up a chair for me. "Your new scarf looks nice."

"Yes, it is nice."

"Your coat looks nice too."

"It's my daughter's."

"It suits you."

"Thank you. I feel good."

"You look like a stylish city lady."

"Do I?"

"Yes. Do you want me to wash your hair? Then a blow-dry?"

"I'm not sure." I felt my hair.

"It'll warm you up."

"Okay."

I closed my eyes and lay back on the shampoo bed. The barber had moved the electric heater near me, so there was some warm, dry air blowing toward my body.

The water was hot. The barber's fingers rubbed between my scalp and my hair. I could feel the shampoo was bubbly and my hair was smooth. The smell of the shampoo was delicate, like flowers.

"Am I the first customer today?" I asked when the barber was switching on the hair dryer.

"Yes. Nobody would go out in such weather."

"People will come as it's going to be Spring Festival soon."

"Not really. You know most families cut each other's hair."

"It's not easy to cut hair."

"It's easy if you're not fussed about styles. Some shavers can measure the length you want, so it's handy for men's hair."

"My husband and his mah-jongg friends sometimes cut hair for each other."

"You know he's been here. His hair isn't bad."

"It's a lot of hassle to cut your own hair."

"Practice also makes perfect."

"I like to have my hair done here."

"It's nice to have you here."

"Your girlfriend's lucky. She doesn't have to pay for hairdos."

"But I don't do her hair."

"Why not?"

"She doesn't like it. She washes her own hair and lets it dry naturally."

"Most people do it that way."

"I don't want to do it for her anyway."

"Why not?"

"I used to wash her hair for her, but she complained that I rubbed her head too hard."

"That was a shame."

"Her hair is thin, and it grows slowly. When she thinks her hair is too long, she holds the ends and cuts it herself."

"By the way, is she coming back home for Spring Festival?"

"I don't know."

I asked after a brief silence, "Are you lonely?"

"What do you think?"

"I don't know."

"I'm not lonely when you're here."

"Do you want to have a cup of tea?" the barber asked after he finished drying my hair.

"Yes, if it's not too much trouble."

"Green tea or black tea? Flower tea?" he said as he moved the heater toward me.

"Some flower tea, please. I've never had flower tea before."

"Flower tea suits you."

When he handed the teacup to me, his fingers touched mine.

I took a sip of tea. "It tastes sweet."

He moved his chair nearer to me. "I've put some honey in it. It's the tea for ladies like you."

"I'm sure it's nice for everyone."

"Do you drink tea at home?"

"I drink green tea."

"Do you drink tea with your husband?"

"He doesn't like tea."

"I drink tea on my own too. It's nice to drink tea with you."
He stroked the backs of my hands lightly and slowly.

"I think I should go home now. It might snow again later."
I stood up.

"I can lend you an umbrella. Or I can walk you home."

I shook my head. "You need to look after your customers."

"You're my only customer."

I turned toward the door.

I felt two hands being placed on my breasts from behind. I
became motionless. The barber's hands stayed on my breasts,
but didn't move.

His fingers pressed my breasts slightly. "Nobody's here, and
nobody's coming."

I touched a couple of his fingers, thinking what he might do
with them. I didn't mind today, since I was wearing my new
bra. My breasts were not beautiful, but with the decoration of
the lacy bra, they wouldn't look ugly. Hopefully he wouldn't
mind their size. They weren't large, but they were still breasts.
Then I wished I'd bought new panties as well. I wouldn't want
him to see my old panties.

I moved his hands away with both of my hands. "I have to
go home."

"No. Don't go."

He pulled my sweater and my layered top up and his hands
searched under my top.

I couldn't see his face, but I could feel his heavy breathing
on my neck, and he was still holding me from behind. I shut
my eyes.

His hands squeezed under the cups of my bra. His fingers
touched my nipples.

I shivered.

"Are you okay?" he asked.

"I don't know."

"Do you want to go upstairs?" he whispered.

I didn't answer.

Slowly, he turned me around. I didn't know when and how, but my bra had already been undone.

He buried his head between my breasts. His lips were warm.

My eyes felt moist after I shut the door behind me. I didn't know whether I would come here to have my hair done again.

The barber wanted to walk me home, but I asked him not to. He said nobody would be out, so nobody would see us. I wanted to walk home myself. It didn't matter whether there were people out or not, I wanted to be on my own for a while.

"Wait."

I turned back.

The barber had rushed out of the barbershop.

He handed a small paper bag to me. "Here's some flower tea for you. Remember to drink it. It's good for your skin."

I took the bag silently.

"We'll go upstairs next time," he said gently.

I looked away.

The barber lifted his hands up and caressed my cheeks.

"I... I love you." He looked into my eyes.

I felt tears running down my cheeks.

"Go back. It's cold outside," I said. He was only wearing a sweater.

"I'm not cold."

"Go back. People will see us."

I watched the barber walking back toward his shop.

He opened the door slowly and entered the shop.

He kept the door ajar for a while and looked my way, before closing it.

I saw the curtains open. He waved to me through the windows.

I didn't wave back.

I turned around, but didn't know where to go.

Where is my home?

37

I'd been awake most of the night.

I'm a bad woman, a Damaged Shoe.

I should have stopped the barber. I didn't want to blame him, since I could have stopped myself. I felt ashamed of myself. At first, I thought about stopping him and leaving, as I felt embarrassed about my panties. He wasn't forcing me to do anything, but when his body was touching mine, I felt too weak to move. I couldn't remember what happened before he pulled my trousers down. Then his eyes were half-shut. He probably didn't notice what my panties looked like.

I had a shower and washed my panties as soon as I arrived home. My body felt fresh under the water. I examined my panties. They were old, but they probably looked okay to the barber when he wasn't concentrating on my clothing.

When the husband walked into the kitchen, I'd already made a pot of flower tea.

"You've got short hair," the husband said.

"I've had it for days. Did you not notice?"

"No." The husband shook his head.

I thought he would apologize, or at least make a comment, but he did neither.

I was wearing my new bra, and I didn't think he had seen me wearing it. In fact, he didn't know I had a new bra.

The flower tea was refreshing. I only took a sip in the barbershop, but now I was enjoying drinking it.

"What are you drinking?" the husband asked.

"Flower tea."

"Flower tea?"

"It tastes sweet."

"Sweet tea? Where did you get it?"

"I bought it in town the other day," I lied.

"In town. After the funeral? That one you weren't paid for?"

"Yes."

"Have they paid you now?"

"Not yet."

"Not yet," he repeated. "They're not going to pay you, you stupid woman."

"It hasn't been long. They will."

"Has water got into your brain?" His voice was louder.

When people said water got into your brain, it meant you were insane. Maybe we all had some water in our brains. Yes, everyone had a lot of water in their brain. He was no exception.

After drinking the flower tea, I picked up the husband's unfinished last outfit to sew.

The earliest stitches were not neat and flat; now, toward the end of making the outfit, I was much better and faster. Once I finished, I would start altering my old skirts.

What about the brother's last outfit? His wife would prepare one for him. Although he was my only sibling, since we had our own families, there wasn't much personal contact or even bond between us.

Suddenly, I wanted to talk to Mum. She had no phone, so I could only pass on messages to her through the brother. After Mum's recent stay, I felt like wanting to say something to her directly. I didn't want to block the brother, but it would make sense for Mum and me to talk to or text each other whenever we wanted or needed. I would buy a phone for her. I would buy one when I was doing my bank account in town. I knew she didn't like to talk on the phone. She said she felt it odd and didn't know what to say to the phone. But she would get used to it.

I would invite Mum to spend some time with us when the daughter came back at Spring Festival. They hadn't seen each other since last Spring Festival. Mum would be happy to see her granddaughter. We would eat hotpot together and I would give her some sausages to take with her when she went back to the brother's.

Thinking about the sausages, I went to the backyard to check on them. I had hung them on the outside of the back door. They were dry and they smelled good.

When I put the sausages on the dining table and divided them into three piles, I realized some of them were missing. I remembered that I had made forty-eight sausages, but there were only thirty-six left. I counted several times, but it was still thirty-six.

There were no foxes or weasels in the area, and there were no thieves in the village; unless I had miscounted, or I didn't hang them all out. I could have remembered the wrong number, but that was unlikely. Twelve sausages was a lot of meat. Each year, I bought the same amount of sausage skin and same amount of pork to make the same number of sausages.

Had the husband taken them and given them to someone? I wouldn't ask him. He would be furious if I did. I didn't mind if he had given some away, but he should have asked me first, or at least told me.

If I had forgotten how many sausages I had made, I would be worried. I might be suffering dementia, like Dad, and becoming an official idiot. Was I too young to have dementia?

The husband was lying on the sofa, watching TV.

"Aren't you going to play mah-jongg today?" I asked.

"I'm tired."

"I feel tired too. I'm getting old."

"I'm getting old too."

"My memory's getting worse too."

"What happened?"

"I thought I had made forty-eight sausages, but there are only thirty-six."

"Are you sure?"

"Yes. I counted."

"It's crazy that you actually counted them."

"I always do. Each year, the same amount of meat and sausage skin."

"But if you made the sausages bigger and longer, then there wouldn't be forty-eight."

"Maybe I didn't count them this year."

"Maybe you didn't. Everyone forgets about something sometimes."

"But it never happened before."

"They're only sausages."

"They're more than sausages to me."

"I don't know what you mean." He shook his head.

"I made them. It was hard work."

I packed the sausages in three paper bags, one for the daughter, one for Mum—effectively for the brother's family—and one for the husband and myself.

The husband was watching TV. The programs must be boring, since he kept changing channels. I didn't watch TV very often, but recently I'd watched some reality shows. You could follow film stars' or pop stars' everyday lives. I didn't know anything about those famous people, as I didn't watch films or listen to music, but watching rich, good-looking people arguing and falling out made me think my life could be worse. It would be nice to watch TV with your family and make comments together, but I didn't want to watch anything with the husband, as he would contradict what I said.

Strangely enough, the husband didn't lose his temper when I told him about the sausages. I was expecting him to call me a "stupid woman," but he didn't. He didn't even become impatient, although he thought it was "crazy" to count the sausages.

The only possible explanation was that he felt guilty. Why would he feel guilty? He wouldn't have felt bad unless he was the one who'd taken the twelve missing sausages.

Had he given the sausages to his mah-jongg friends? Unlikely. Had he given them to Hotpot? No, she didn't live here anymore. But she must have told him her address. When he wasn't home, I always thought he had gone out to play mah-jongg. He could well have gone to visit her and come back on the same day. I never checked on him, so he could easily do that. So he had stolen the sausages for Hotpot.

Then there was that necklace, the shiny golden necklace my rich client gave me. I was going to post it to the daughter, but I couldn't find it. I didn't give it a second thought at the time, as I thought I must have forgotten where I had put it. Although I thought it was a cheap necklace, I could be wrong. Had he stolen it and given it to Hotpot when he slept with her? Did he also give her Mum's bone china bowl?

"The sausage-fried snow peas are delicious." The husband chomped noisily.

"I'm glad you like the sausages."

"Hotpot liked them too." He nodded.

"Hotpot? Has she eaten my sausages?"

"No, I mean we can use sausages in hotpot."

"Sausages in hotpot. Are you mad?"

"Why not? You can boil anything in the hotpot soup."

"I imagine so. Talking of Hotpot, how is she now? The woman Hotpot, not the soup hotpot."

"I don't know."

"I hope she's fine. Maybe we should go and visit her. We can give her some sausages and cabbage."

"Some snow peas too. They're free, aren't they?"

"They're not free. I grew them."

"They're cheaper than the shop ones."

"I'm not sure they're cheaper. I know they're better. What else do you think we should give her?"

He stared at me. "Do you mean it?"

"What do you think?" I asked.

I had nearly finished the husband's last outfit. I'd used his old clothes to measure the size briefly. He had been different sizes over the years. To be honest, as the wife, I didn't know his current size. The only thing I would like to check was his waist. If the waist wasn't right, it would be tricky to put the last outfit on. I was going to ask him to try them on, then I remembered Mum said, *you should never try your last outfit on.*

"Hey," I said.

"What?"

"I need to measure your waist."

"Why?" he asked.

"Are the trousers you're wearing the right size for you?"

"They're a bit loose, but I've got a belt. Why?"

"Can you take them off?"

"Why?"

"I need to know the size of your waist."

"I don't have a waist."

"Look at these trousers I'm making for you."

"Oh, the trousers I'm going to wear after I die." He sounded indifferent.

"If the waist of the trousers is too loose, you know, they'll fall off."

"Fall off." He laughed. "Do you think I can still stand up when I'm dead?"

"No."

"I imagine I'll be very thin when I die. I'll be ill and I'll lose weight before I die, so you don't need to worry about my size."

"All right. You don't need to take your trousers off."

"I will. I'll take my trousers off. I'll also take my underwear off."

The husband smelled of something I wasn't familiar with, a bit like soap and a bit like trees or bamboo. Where did he get the smell from? Maybe he smelled like he always did, and who would care how he smelled?

The barber smelled different from the husband. I couldn't say what the barber smelled of, but even when my eyes were shut, I could tell who was holding me. Maybe different men smelled different.

Recently, I'd been thinking of getting myself some perfume, the smell of flowers, so I would smell like flowers. I had seen air fresheners in town several times, but I had never thought about buying any. What was the point in spraying some smell in the house? Now that I wanted to smell nice, I would like the house to smell nice too. If only I could spray the air freshener in the village, then the village wouldn't smell of pig poo and chicken poo.

The husband took my panties off after he took his underwear off. His hands were still awkward, but he wasn't too impatient.

THE FUNERAL CRYER   309

I closed my eyes, imagining the barber was on top of me. Had the barber lasted a little longer?

Was the husband imagining someone else underneath him?

The husband was snoring, and I was missing the barber. I missed his gentle whisper and his patient fingers. I had never been touched by the husband the way he touched me.

I wanted to go back to the barbershop, but not for my hair. I wanted to go to his upstairs room.

I wanted to hear the barber say *I love you* again. Would he say it without hesitation?

Did he want to hear me say *I love you*? I had never said it in my life.

38

"The last outfit you've made for me doesn't look bad," the husband said. "I wouldn't mind wearing it as my normal clothes..."

"You're mad," I snapped.

"Then you'd have to make another last outfit for me."

"I need to be alive to be able to make it for you."

"I want to die first."

"Why?"

"It's better to die first."

"Why?"

"I want you to cry at my funeral."

"I hope we can both live for a long time," I said.

"You know the saying—good people die young, bad people live for one thousand years."

"I wouldn't mind being a bad person if I only had to live for one hundred years."

I redivided the sausages into five piles—one of ten for Mum and the brother, one of eight for the daughter, and two of six for Hotpot and the barber. There were only four left for the husband and me after I cooked two, but I didn't mind. I could make more for myself whenever I wanted. I also packed some pickled mooli. Mum had made a large jar of it while she was staying. The pickle was sweet, sour and spicy, good company for rice porridge or noodles. Chopped pickled mooli was tasty with omelette, hearty food for us countryside people. I checked the snow peas in the backyard. There were not many left, so I would keep them for Mum.

When I was on my way to the barbershop, I tried to think what I should say to him. We hardly talked before and after we were together, and I was too embarrassed to tell him how I felt. Would he think I was a bad woman if I told him he had made me happy?

At some point, he was going to kiss me. But I felt I wasn't ready for kisses. My lips had been untouched for many years. Next time, I would let him kiss me.

The barber seemed to be capable of looking after himself, but I felt I would like to do something for him. Perhaps I could cook a meal for him. Now we had slept together, he was my man as well as my barber. I still didn't know what his name was, and he hadn't asked mine either. Neither did we know each other's ages. We were just a man and a woman who wanted to be together.

But was he my man? Nobody had taught me, but I knew I wasn't supposed to have two men at a time unless I was a Damaged Shoe. The husband had been my husband for over twenty years, so he was naturally my man. How did women decide who was their man? The one you liked or loved most? Or the man you had been together with the longest?

Nobody was in the barbershop. I knocked on the door several times, but there was no answer. The curtains were drawn.

I was disappointed. I'd wanted to see the barber's happy face.

I would show him the sausages and pickled mooli. I didn't know whether we could be together again. He had a girlfriend and I had a husband, so things would be complicated if we were found out. However, being naked with a man was like a promise for me. Then I became nervous. I couldn't recall whether the curtains were drawn tight. Could anybody have seen us? Yes, the curtains were drawn. I remembered seeing him opening the curtains when he waved me goodbye.

To be fair, the barber might not be especially unhappy with his girlfriend. You wouldn't know whether other people were happy or not. Happiness wasn't something we talked about in our village. Life was more about what was happening, not about what we were thinking about. As long as we were not too unhappy, life was normal. More money and a bigger house, some children and grandchildren were the most important things for most people.

I remembered the legendary Great-Great-Grandma. She would be remembered by the village for many years, since her life was the perfect reflection of a successful personal life. But had anybody asked if she had been happy? No. Had anybody even cared whether she was happy or not? Who would have known? She'd had a life of such rare fulfilment. Compared to her achievements for her family, happiness had been nothing.

Sometimes I thought happiness was too profound for me to understand, but other times it was the simplest thing, like a dumpling with some delicious filling.

When I was reluctantly walking back home, some snowflakes were floating around slowly in the air. The sun was shimmering in the distant mist. It looked tired and thin, and soon it would disappear into the unknown distance. When the snow took over, the sun would be forgotten.

Where could the barber be? He had always been there when I went to see him for my hair. Was I too early today? No. It was nearly lunchtime. He could have well been in a different room, or he could have gone out. He could be in his grocery shop. He could even have gone away to see his girlfriend. It would be Spring Festival soon, so they would have to be together. It could be something else. Did he have another woman, one like me?

Maybe I should go back to the barbershop later. If he was in, we could drink some tea together. Would he invite me to his upstairs room?

The husband wasn't home. He wouldn't know where I had been and he wouldn't care. No, he would mind if he knew I had been to the barbershop, as there were curtains there and they could be drawn. Although the husband said no man wanted to sleep with me, he didn't want me to be with a man in a dark room.

After dinner, the husband was lying on the sofa watching TV. I walked to the living room after I did the washing up. The husband was surprised when I handed him a bag of sausages and pickled mooli for Hotpot.

"I thought you wouldn't give Hotpot anything. You actually meant it."

"Why not? Because you've slept with her?" I didn't know why I said that.

"Do you think I sleep with her?"

"Do you sleep with her?"

He shook his head. "I don't know why you think so."

"You do. I know you do. You don't need to admit it."

"Do you sleep with the barber?" he asked casually.

"No," I shouted.

"You can't prove you don't."

"I don't need to prove it."

"Why do you go to the barbershop all the time?"

"I go there to have my hair done."

"You don't need to go there so often."

"I do."

"You gave him our old curtains."

"So what?"

"The curtains can hide what you do together."

"We haven't done anything."

"You know whether you are lying."

"You know whether *you* are lying."

The next morning, I picked some snow peas in the back-yard and packed them with the sausages and pickled mooli for Hotpot.

The husband took a handful of snow peas from the table and put one into his mouth. "Are you sure you're giving her these snow peas too?"

"Yes, sausages and snow peas are a good match."

"You're kind, but…"

"She'll like them."

"Do you hate her?"

"Why?"

"You think I sleep with her."

"Maybe you do."

"If you think I sleep with her, you must hate her."

"I don't."

"It's odd you don't hate her."

"She's a lonely widow."

The husband had gone with the food for Hotpot. They would sleep together, but I didn't care. I had my own man. He said *I love you* to me.

I had a crying job in a nearby village. I would be collected by a moped.

The bag of sausages and pickled mooli for the barber was on the floor of the kitchen. I wouldn't finish my work until late afternoon, and it would be dark by the time I returned home. Perhaps I could try my luck in the barbershop again the next day.

My hair didn't look bad. When I didn't need a bun, there was almost no need to go to the barbershop. The husband wasn't wrong.

The daughter texted while I was waiting to cry.

"I still haven't got train tickets. I'll keep trying. Do you want me to buy anything for you? I'll post them to you if I can't come home this year."

I knew how difficult it was to get ahold of tickets, but she could have tried earlier. From her message, I couldn't sense any emotion. It was matter-of-fact. She wasn't bothered phoning me and explaining the situation. There was no "sorry" in her tone.

And what did I want? She knew I wouldn't ask her to buy anything for me. I wanted some pretty panties, and I would buy them myself.

If I can't come home. What she really meant was she wouldn't come home for Spring Festival. Would she go to her boyfriend's hometown? Had they split up again? I couldn't always believe what she said these days. Some mums would want their daughters to find rich boyfriends, but I had never forced her. I would be happy if she had a Shanghainese boyfriend, but I had never said she must. She could mostly do whatever she wanted, as I didn't want to be told to do things I didn't like myself. She didn't like to tell me her thoughts or opinions. She preferred to tell me what happened.

Maybe this was life. I didn't tell people my thoughts. I didn't believe what the husband said, and he probably didn't believe what I said.

Nobody believed each other. Should I believe the barber? It didn't matter whatever else he lied about, as long as his *I love you* was genuine. But how could I tell whether his *I love you* was genuine? If I believed him, *love* was there. If I didn't believe him, *love* wasn't there and he was a liar.

I was tipped some extra cash for the crying job. It was nearer Spring Festival, so it was a small "thank-you" token. Although I didn't know the deceased, I was invited to stay for dinner. There was too much food, of course, when Spring Festival was approaching.

It was a true banquet, far better than my normal Spring Festival Eve dinner. Banquets were for big families or groups. If there were fewer than a dozen dishes, you couldn't call it a banquet. But how could two or three people eat even half a dozen dishes in my house?

I was preoccupied while I was eating the tofu banquet. I didn't have a good appetite. I wanted to go home. No. I wanted to go back to my village. There was a man waiting for me. He wanted me and I wanted him.

It was dark and cold when I entered the house. The husband wasn't home. I didn't expect him to be home.

I turned the stove on and had a shower before I went to bed. It took a while to warm up the duvet. I lay in bed quietly and started thinking about doing some Spring Festival shopping, and I would also buy some new panties. When the barber and I were together next time, maybe we wouldn't be in a hurry. Would he want to look at my bra and panties closely?

I'd checked the weather forecast, and I was happy to know that it would be sunny for the next few days. I would go to town after taking the food to the barber. I would go to the bank and do some shopping afterward. Then I remembered the money the arguing families still owed me. Maybe I had been stupid to trust them. I should contact them for payment. I hoped they would pay me. If not, at least I didn't owe anything to anyone.

I didn't switch off the lights in the living room or the bedroom. I didn't know when the husband would be home, and I didn't want to climb out of my bed in the cold and dark to open the door for him. He would probably have had dinner with Hotpot. They would eat the food I had prepared, and then he would climb into her bed.

I couldn't get up in the morning. I had a bad headache and my forehead felt warm.

I wanted to drink some hot water, but didn't have the energy to move.

I felt so tired that I fell asleep again.

I didn't know how long I had been asleep. When I opened my eyes again, I saw the husband sitting on the edge of the bed.

"How are you feeling?" he asked.

I tried to sit up. "I've got a headache. Can you get me some hot water?"

"Okay. I'll boil the kettle for you."

When the husband handed me the water, he said, "I thought you were dead too."

"What? Who died?"

"The barber."

I dropped the cup.

39

The barber was dead.

Somebody—the husband told me the story, and he didn't know who that somebody was—had found the barber's body in the barbershop.

"Terrible." The husband shook his head. "Two police vans are still outside the barbershop."

"How did he die?"

"He committed suicide."

"Do the police know when he died?"

"I don't know. I mean, I don't know whether they know or not," he said.

"He definitely wasn't murdered?"

"No."

"I can't believe he killed himself."

"I can't believe that either. He never looked unhappy," the husband said.

"Where were you last night?" I changed the subject.

"I was tired, and I fell asleep on Hotpot's sofa."

"You didn't sleep in her bed?"

"No, I didn't. You don't believe me."

"It doesn't matter." I lay back down.

"I'll go and find out more about the barber's death. I saw lots of people watching outside the police cordon."

So the barber had killed himself. Why?

I had moved myself to the sofa. I didn't want to stay in bed. I was worried I would fall asleep in bed and die. My headache was still bad, and I was hungry. I felt dizzy, but couldn't keep the barber out of my head.

Could I have saved him if I'd gone into the barbershop that last time, or if I'd visited him before I went away for my crying job?

Did he not want to see me again? Did he have nothing to say to me when he decided to die? Did he miss me when he was dying?

I should have phoned him. I had his phone number.

I felt angry. There was anger toward the barber, there was anger because he didn't let me share his sadness, and there was anger because I didn't have a chance to help him. Why didn't he let me share his sadness? He didn't like me. He didn't like me enough to tell me about his sadness. He slept with me because he was on his own and he was lonely. He wanted to touch a woman and I was there. That was why he didn't say anything when he was moving on top of me.

Did he not enjoy sex with me? Did he not want to sleep with me again?

Why did he say *I love you* to me?

I couldn't think anymore. My headache was getting worse. I wanted something to eat...

When I woke up, I found myself lying in bed.

The husband was sitting on the floor next to the bed. "Sorry I didn't give you any food. You fainted. You're fine now."

"Am I going to die?" My head felt light.

"No, you're not." The husband shook his head.

"I don't want to die."

"You won't die."

"I want to get up."

"You need to stay in bed for a couple of days."

"If I die, you know where my last outfit is."

"I don't want to talk about that."

"It's with your last outfit."

"You're not going to die. Close your eyes. Have a rest." He stroked my cheek.

"I've had a rest. I slept, but I…"

"What?"

"I had a dream. It was scary."

"A nightmare."

"The barber died. The barber in our village."

"It wasn't a dream. Yes, he died."

"How?"

"He killed himself."

The husband had cooked dinner. He had made two dishes— sausage slices with scrambled eggs and carrot fried with snow peas.

I picked at the rice slowly with my chopsticks and said, "Dinner's delicious."

"The police dug his backyard up and found his girlfriend's body. I thought she was the wife," the husband said. "Nobody knew when he killed her or why."

I listened.

"He left a suicide note on the dressing table."

"What did he say in the note?" I asked.

"I don't know. The police wouldn't tell anyone."

"It'll be in the news, on TV and in the newspapers."

"Yes. Maybe there's no suicide note. It's all hearsay. I don't know."

"Where is he now? His body?"

"They took his body away in an ambulance."

"Did anyone see that?"

"I don't know. I didn't."

"What are they going to do with him?"

"Do you mean for a funeral? I don't know."

"By the way, how did he kill himself?"

"He hanged himself on the door frame."

"How?"

"With a scarf."

"A scarf?" My heart skipped a beat.

"Maybe it was his wife's, his girlfriend's, scarf. I heard it was a hand-knitted scarf, long and stretchy, so it didn't snap."

"How could a scarf kill him?" My chopsticks paused in the air.

The barber hanged himself with my scarf. Did he choose it on purpose? Maybe he couldn't find any rope? It was easy. He had many cables in the barbershop. The cables would have been easier to kill himself with than the scarf.

While the husband was doing the washing up, I was resting on the sofa.

Since we got married, I had never been properly ill. I had had colds and headaches, but had never needed to stay in bed. This time, the husband had thought I was going to die. It was the first time that I felt he cared about me.

When the husband helped me climb onto the sofa, he looked nervous.

"You should stay in bed," he said.

"No. It makes me feel I'm ill if I stay in bed."

"You are ill."

"Don't worry. I'm not going to die."

He put a blanket on me. "I don't want to move to town any-more."

"Why not?"

"I'll buy some piglets and chicks to raise in the backyard."

"They're too dirty and smelly for you."

"It doesn't matter. I want to start making a regular income."

I thought of the ancient proverbs: *when the rabbit dies, the fox has self-pity.* Everyone would take their turn to suffer. *Every cloud has a silver lining.* The barber's and his girlfriend's deaths made us realize how fragile life could be and how we had to look after each other.

Would the husband change his mind once I recovered?

We hadn't told Mum and the brother about the suicide and the suspected murder. They would hear from other people. When the husband didn't notice, I would throw away the food I was going to give the barber. I wouldn't have the stomach to eat it myself and it wouldn't be good to offer it to someone else. I might throw my new bra away as well.

I hadn't cried since the barber died. I might not be able to cry for him at all. His life ended as a total failure, and he would be remembered as a cold-blooded, evil man by many people for many years to come.

I wanted to know: why did the barber kill his girlfriend? What happened between them? Did he kill her on purpose or by accident?

Had he killed anyone else before that? Had he ever wanted to kill me? Would he have killed me if I had gone to his upstairs room?

I felt shattered and ashamed of myself. How could I fall for a murderer?

What had I done?

40

The husband cooked and did all the housework when I was ill. He didn't shout at me at all. I didn't know whether he still liked me or he just didn't want me to die because he wanted me to earn money and look after him.

I was going to invite Mum to have Spring Festival Eve dinner with us. If the brother wanted her to stay with them, it was fine. We still didn't know whether the daughter was able to come. If both Mum and the daughter came, we would have hotpot. If neither of them came, it would be the husband and me only, but we would still have hotpot. Hotpot was everyone's comfort food, especially when the weather was gloomy. I didn't know anyone who didn't like hotpot.

To make a festive hotpot, a wide variety of ingredients was required. I would have gone to the grocery shop for most of the food I needed for the hotpot, but right now I didn't feel like going there. The shop had been partly owned by the barber, and I didn't want to be reminded of him or hear any gossip about him in the shop. On the other hand, I was wondering whether the shop was still open. I could find out from the husband, but I didn't want to.

It would be easy to avoid seeing the barbershop on the way to the bus stop outside the village. The police vans, or the cordon lines, or people standing watching—none of these were things I would like to see. I imagined there would be men wearing white overalls and masks going in and out of the house, and black bin bags, something like that. I had seen all that in films. Everything would look surreal except for the curtains, my curtains.

I had thought I had made the barber happy, although he didn't say anything. I wasn't upset at the time since I assumed we would meet again soon and we would talk when we were together. He must have been happy, otherwise he wouldn't have said *I love you* when I was leaving.

I thought we were going to have chances to spend some time in his *nice* upstairs room. Had he already decided to kill himself before we had sex?

I felt hurt and angry, but if that was what he had wanted, that was fate. I happened to be there, and it was his chance to enjoy sex for the last time before he died. I didn't lose anything.

"Is there anything you'd like me to buy in town?" I asked the husband when we were eating breakfast. It was pancake and rice porridge with pickled mooli.

"You can buy some snacks. Peanuts, sunflower seeds, or beer if it's not too heavy."

"I'll try."

"By the way, they say the barber didn't kill his girlfriend."

"Who are 'they'?"

"People."

"Who killed her, then?"

"Nobody. It was an accident."

I stopped eating. "But he buried her in the backyard."

THE FUNERAL CRYER   325

"Yes. Maybe he did kill her."

"If he didn't kill her, he should have called the police."

"Maybe he should. He must have been worried that they'd think he'd killed her."

"But it cost him his own life in the end." I could feel my throat was dry.

"Who knows what happened."

"The police will find out."

"They don't always."

"Whatever happened, he shouldn't have killed himself." I knew I must have sounded angry. I was.

The husband took a look at me. "It was sad. He was ill, though."

"What?" I was surprised. No, I wasn't.

"They... People say he was ill and he wouldn't live for too long."

"People."

"He mentioned it in his suicide note. He must have felt guilty for causing his girlfriend's death."

"But he said he didn't kill her. How senseless of him to kill himself." My hand was shaking so much that I dropped the chopsticks.

"I know."

"He's dead." I left the table.

The husband didn't go into town with me. He was with his mah-jongg friends. The husband said that a bit of mah-jongg was a bit of gambling, and was a bit of fun in a boring life, and there was no harm. Perhaps he was right. I just hoped he would remember to buy some piglets and chicks.

When someone in the village died, everyone would be affected, especially if there was murder involved. However, if they were not your friend or a member of your family, you would recover quickly. The husband seemed to have been in shock for a while, but now his daily routine was back to normal. I remembered the time after Butcher had died and how we helped Hotpot. It was like Butcher had left something behind to remind us of him and there was sympathy whenever people mentioned him. For the barber, what was there left? A murder mystery?

It didn't take long for people to forget about the barber. After all, he had been an outsider. I also wondered how many people had known his girlfriend well. And did anyone in the village know his name?

The town was busy, but the bank was almost empty. It took me no more than fifteen minutes to apply for a bank card. Then I was told the card would be posted to my home address within five working days.

Before I went food shopping, I bought a couple of pairs of pretty panties.

I also found a phone for Mum. It wasn't a smartphone, but it looked neat and it was surprisingly cheap. Mum would like it, and it came with a free sim card.

Although I didn't need to cook dozens of hot dishes, I bought more food than we would need. Whatever else I cooked, I couldn't skip making dumplings. Spring Festival wasn't Spring Festival without dumplings. The husband had made a big ball of dough before he went out for mah-jongg.

Dumplings were the only staple food that had a warm inside. The warmth made your taste buds grateful, and you swallowed the warmth into your stomach and it stayed inside you. Eating dumplings required some solidarity. It was dull to eat them on your own, so you had to share them with people, the people whom you cared about and the people who cared about you. In a way, dumplings and hotpot were a pair.

Once my bank card arrived, I would call the brother to ask Mum to come. I hoped she had done her card by then. Then we could go to Dalian together. She would also be delighted to see the new phone I had bought for her.

The daughter might not come. She said she couldn't get tickets, but maybe she didn't want to come home.

Spring Festival was just around the corner, so I hoped that nobody would die now, or soon. The crematorium needed a break too. But surely it couldn't, as there were people dying every day, every hour and every minute...

Funerals took place every day, and I would never be out of work.

What about the barber? What about his funeral? Would he be burned in the furnace like rubbish? Nobody would keep his ashes.

I realized why the barber decided to take his own life near Spring Festival. It would be suspicious if his girlfriend didn't turn up. Was she the woman who argued with him over *me*, or another woman who wore tight jeans? I heard the banging of furniture and rushed away. Did she die then? Or did they continue to fight and she died accidentally? How?

The husband said the barber was ill. When I once saw the barber in town, he had some medicine from the hospital. Maybe I should have found out how unwell he was.

There probably wouldn't be a funeral for him. It wouldn't be easy to find his next of kin. If there was a funeral, there would hardly be any attendees. Who would want to mourn for an accidental murderer? As a funeral cryer, I was paid to go to funerals, but nobody would pay me to cry for him.

On the other hand, although I was a married woman, I was also his *lover*. I wanted to bid him farewell. I would like to take a last look at his handsome face. But how? I didn't know where his body was. And the fact that I didn't even know his name hurt me deeply.

I was still angry toward the barber. If he'd told me about his girlfriend's accident, I would have gone to the police with him.

If he had to go to prison, I would wait for him. I didn't know how to cut hair, but at least I would help run the shop. People in the village, especially the husband, would have thought I was a bad woman, but I wouldn't have cared.

I had a shower and put on my new panties and nearly new bra. I wouldn't throw my beautiful bra away. My belly wasn't firm and flat, but I didn't look too bad. My breasts looked like little hills under my clothes. I combed my damp hair and waited for it to dry naturally. When I was next in town, I should remember to buy a hair dryer. There wasn't a barbershop in the village anymore, and I would do my hair myself.

I made the pork and dill dumplings and displayed them on the trays. I counted the dumplings, like I used to do when I was a little girl. I would cook some when the husband was home from his mah-jongg, and put most of them in containers and keep them in the freezer.

I dozed off after I tidied up and cleaned the house. Then I was awoken by my phone. It must be a message from the daughter.

I picked up my phone from the coffee table. It wasn't from the daughter.

I sat up. It was a message from the barber's number. Although I had never phoned him or texted him, I had seen his number many times.

No. It couldn't be him. He was dead.

The message read like this: "I'm his stepson. I have no idea what happened. I don't know whether he killed my mother or not, but he is responsible for her death. He was a good stepfather to me, and he used to love my mother too, but it doesn't matter. He destroyed our family. He doesn't deserve a decent funeral. I hate him, but I still want to arrange a send-off for him. Everyone needs a funeral to say goodbye to the human world. I might not be able to cry for him; nobody in our family will cry for him.

"He left a suicide note and he mentioned you. He said if there was a funeral for him, he would like you to be his funeral cryer. He said you were the best."

He said you were the best.

My eyes filled with tears.

Would I cry for him?

★ ★ ★ ★ ★

Acknowledgments

I would like to start my acknowledgments by thanking my husband, Dr. Mark Elliott. Mark has supported and encouraged me throughout, not because he thinks I can write, but because writing is what I want to do.

I am grateful to my tutors in my MSt in Creative Writing and Postgraduate Certificate in Teaching Creative Writing courses from the University of Cambridge. I received advice and guidance from Dr. Sarah Burton, Professor Jem Poster, Dr. Midge Gillies, Dr. Jenny Bavidge and Dr. Lucy Durneen on my writing; they also helped me with my confidence. I learned from my fellow classmates in the courses as well.

After being long-listed for the SI Leeds Literary Prize in 2018 and the Bridport Prize in 2019 with my historical novel *The Martyr's Hymn*, I won the SI Leeds Literary Prize in 2020 with my novel *The Funeral Cryer*. I will forever owe my gratitude to Niki Chang, chair of the judging panel; the other judges, Malika Booker, Kadija George and Yvonne Singh; and Fiona Goh, director of the prize.

Many thanks to my agent, Kemi Ogunsanwo, and her colleagues at the Good Literary Agency, led by Nikesh Shukla and Julia Kingsford. They showed passion and faith in *The Funeral Cryer* even before I won the SI Leeds Literary Prize, and Kemi provides me with invaluable advice and strategies, ensuring all the teamwork related to my book runs smoothly. I was also extremely fortunate to be advised by Arzu Tahsin, who had confidence in my writing. Callen Martin and Gyamfia Osei have been helpful in terms of providing different pairs of eyes in reading as well as helping with logistics.

Without the hard work of Editorial Director Peter Joseph, Editorial Assistant Eden Railsback and their team at Hanover Square Press of HarperCollins, the publication of *The Funeral Cryer* in the US and Canada would not have been possible. Thank you to copy editor Gina Macedo, typesetter Nelson Gonzalez, proofreaders Vicki So and Sasha Regehr, and the behind-the-scenes team, including Sara Watson, Angela Hill, Gina Macdonald, and Tamara Shifman. Special thanks go to my former student Dr. Yuting Cao, whose beautiful painting is the inspiration for the cover of *The Funeral Cryer*. Also thanks to the cover designer Holly Battle.

I would also like to thank Professor Robert Macfarlane for his encouragement during the early stages of my writing.

Lastly, I want to thank my amazing children, Sean and Carys, and my parents for their love and belief in me.